THE ALLYN & BACON LITERATURE SERIES

ALLYN and BACON, INC.

Boston Rockleigh, N.J. Atlanta Dallas Belmont, Calif.

20th CENTURY AMERICAN SHORT STORIES

Theodore W. Hipple, *Series Editor*

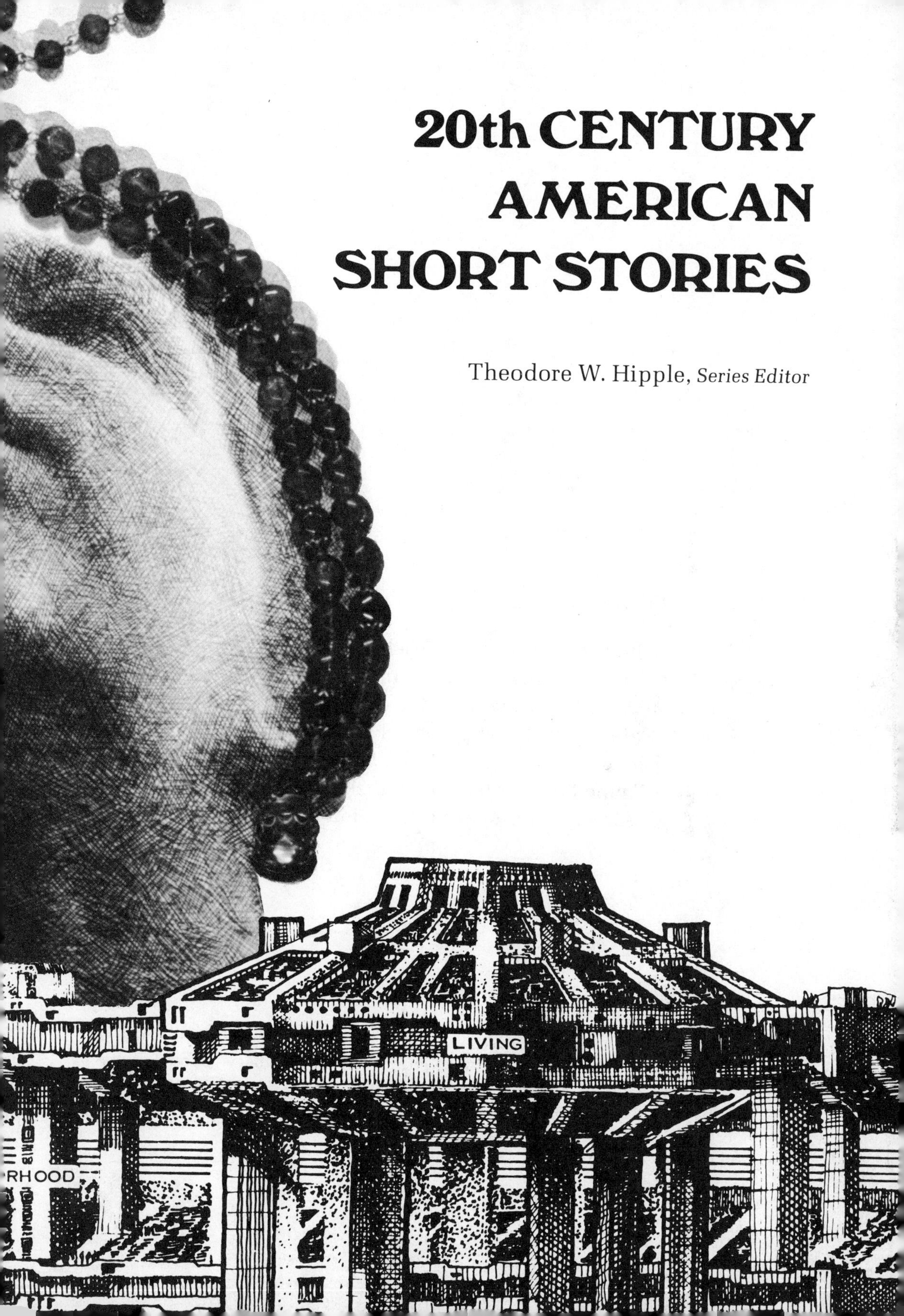

About the Author

A former high school English teacher, Dr. Ted Hipple has been associated with English teacher training at the Universities of Illinois and South Carolina, and is currently at the University of Florida, Gainesville. Dr. Hipple is chairperson of the Conference on English Education. He is on the Executive Committee of the National Council of Teachers of English, and is past president of ALAN (Assembly on Literature for Adolescents of NCTE).

Library of Congress Catalog Card No. 76-43398

Printed in the United States of America.
6 7 8 9 85 84 83

INTRODUCTION

The short story is probably the oldest literary form, most likely first used in the days before writing, when people entertained themselves by telling tales, some based on the actual events of their own lives or on the lives of their ancestors, some created out of a heightened imagination. Stories figured prominently in the Bible and in the Greek epics of Homer. Stories formed what we now call *The Arabian Nights*, were principal elements in Boccaccio's *Decameron* in Italy and Chaucer's *Canterbury Tales* in England, and continued their popularity in Renaissance and post-Renaissance literature. There were often short stories within the earliest novels, such as Cervantes' *Don Quixote* and Fielding's *Tom Jones*. And, of course, there are the famous American short story writers of the nineteenth century, literary giants such as Irving, Hawthorne, Poe, Twain, and Bret Harte, to name only a few. Twentieth century America may lay claim to having produced some of the greatest writings in the history of the short story. A number of these are included in the present volume.

One way of looking at fiction is to consider its elements: plot, characters, setting (including time and place), themes, and style. Prior to the twentieth century, plot seemed the predominant characteristic of short stories, with other features playing less significant roles. (The chief exception to this generalization is the work of Edgar Allan Poe.) In the twentieth century, however, all elements of the short story became important. Authors discovered that a story could concentrate on profound characterization, could reveal an important setting, could explore a significant theme, could demonstrate a compelling style. They studied their craft as writers of the short story, took risks with it, tried to alter its shape. In fact, they enlarged it.

We have their results today, marvelous stories that stay with us well beyond the twenty minutes or so it takes to read them. Most readers will feel strongly the biting cold that is almost another character in "To Build a Fire," or the fragile yet durable thing that love is in "The Vase." What happens to Pepé in "Flight" is not easily forgotten or ignored, nor are the haunting pictures of burnt-out lives found in "A Summer Tragedy."

And these are but a few of the stories you'll remember from this volume. There are others, equally good, by O. Henry, Langston Hughes, William Faulkner, F. Scott Fitzgerald, Jesse Stuart, Ernest Hemingway, Sherwood Anderson, Shirley Jackson, Katherine Anne Porter, Kurt Vonnegut, Jr., Bernard Malamud, Dorothy Parker, and Willa Cather. Their stories differ markedly. Yet all of these authors share a considerable artistry and all of them have achieved excellence in the short story as a written form of literature. Their heritage as writers of short stories is a long and cherished one, extending from the earliest times and to other countries. They have honored this heritage most ably, as you will discover for yourself when you read the stories in this book.

Thematic approach to the study of the stories in this book?

CONTENTS

Acknowledgments

"The Sculptor's Funeral"	Reprinted from *Youth and the Bright Medusa*, by Willa Cather, courtesy of Alfred A. Knopf, Inc.
"To Build a Fire"	© Copyright, Irving Shepard.
"Sophistication"	From *Winesburg, Ohio* by Sherwood Anderson. Copyright 1919 by B.W. Huebsch, Inc. Copyright © renewed 1947 by Eleanor Copenhaver Anderson. Reprinted by permission of the Viking Press, Inc.
"Rope"	Copyright © 1930, 1958, by Katherine Anne Porter. Reprinted from her volume, *Flowering Judas and Other Stories*, by permission of Harcourt Brace Jovanovich, Inc.
"The Waltz"	From *The Portable Dorothy Parker*. Copyright 1933, Copyright © 1961 by Dorothy Parker. Reprinted by permission of The Viking Press, Inc. Originally appeared in *The New Yorker*.
"Winter Dreams"	"Winter Dreams" (Copyright © 1922 Frances Scott Fitzgerald Lanahan) is reprinted by permission of Charles Scribner's Sons from *All the Sad Young Men* by F. Scott Fitzgerald.
"The Tall Men"	Copyright © 1941 and renewed 1969 by Estelle Faulkner and Jill Faulkner Summers. Reprinted from *Collected Stories of William Faulkner*, by permission of Random House, Inc.
"In Another Country"	"In Another Country" (Copyright © 1927 Charles Scribner's Sons) is reprinted by permission of Charles Scribner's Sons from *Men without Women* by Ernest Hemingway.
"A Summer Tragedy"	Reprinted by permission of Dodd, Mead and Company, Inc. from *The Old South* by Arna Bontemps. Copyright 1933, 1961 by Arna Bontemps. Copyright © 1973 by Alberta Bontemps, Executrix.
"Flight"	From *The Long Valley* by John Steinbeck. Copyright 1938, Copyright © renewed 1966 by John Steinbeck. Reprinted by permission of The Viking Press, Inc.
"Thank You, M'am"	Reprinted by permission of Harold Ober Associates Incorporated. Copyright © 1958 by Langston Hughes.
"Land of Our Enemies"	© Copyright, Jesse Stuart.
"The Vase"	From *The Friendly Persuasion*, copyright ©, 1945, 1973, by Jessamyn West. Reprinted by permission of Harcourt Brace Jovanovich, Inc.
"A Summer's Reading"	Reprinted with the permission of Farrar, Straus and Giroux, Inc. From *The Magic Barrel* by Bernard Malamud, Copyright © 1956 by Bernard Malamud. "A Summer's Reading" originally appeared in *The New Yorker*.
"Charles"	Reprinted with the permission of Farrar, Straus and Giroux, Inc. From *The Lottery* by Shirley Jackson, Copyright © 1948, 1949 by Shirley Jackson.
"Tomorrow and Tomorrow and Tomorrow"	"Tomorrow and Tomorrow and Tomorrow" is by Kurt Vonnegut, Jr. Copyright © 1954 by Kurt Vonnegut, Jr. Originally published in *Galaxy* as "The Big Trip Up Yonder." Reprinted from the book, *Welcome to the Monkey House*, by Kurt Vonnegut, Jr. with permission of the publisher, Delacorte Press, Seymour Lawrence.

ILLUSTRATIONS

George Bellerose, Stock Boston, page 150; Patrick Blackwell, page 68; Fredrik D. Bodin, pages i, 178, 188; Bobbi Carrey, pages 157, 196; Bernie Colonna, pages 22, 40; Judy De Luca, page 168; Jeremy Elkin, pages 42, 180; Jack Freas, pages 62, 152; John Ham, pages 6, 190; Peter Harritos, pages xii, 4, 94, 109, 130; Historical Pictures Service, Chicago, pages 93; Robin Perry, cover photo; Ruth Sanderson, pages 52, 60; Ben Shahn, Courtesy Library of Congress, page 109; Paolo Soleri, Reprinted from Arcology: The City in the Image of Man by Paoli Soleri by permission of The M.I.T. Press, Cambridge, Ma., pages ii—iii, 214; L. Christopher Valente, page 129; Victor Valla, pages 158, 166; Charles Waller, pages 110, 116, 118, 198

20th CENTURY AMERICAN SHORT STORIES

AFTER TWENTY YEARS

O. HENRY

THE policeman on the beat moved up the avenue impressively. The impressiveness was habitual and not for show, for spectators were few. The time was barely 10 o'clock at night, but chilly gusts of wind with a taste of rain in them well nigh depeopled the streets.

Trying doors as he went, twirling his club with many intricate and artful movements, turning now and then to cast his watchful eye adown the pacific thoroughfare, the officer, with his stalwart form and slight swagger, made a fine picture of a guardian of the peace. The vicinity was one that kept early hours. Now and then you might see the lights of a cigar store or of an all-night lunch counter; but the majority of the doors belonged to business places that had long since been closed.

When about midway of a certain block the policeman suddenly slowed his walk. In the doorway of a darkened hardware store a man leaned, with an unlighted cigar in his mouth. As the policeman walked up to him the man spoke up quickly.

"It's all right, officer," he said, reassuringly. "I'm just waiting for a friend. It's an appointment made twenty years ago. Sounds a little funny to you, doesn't it? Well, I'll explain if you'd like to make certain it's all straight. About that long ago there used to be a restaurant where this store stands — 'Big Joe' Brady's restaurant."

"Until five years ago," said the policeman. "It was torn down then."

The man in the doorway struck a match and lit his cigar. The light showed a pale, square-jawed face with keen eyes, and a little white scar near his right eyebrow. His scarfpin was a large diamond, oddly set.

"Twenty years ago to-night," said the man, "I dined here at 'Big Joe' Brady's with Jimmy Wells, my best chum, and the finest chap in the world. He and I were raised here in New York, just like two brothers, together. I was eighteen and Jimmy was twenty. The next morning I was to start for the West to make my fortune. You couldn't have dragged Jimmy out of New York; he thought it was the only place on earth. Well, we agreed that night that we would meet here again exactly twenty years from that date and time, no matter what our conditions might be or from what distance we might have to come. We figured that in twenty years each of us ought to have our destiny worked out and our fortunes made, whatever they were going to be."

"It sounds pretty interesting," said the policeman. "Rather a long time between meets, though, it seems to me. Haven't you heard from your friend since you left?"

"Well, yes, for a time we corresponded," said the other. "But after a year or two we lost track of each other. You see, the West is a pretty big proposition, and I kept hustling around over it pretty lively. But I know Jimmy will meet me here if he's alive, for he always was the truest, stanchest old chap in the world. He'll never forget. I came a thousand miles to stand in this door to-night, and it's worth it if my old partner turns up."

The waiting man pulled out a handsome watch, the lids of it set with small diamonds.

"Three minutes to ten," he announced. "It was exactly ten o'clock when we parted here at the restaurant door."

"Did pretty well out West, didn't you?" asked the policeman.

"You bet! I hope Jimmy has done half as well. He was a kind of plodder, though, good fellow as he was. I've had to compete with some of the sharpest wits going to get my pile. A man gets in a groove in New York. It takes the West to put a razor-edge on him."

The policeman twirled his club and took a step or two.

"I'll be on my way. Hope your friend comes around all right. Going to call time on him sharp?"

"I should say not!" said the other. "I'll give him half an hour at least. If Jimmy is alive on earth he'll be here by that time. So long, officer."

"Good-night, sir," said the policeman, passing on along his beat, trying doors as he went.

There was now a fine, cold drizzle falling, and the wind had risen from its uncertain puffs into a steady blow. The few foot passengers astir in that quarter hurried dismally and silently along with coat collars turned high and pocketed hands. And in the door of the hardware store the man who had come a thousand miles to fill an appointment, uncertain almost to absurdity, with the friend of his youth, smoked his cigar and waited.

About twenty minutes he waited, and then a tall man in a long overcoat, with collar turned up to his ears, hurried across from the opposite side of the street. He went directly to the waiting man.

"Is that you, Bob?" he asked, doubtfully.

"Is that you, Jimmy Wells?" cried the man in the door.

"Bless my heart!" exclaimed the new arrival, grasping both the other's hands with his own. "It's Bob, sure as fate. I was certain I'd find you here if you were still in existence. Well, well, well! — twenty years is a long time. The old restaurant's gone, Bob; I wish it had lasted, so we could have had another dinner there. How has the West treated you, old man?"

"Bully; it has given me everything I asked it for. You've changed lots, Jimmy. I never thought you were so tall by two or three inches."

"Oh, I grew a bit after I was twenty."

"Doing well in New York, Jimmy?"

"Moderately. I have a position in one of the city departments. Come on, Bob; we'll go around to a place I know of, and have a good long talk about old times."

The two men started up the street, arm in arm. The man from the West, his egotism enlarged by success, was beginning

to outline the history of his career. The other, submerged in his overcoat, listened with interest.

At the corner stood a drug store, brilliant with electric lights. When they came into this glare each of them turned simultaneously to gaze upon the other's face.

The man from the West stopped suddenly and released his arm.

"You're not Jimmy Wells," he snapped. "Twenty years is a long time, but not long enough to change a man's nose from a Roman to a pug."

"It sometimes changes a good man into a bad one," said the tall man. "You've been under arrest for ten minutes, 'Silky' Bob. Chicago thinks you may have dropped over our way and wires us she wants to have a chat with you. Going quietly, are you? That's sensible. Now, before we go to the station here's a note I was asked to hand to you. You may read it here at the window. It's from Patrolman Wells."

The man from the West unfolded the little piece of paper handed him. His hand was steady when he began to read, but it trembled a little by the time he had finished. The note was rather short.

Bob: I was at the appointed place on time. When you struck the match to light your cigar I saw it was the face of the man wanted in Chicago. Somehow I couldn't do it myself, so I went around and got a plain clothes man to do the job.

JIMMY.

Assignment: gave classes 15 minutes (in class) to write their personal reactions to the ending of the story (no grade; credit only).

THE SCULPTOR'S FUNERAL

WILLA CATHER

A group of the townspeople stood on the station siding of a little Kansas town, awaiting the coming of the night train, which was already twenty minutes overdue. The snow had fallen thick over everything; in the pale starlight the line of bluffs across the wide, white meadows south of the town made soft, smoke-colored curves against the clear sky. The men on the siding stood first on one foot and then on the other, their hands thrust deep into their trousers pockets, their overcoats open, their shoulders screwed up with the cold; and they glanced from time to time toward the southeast, where the railroad track wound along the river shore. They conversed in low tones and moved about restlessly, seeming uncertain as to what was expected of them. There was but one of the company who looked as if he knew exactly why he was there, and he kept conspicuously apart; walking to the far end of the platform, returning to the station door, then pacing up the track again, his chin sunk in the high collar of his overcoat, his burly shoulders drooping forward, his gait heavy and dogged. Presently he was approached by a tall, spare, grizzled man clad in a faded Grand Army suit, who shuffled out from the group and advanced with a certain deference, craning his neck forward until his back made the angle of a jackknife three-quarters open.

"I reckon she's a-goin' to be pretty late again tonight, Jim," he remarked in a squeaky falsetto. "S'pose it's the snow?"

"I don't know," responded the other man with a shade of annoyance, speaking from out an astonishing cataract of red beard that grew fiercely and thickly in all directions.

The spare man shifted the quill toothpick he was chewing to the other side of his mouth. "It ain't likely that anybody from the East will come with the corpse, I s'pose," he went on reflectively.

"I don't know," responded the other, more curtly than before.

"It's too bad he didn't belong to some lodge or other. I like an order funeral myself. They seem more appropriate for people of some reputation," the spare man continued, with an ingratiating concession in his shrill voice, as he carefully placed his toothpick in his vest pocket. He always carried the flag at the G. A. R. funerals in the town.

The heavy man turned on his heel without replying and walked up the siding. The spare man rejoined the uneasy group. "Jim's ez full ez a tick, ez ushel," he commented commiseratingly.

Just then a distant whistle sounded, and there was a shuffling of feet on the platform. A number of lanky boys, of all ages, appeared as suddenly and slimily as eels wakened by the crack of thunder; some came from the waiting room, where they had been warming themselves by the red stove, or half asleep on the slat benches; others uncoiled themselves from baggage trucks or slid out of express wagons. Two clambered down from the driver's seat of a hearse that stood backed up against the siding. They straightened their stooping shoulders and lifted their heads, and a flash of momentary animation kindled their dull eyes at that cold, vibrant scream, the world-wide call for men. It stirred them like the note of a trumpet; just as it had often stirred the man who was coming home tonight, in his boyhood.

The night express shot, red as a rocket, from out the eastward marsh lands and wound along the river shore under the long lines of shivering poplars that sentineled the meadows, the escaping steam hanging in gray masses against the pale sky and blotting out the Milky Way. In a moment the red glare from the headlight streamed up the snow-covered track before the siding and glittered on the wet, black rails. The burly man with the disheveled red beard walked swiftly up the platform toward the approaching train, uncovering his head as he went. The group of men behind him hesitated, glanced questioningly at one another, and awkwardly followed his example. The train stopped, and the crowd shuffled up to the express car just as the door was thrown open, the man in the G. A. R. suit thrusting his head forward with curiosity. The express messenger appeared in the doorway, accompanied by a young man in a long ulster and traveling cap.

"Are Mr. Merrick's friends here?" inquired the young man.

The group on the platform swayed uneasily. Philip Phelps, the banker, responded with dignity: "We have come to take charge of the body. Mr. Merrick's father is very feeble and can't be about."

"Send the agent out here," growled the express messenger, "and tell the operator to lend a hand."

The coffin was got out of its rough box and down on the snowy platform. The townspeople drew back enough to make room for it and then formed a close semicircle about it, looking curiously at the palm leaf which lay across the black cover. No one said anything. The baggage man stood by his truck, waiting to get at the trunks. The engine panted heavily, and the fireman dodged in and out among the wheels with his yellow torch and long oil can, snapping the spindle boxes. The young Bostonian, one of the dead sculptor's pupils who had come with the body, looked about him helplessly. He turned to the banker, the only one of that black, uneasy, stoop-shouldered group who seemed enough of an individual to be addressed.

"None of Mr. Merrick's brothers are here?" he asked, uncertainly.

The man with the red beard for the first time stepped up and joined the others. "No, they have not come yet; the family is scattered. The body will be taken directly to the house." He stooped and took hold of one of the handles of the coffin.

"Take the long hill road up, Thompson; it will be easier on the horses," called the liveryman as the undertaker snapped the door of the hearse and prepared to mount to the driver's seat.

Laird, the red-bearded lawyer, turned again to the stranger. "We didn't know whether there would be anyone with him or not," he explained. "It's a long walk, so you'd better go up in the hack." He pointed to a single battered conveyance, but the young man replied stiffly: "Thank you, but I think I will go up with the hearse. If you don't object," turning to the undertaker, "I'll ride with you."

They clambered up over the wheels and drove off in the starlight up the long, white hill toward the town. The lamps in the still village were shining from under the low, snow-burdened roofs; and beyond, on every side, the plains reached out into emptiness, peaceful and wide as the soft sky itself, and wrapped in a tangible, white silence.

When the hearse backed up to a wooden sidewalk before a naked, weather-beaten frame house, the same composite, ill-defined group that had stood upon the station siding was huddled about the gate. The front yard was an icy swamp, and a couple of warped planks, extending from the sidewalk to the door, made a sort of rickety footbridge. The gate hung on one hinge, and was opened wide with difficulty. Steavens, the young stranger, noticed that something black was tied to the knob of the front door.

The grating sound made by the casket, as it was drawn from the hearse, was answered by a scream from the house; the front door was wrenched open, and a tall, corpulent woman rushed out bareheaded into the snow and flung herself upon the coffin, shrieking: "My boy, my boy! And this is how you've come home to me!"

As Steavens turned away and closed his eyes with a shudder of unutterable repulsion, another woman, also tall, but flat and angular, dressed entirely in black, darted out of the house and caught Mrs. Merrick by the shoulders, crying sharply: "Come, come, Mother; you mustn't go on like this!" Her tone changed to one of obsequious solemnity as she turned to the banker. "The parlor is ready, Mr. Phelps."

The bearers carried the coffin along the narrow boards, while the undertaker ran ahead with the coffin-rests. They bore it into a large, unheated room that smelled of dampness and disuse and furniture polish, and set it down under a hanging lamp ornamented with jingling glass prisms and before a "Rogers group" of John Alden and Priscilla, wreathed with smilax. Henry Steavens stared about him with the sickening conviction that there had been a mistake and that he had somehow arrived at the wrong destination. He looked at the clover-green Brussels, the fat plush upholstery, among the hand-painted china plaques and panels and vases, for some mark of identification — for something that might once conceivably have belonged to Harvey Merrick. It was not until he recognized his friend in the crayon portrait of a little boy in kilts and curls, hanging above the piano, that he felt willing to let any of these people approach the coffin.

"Take the lid off, Mr. Thompson. Let me see my boy's face," wailed the elder woman between her sobs. This time Steavens looked fearfully, almost beseechingly into her face, red and swollen under its masses of strong, black, shiny hair. He flushed, dropped his eyes, and then, almost incredulously, looked again. There was a kind of power about her face — a kind of brutal handsomeness, even; but it was scarred and furrowed by violence, and so colored and coarsened by fiercer passions that grief seemed never to have laid a gentle finger there. The long nose was distended and knobbed at the end, and there were deep lines on either side of it; her heavy black brows almost met across her forehead, her teeth were large and square and set far apart — teeth that could tear. She filled the room; the men were obliterated, seemed tossed about like twigs in an angry water, and even Steavens felt himself being drawn into the whirlpool.

The daughter — the tall, raw-boned woman in crepe, with a mourning comb in her hair which curiously lengthened her long face — sat stiffly upon the sofa, her hands, conspicuous for their large knuckles, folded in her lap, her mouth and eyes drawn down, solemnly awaiting the opening of the coffin. Near the door stood a mulatto woman, evidently a servant in the house, with a timid bearing and an emaciated face pitifully sad and gentle. She was weeping silently, the corner of her calico apron lifted to her eyes, occasionally suppressing a long, quivering sob. Steavens walked over and stood beside her.

Feeble steps were heard on the stairs, and an old man, tall and frail, odorous of pipe smoke, with shaggy, unkempt gray hair and a dingy beard, tobacco-stained about the mouth, entered uncertainly. He went slowly up to the coffin and stood rolling a blue cotton handkerchief between his hands, seeming so pained and embarrassed by his wife's orgy of grief that he had no consciousness of anything else.

"There, there, Annie, dear, don't take on so," he quavered timidly, putting out a shaking hand and awkwardly patting her elbow. She turned and sank upon his shoulder with such violence that he tottered a little. He did not even glance toward the coffin, but continued to look at her with a dull, frightened, appealing expression, as a spaniel looks at the whip. His sunken cheeks slowly reddened and burned with miserable shame. When his wife rushed from the room, her daughter strode after her with set lips. The servant stole up to the coffin, bent over it for a moment, and then slipped away to the kitchen, leaving Steavens, the lawyer, and the father to themselves. The old man stood looking down at his dead son's face. The sculptor's splendid head seemed even more noble in its rigid stillness than in life. The dark hair had crept down upon the wide forehead; the face seemed strangely long, but in it there was not that repose we expect to find in the faces of the dead. The brows were so drawn that there were two deep lines above the beaked nose, and the chin was thrust forward defiantly. It was as though the strain of life had been so sharp and bitter that death could not at once relax the tension and smooth the countenance into perfect peace — as though he were still guarding something precious, which might even yet be wrested from him.

The old man's lips were working under his stained beard. He turned to the lawyer with timid deference: "Phelps and the rest are comin' back to set up with Harve, ain't they?" he asked. "Thank 'ee, Jim, thank 'ee." He brushed the hair back gently from his son's forehead. "He was a good boy, Jim; always a good boy. He was ez gentle ez a child and kindest of 'em all — only we didn't none of us ever onderstand him." The tears trickled slowly down his beard and dropped upon the sculptor's coat.

"Martin! Martin! Oh, Martin! come here," his wife wailed from the top of the stairs. The old man started timorously: "Yes, Annie, I'm coming." He turned away, hesitated, stood for a moment in miserable indecision; then reached back and patted the dead man's hair softly, and stumbled from the room.

"Poor old man, I didn't think he had any tears left. Seems as if his eyes would have gone dry long ago. At his age nothing cuts very deep," remarked the lawyer.

Something in his tone made Steavens glance up. While the mother had been in the room, the young man had scarcely seen anyone else; but now, from the moment he first glanced into Jim Laird's florid face and bloodshot eyes, he knew that he had found what he had been heartsick at not finding before — the feeling, the understanding that must exist in someone, even here.

The man was red as his beard, with features swollen and blurred by dissipation, and a hot, blazing blue eye. His face was strained — that of a man who is controlling himself with difficulty — and he kept plucking at his beard with a sort of fierce resentment. Steavens, sitting by the window, watched him turn down the glaring lamp, still its jangling pendants with an angry gesture, and then stand with his hands locked behind him, staring down into the master's face. He could not help wondering what link there had been between the porcelain vessel and so sooty a lump of potter's clay.

From the kitchen an uproar was sounding; when the dining-room door opened, the import of it was clear. The mother was abusing the maid for having forgotten to make the dressing for the chicken salad which had been prepared for the watchers. Steavens had never heard anything in the least like it; it was injured, emotional, dramatic abuse, unique and masterly in its excruciating cruelty, as violent and unrestrained as had been her grief of twenty minutes before. With a shudder of disgust the lawyer went into the dining room and closed the door into the kitchen.

"Poor Roxy's getting it now," he remarked when he came back. "The Merricks took her out of the poorhouse years ago; and if her loyalty would let her, I guess the poor old thing could tell tales that would curdle your blood. She's the mulatto woman who was standing in here a while ago, with her apron to her eyes. The old woman is a fury; there never was anybody like her. She made Harvey's life a hell for him when he lived at home; he was so sick ashamed of it. I never could see how he kept himself sweet."

"He was wonderful," said Steavens slowly, "wonderful; but until tonight I have never known how wonderful."

"That is the eternal wonder of it, anyway; that it can come even from such a dung heap as this," the lawyer cried, with a sweeping gesture which seemed to indicate much more than the four walls within which they stood.

"I think I'll see whether I can get a little air. The room is so close I am beginning to feel rather faint," murmured Steavens, struggling with one of the windows. The sash was stuck, however, and would not yield, so he sat down dejectedly and began pulling at his collar. The lawyer came over, loosened the sash with one blow of his red fist and sent the window up a few inches. Steavens thanked him, but the nausea which had been gradually climbing into his throat for the last half hour left him with but one desire — a desperate feeling that he must get away from this place with what was left of Harvey Merrick. Oh, he comprehended well enough now the quiet bitterness of the smile that he had seen so often on his master's lips!

Once when Merrick returned from a visit home, he brought with him a singularly feeling and suggestive bas-relief of a thin, faded old woman, sitting and sewing something pinned to her knee; while a full-lipped, full-blooded little urchin, his trousers held up by a single gallows, stood beside her, impatiently twitching her gown to call her attention to a butterfly he had caught. Steavens, impressed by the tender and delicate modeling of the thin, tired face, had asked him if it were his mother. He remembered the dull flush that had burned up in the sculptor's face.

The lawyer was sitting in a rocking chair beside the coffin, his head thrown back and his eyes closed. Steavens looked at him earnestly, puzzled at the line of the chin, and wondering why a man should conceal a feature of such distinction under that disfiguring shock of beard. Suddenly, as though he felt the young sculptor's keen glance, Jim Laird opened his eyes.

"Was he always a good deal of an oyster?" he asked abruptly. "He was terribly shy as a boy."

"Yes, he was an oyster, since you put it so," rejoined Steavens. "Although he could be very fond of people, he always gave one the impression of being detached. He disliked violent emotion; he was reflective, and rather distrustful of himself — except, of course, as regarded his work. He was sure enough there. He distrusted men pretty thoroughly and women even more, yet somehow without believing ill of them. He was determined, indeed, to believe the best; but he seemed afraid to investigate."

"A burnt dog dreads the fire," said the lawyer grimly, and closed his eyes.

Steavens went on and on, reconstructing that whole miserable boyhood. All this raw, biting ugliness had been the portion of the man whose mind was to become an exhaustless gallery of beautiful impressions — so sensitive that the mere shadow of a poplar leaf flickering against a sunny wall would be etched and held there for ever. Surely, if ever a man had the magic word in his finger tips, it was Merrick. Whatever he touched, he revealed its holiest secret; liberated it from enchantment and restored it to its pristine loveliness. Upon whatever he had come in contact with, he had left a beautiful record of the experience — a sort of ethereal signature; a scent, a sound, a color that was his own.

Steavens understood now the real tragedy of his master's life; neither love nor wine, as many had conjectured, but a blow which had fallen earlier and cut deeper than anything else could have done — a shame not his, and yet so unescapably his, to hide in his heart from his very boyhood. And without — the frontier warfare; the yearning of a boy, cast ashore upon a desert of newness and ugliness and sordidness, for all that is chastened and old, and noble with traditions.

At eleven o'clock the tall, flat woman in black announced that the watchers were arriving, and asked them to "step into the dining room." As Steavens rose, the lawyer said, dryly: "You go on — it'll be a good experience for you. I'm not equal to that crowd tonight; I've had twenty years of them."

As Steavens closed the door after him he glanced back at the lawyer, sitting by the coffin in the dim light, with his chin resting on his hand.

The same misty group that had stood before the door of the express car shuffled into the dining room. In the light of the kerosene lamp they separated and became individuals. The minister, a pale, feeble-looking man with white hair and blond chin whiskers, took his seat beside a small side table and placed his Bible upon it. The Grand Army man sat down behind the stove and tilted his chair back comfortably against the wall, fishing his quill toothpick from his waistcoat pocket. The two bankers, Phelps and Elder, sat off in a corner behind the dinner table, where they could finish their discussion of the new usury law and its effect on chattel security loans. The real-estate agent, an old man with a smiling, hypocritical face, soon joined them. The coal and lumber dealer and the cattle shipper sat on opposite sides of the hard-coal burner, their feet on the nickelwork. Steavens took a book from his pocket and began to read. The talk around him ranged through various topics of local interest while the house was quieting down. When it was clear that the members of the family were in bed, the Grand Army man hitched his shoulders and, untangling his long legs, caught his heels on the rounds of his chair.

"S'pose there'll be a will, Phelps?" he queried in his weak falsetto.

The banker laughed disagreeably, and began trimming his nails with a pearl-handled pocket knife.

"There'll scarcely be any need for one, will there?" he queried in his turn.

The restless Grand Army man shifted his position again, getting his knees still nearer his chin. "Why, the ole man says Harve's done right well lately," he chirped.

The other banker spoke up. "I reckon he means by that Harve ain't asked him to mortgage any more farms lately, so as he could go on with his education."

"Seems like my mind don't reach back to a time when Harve wasn't bein' edycated," tittered the Grand Army man.

There was a general chuckle. The minister took out his handkerchief and blew his nose sonorously. Banker Phelps closed his knife with a snap. "It's too bad the old man's sons didn't turn out better," he remarked with reflective authority. "They never hung together. He spent money enough on Harve to stock a dozen cattle farms, and he might as well have poured it into Sand Creek. If Harve had stayed at home and helped nurse what little they had, and gone into stock on the old man's bottom farm, they might all have been well fixed. But the old man had to trust everything to tenants and was cheated right and left."

"Harve never could have handled stock none," interposed the cattleman. "He hadn't it in him to be sharp. Do you remember when he bought Sander's mules for eight-year-olds, when everybody in town knew that Sander's father-in-law give 'em to his wife for a wedding present eighteen years before, an' they was full-grown mules then?"

The company laughed discreetly, and the Grand Army man rubbed his knees with a spasm of childish delight.

"Harve never was much account for anything practical, and he shore was never fond of work," began the coal and lumber dealer. "I mind the last time he was home; the day he left, when the old man was out to the barn helpin' his hand hitch up to take Harve to the train, and Cal Moots was patchin' up the fence; Harve, he come out on the step and sings out, in his ladylike voice, 'Cal Moots! Cal Moots! please come cord my trunk.' "

"That's Harve for you," approved the Grand Army man. "I kin hear him howlin' yet, when he was a big feller in long pants and his mother used to whale him with a rawhide in the barn for lettin' the cows get foundered in the cornfield when he was drivin' 'em home from pasture. He killed a cow of mine that-a-way onct — a pure Jersey and the best milker I had, an' the old man had to put up for her. Harve, he was watchin' the sun set acrost the marshes when the anamile got away."

"Where the old man made his mistake was in sending the boy East to school," said Phelps, stroking his goatee and speaking in a deliberate, judicial tone. "There was where he got his head full of nonsense. What Harve needed, of all people, was a course in some first-class Kansas City business college."

The letters were swimming before Steavens's eyes. Was it possible that these men did not understand, that the palm on the coffin meant nothing to them? The very name of their town would have remained forever buried in the postal guide had it not been now and again mentioned in the world in connection with Harvey Merrick's. He remembered what his master had said to him on the day of his death, after the congestion of both lungs had shut off any probability of recovery, and the sculptor had asked his pupil to send his body home. "It's not a pleasant place to be lying while the world is moving and doing and bettering," he had said with a feeble smile, "but it rather seems as though we ought to go back to the place we came from, in the end. The townspeople will come in for a look at me; and after they have had their say, I shan't have much to fear from the judgment of God!"

The cattleman took up the comment. "Forty's young for a Merrick to cash in; they usually hang on pretty well. Probably he helped it along with whisky."

"His mother's people were not long-lived, and Harvey never had a robust constitution," said the minister mildly. He would have liked to say more. He had been the boy's Sunday-school teacher and had been fond of him; but he felt that he was not in a position to speak. His own sons had turned out badly, and it was not a year since one of them had made his last trip home in the express car, shot in a gambling house in the Black Hills.

"Nevertheless, there is no disputin' that Harve frequently looked upon the wine when it was red, also variegated, and it shore made an oncommon fool of him," moralized the cattleman.

Just then the door leading into the parlor rattled loudly and everyone started involuntarily, looking relieved when only Jim Laird came out. The Grand Army man ducked his head when he saw the spark in his blue, bloodshot eye. They were all afraid of Jim; he was a drunkard, but he could twist the law to suit his client's needs as no other man in all western Kansas could do, and there were many who tried. The lawyer closed the door behind him, leaned back against it, and folded his arms, cocking his head a little to one side. When he assumed this attitude in the courtroom, ears were always pricked up, as it usually foretold a flood of withering sarcasm.

"I've been with you gentlemen before," he began in a dry, even tone, "when you've sat by the coffins of boys born and raised in this town; and, if I remember rightly, you were never any too well satisfied when you checked them up. What's the matter, anyhow? Why is it that reputable young men are as scarce as millionaires in Sand City? It might almost seem to a stranger that there was, some way, something the matter with your progressive town. Why did Reuben Sayer, the brightest young lawyer you ever turned out, after he had come home from the university as straight as a die, take to drinking and forge a check and shoot himself? Why did Bill Merrit's son die of the shakes in a saloon in Omaha? Why was Mr. Thomas's son, here, shot in a gambling house? Why did young Adams burn his mill to beat the insurance companies and go to the pen?"

The lawyer paused and unfolded his arms, laying one clenched fist quietly on the table. "I'll tell you why. Because you drummed nothing but money and knavery into their ears from the time they wore knickerbockers; because you carped away at them as you've been carping here tonight, holding our friends Phelps and Elder up to them for their models, as our grandfathers held up George Washington and John Adams. But the boys were young, and raw at the business you put them to, and how could they match coppers with such artists as

Phelps and Elder? You wanted them to be successful rascals; they were only unsuccessful ones — that's all the difference. There was only one boy ever raised in this borderland between ruffianism and civilization who didn't come to grief, and you hated Harvey Merrick more for winning out than you hated all the other boys who got under the wheels. Lord! Lord, how you did hate him! Phelps, here, is fond of saying that he could buy and sell us all out any time he's a mind to; but he knew Harve wouldn't have given a . . . for his bank and all his cattle farms put together; and a lack of appreciation, that way, goes hard with Phelps.

"Old Nimrod thinks Harve drank too much; and this from such as Nimrod and me!

"Brother Elder says Harve was too free with the old man's money — fell short in filial consideration, maybe. Well, we can all remember the very tone in which brother Elder swore his own father was a liar, in the county court; and we all know that the old man came out of that partnership with his son as bare as a sheared lamb. But maybe I'm getting personal, and I'd better be driving ahead at what I want to say."

The lawyer paused a moment, squared his heavy shoulders, and went on: "Harvey Merrick and I went to school together, back East. We were dead in earnest, and we wanted you all to be proud of us some day. We meant to be great men. Even I, and I haven't lost my sense of humor, gentlemen, I meant to be a great man. I came back here to practice, and I found you didn't in the least want me to be a great man. You wanted me to be a shrewd lawyer — oh, yes! Our veteran here wanted me to get him an increase of pension, because he had dyspepsia; Phelps wanted a new county survey that would put the widow Wilson's little bottom farm inside his south line; Elder wanted to lend money at five per cent a month, and get it collected; and Stark here wanted to wheedle old women up in Vermont into investing their annuities in real-estate mortgages that are not worth the paper they are written on. Oh, you needed me hard enough, and you'll go on needing me!

"Well, I came back here and became the . . . shyster you wanted me to be. You pretend to have some sort of respect for me; and yet you'll stand up and throw mud at Harvey Merrick, whose soul you couldn't dirty and whose hands you couldn't tie. Oh, you're a discriminating lot of Christians! There have been times when the sight of Harvey's name in some Eastern paper has made me hang my head like a whipped dog; and, again, times when I liked to think of him off there in the world, away from all this hog-wallow, climbing the big, clean up-grade he'd set for himself.

"And we? Now that we've fought and lied and sweated and stolen, and hated as only the disappointed strugglers in a bitter, dead little Western town know how to do, what have we got to show for it? Harvey Merrick wouldn't have given one sunset over your marshes for all you've got put together, and you know it. It's not for me to say why, in the inscrutable wisdom of God, a genius should ever have been called from this place of hatred and bitter waters; but I want this Boston man to know that the drivel he's been hearing here tonight is the only tribute any truly great man could have from such a lot of sick, side-tracked, burnt-dog, land-poor sharks as the here-present financiers of Sand City—upon which town may God have mercy!"

The lawyer thrust out his hand to Steavens as he passed him, caught up his overcoat in the hall, and had left the house before the Grand Army man had had time to lift his ducked head and crane his long neck about at his fellows.

Next day Jim Laird was drunk and unable to attend the funeral services. Steavens called twice at his office, but was compelled to start East without seeing him. He had a presentiment that he would hear from him again, and left his address on the lawyer's table; but if Laird found it, he never acknowledged it. The thing in him that Harvey Merrick had loved must have gone underground with Harvey Merrick's coffin; for it never spoke again, and Jim got the cold he died of driving across the Colorado mountains to defend one of Phelps's sons who had got into trouble out there by cutting government timber.

Assignment: see teacher's manual – page 19 (bottom) – one about obituaries.

Read: 4/22/87, 4/27/88, 6/16/92, 6/22/93, 1/27/98

Read: 4/28/86,

Due: 1-28-85

TO BUILD A FIRE

JACK LONDON

DAY had broken cold and gray, exceedingly cold and gray, when the man turned aside from the main Yukon trail and climbed the high earth bank, where a dim and little-traveled trail led eastward through the fat spruce timber-land. It was a steep bank, and he paused for breath at the top, excusing the act to himself by looking at his watch. It was nine o'clock. There was no sun or hint of sun, though there was not a cloud in the sky. It was a clear day, and yet there seemed an intangible pall over the face of things, a subtle gloom that made the day dark, and that was due to the absence of sun. This fact did not worry the man. He was used to the lack of sun. It had been days since he had seen the sun, and he knew that a few more days must pass before that cheerful orb, due south, would just peep above the sky line and dip immediately from view.

The man flung a look back along the way he had come. The Yukon lay a mile wide and hidden under three feet of ice. On top of this ice were as many feet of snow. It was all pure white, rolling in gentle undulations where the ice jams of the freeze-up had formed. North and south, as far as his eye could see, it was unbroken white, save for a dark hairline that curved and twisted from around the spruce-covered island to the south, and that curved and twisted away into the north, where it disappeared behind another spruce-covered island. This dark hairline was the trail — the main trail — that led south five hundred miles to the Chilkoot Pass, Dyea, and salt water; and that led north seventy miles to Dawson, and still on to the north a thousand miles to Nulato, and finally to St. Michael on Bering Sea, a thousand miles and half a thousand more.

But all this — the mysterious, far-reaching hairline trail, the absence of sun from the sky, the tremendous cold, and the strangeness and weirdness of it all — made no impression on the man. It was not because he was long used to it. He was a newcomer in the land, a cheechako, and this was his first winter. The trouble with him was that he was without imagination. He was quick and alert in the things of life, but only in the things, and not in the significances. Fifty degrees below zero meant eighty-odd degrees of frost. Such fact impressed him as being cold and uncomfortable, and that was all. It did not lead him to meditate upon his frailty as a creature of temperature, and upon man's frailty in general, able only to live within certain narrow limits of heat and cold, and from there on it did not lead him to the conjectural field of immortality and man's place in the universe. Fifty degrees below zero stood for a bite of frost that hurt and that must be guarded against by the use of mittens, ear flaps, warm moccasins, and thick socks. Fifty degrees below zero was to him just precisely fifty degrees below zero. That there should be anything more to it than that was a thought that never entered his head.

As he turned to go on, he spat speculatively. There was a sharp, explosive crackle that startled him. He spat again. And again, in the air, before it could fall to the snow, the spittle crackled. He knew that at fifty below spittle crackled on the snow, but his spittle had crackled in the air. Undoubtedly it was colder than fifty below — how much colder he did not know. But the temperature did not matter. He was bound for the old claim on the left fork of Henderson Creek, where the boys were already. They had come over across the divide from the Indian Creek country, while he had come the roundabout way to take a look at the possibilities of getting out logs in the spring from the islands in the Yukon. He would be into camp by six o'clock; a bit after dark, it was true, but the boys would be there, a fire would be going, and a hot supper would be ready. As for lunch, he pressed his hand against the protruding bundle under his jacket. It was also under his shirt, wrapped up in a handkerchief and lying against the naked skin. It was the only way to keep the biscuits from freezing. He smiled agreeably to himself as he thought of those biscuits, each cut open and sopped in bacon grease, and each enclosing a generous slice of fried bacon.

He plunged in among the big spruce trees. The trail was faint. A foot of snow had fallen since the last sled had passed over, and he was glad he was without a sled, traveling light. In fact, he carried nothing but the lunch wrapped in the handkerchief. He was surprised, however, at the cold. It certainly was cold, he concluded, as he rubbed his numb nose and cheekbones with his mittened hand. He was a warm-whiskered man, but the hair on his face did not protect the high cheekbones and the eager nose that thrust itself aggressively into the frosty air.

At the man's heels trotted a dog, a big native husky, the proper wolf dog, gray-coated and without any visible or temperamental difference from its brother, the wild wolf. The animal was depressed by the tremendous cold. It knew that it was no time for traveling. Its instinct told it a truer tale than was told to the man by the man's judgment. In reality, it was not merely colder than fifty below zero; it was colder than sixty below, than seventy below. It was seventy-five below zero. Since the freezing point is thirty-two above zero; it meant that one hundred and seven degrees of frost obtained. The dog did not know anything about thermometers. Possibly in its brain there was no sharp consciousness of a condition of very cold such as was in the man's brain. But the brute had its instinct. It experienced a vague but menacing apprehension that subdued it and made it slink along at the man's heels and that made it question eagerly every unwonted movement of the man, as if expecting him to go into camp or to seek shelter somewhere and build a fire. The dog had learned fire, and it wanted fire, or else to burrow under the snow and cuddle its warmth away from the air.

The frozen moisture of its breathing had settled on its fur in a fine powder of frost, and especially were its jowls, muzzle, and eyelashes whitened by its crystaled breath. The man's red beard and mustache were likewise frosted, but more solidly, the deposit taking the form of ice and increasing with every warm, moist breath he exhaled. Also, the man was chewing tobacco, and the muzzle of ice held his lips so rigidly that he was unable to clear his chin when he expelled the juice. The result was that a crystal beard of the color and solidity of amber was increasing its length on his chin. If he fell down it would shatter itself, like glass, into brittle fragments. But he did not mind the appendage. It was the penalty all tobacco chewers paid in that country, and he had been out before in two cold snaps. They had not been so cold as this, he knew, but by the spirit thermometer at Sixty Mile he knew they had been registered at fifty below and at fifty-five.

He held on through the level stretch of woods for several miles, crossed a wide flat, and dropped down a bank to the frozen bed of a small stream. This was Henderson Creek, and he knew he was ten miles from the forks. He looked at his watch. It was ten o'clock. He was making four miles an hour, and he calculated that he would arrive at the forks at half-past twelve. He decided to celebrate that event by eating his lunch there.

The dog dropped in again at his heels, with a tail drooping discouragement, as the man swung along the creek bed. The furrow of the old sled trail was plainly visible, but a dozen inches of snow covered the marks of the last runners. In a month no man had come up or down that silent creek. The man held steadily on. He was not much given to thinking, and just then particularly he had nothing to think about save that he would eat lunch at the forks and that at six o'clock he would be in camp with the boys. There was nobody to talk to; and, had there been, speech would have been impossible because of the ice muzzle on his mouth. So he continued monotonously to chew tobacco and to increase the length of his amber beard.

Once in a while the thought reiterated itself that it was very cold and that he had never experienced such cold. As he walked along he rubbed his cheekbones and nose with the back of his mittened hand. He did this automatically, now and again changing hands. But rub as he would, the instant he stopped his cheekbones went numb, and the following instant the end of his nose went numb. He was sure to frost his cheeks; he knew that, and experienced a pang of regret that he had not devised a nose strap of the sort Bud wore in cold snaps. Such a strap passed across the cheeks, as well, and saved them. But it didn't matter much, after all. What were frosted cheeks? A bit painful, that was all; they were never serious.

Empty as the man's mind was of thought, he was keenly observant, and he noticed the changes in the creek, the curves and bends and timber jams, and always he sharply noted where he placed his feet. Once, coming around a bend, he shied abruptly, like a startled horse, curved away from the place where he had been walking, and retreated several paces back along the trail. The creek, he knew, was frozen clear to the bottom — no creek could contain water in that arctic winter — but he knew also that there were springs that bubbled out from the hillsides and ran along under the snow and on top of the ice of the creek. He knew that the coldest snaps never froze these springs, and he knew likewise their danger. They were traps. They hid pools of water under the snow that might be three inches deep, or three feet. Sometimes a skin of ice half an inch thick covered them, and in turn was covered by the snow. Sometimes there were alternate layers of water and ice skin, so that when one broke through he kept on breaking through for a while, sometimes wetting himself to the waist.

That was why he had shied in such panic. He had felt the give under his feet and heard the crackle of a snow-hidden ice skin. And to get his feet wet in such a temperature meant trouble and danger. At the very least it meant delay, for he would be forced to stop and build a fire, and under its protection to bare his feet while he dried his socks and moccasins. He stood and studied the creek bed and its banks, and decided that the flow of water came from the right. He reflected a while, rubbing his nose and cheeks, then skirted to the left, stepping gingerly and testing the footing for each step. Once clear of the danger, he took a fresh chew of tobacco and swung along at his four-mile gait.

In the course of the next two hours he came upon several similar traps. Usually the snow above the hidden pools had a sunken, candied appearance that advertised the danger. Once again, however, he had a close call; and once, suspecting danger, he compelled the dog to go on in front. The dog did not want to go. It hung back until the man shoved it forward, and then it went quickly across the white, unbroken surface. Suddenly it broke through, floundered to one side; and got away to firmer footing. It had wet its forefeet and legs, and almost immediately the water that clung to it turned to ice. It made quick efforts to lick the ice off its legs, then dropped down in the snow and began to bite out the ice that had formed between the toes. This was a matter of instinct. To permit the ice to remain would mean sore feet. It did not know this. It merely obeyed the mysterious prompting that arose from the deep crypts of its being. But the man knew, having achieved a judgment on the subject, and he removed the mitten from his right hand and helped tear out the ice particles. He did not expose his fingers more than a minute, and was astonished at the swift numbness that smote them. It certainly was cold. He pulled on the mitten hastily, and beat the hand savagely across his chest.

At twelve o'clock the day was at its brightest. Yet the sun was too far south on its winter journey to clear the horizon. The bulge of the earth intervened between it and Henderson Creek, where the man walked under a clear sky at noon and cast no shadow. At half-past twelve, to the minute, he arrived at the forks of the creek. He was pleased at the speed he had made. If he kept it up, he would certainly be with the boys by six. He unbuttoned his jacket and shirt and drew forth his lunch. The action consumed no more than a quarter of a minute, yet in that brief moment the numbness laid hold of the exposed fingers. He did not put the mitten on, but, instead, struck the fingers a dozen sharp smashes against his leg. Then he sat down on a snow-covered log to eat. The sting that followed upon the striking of his fingers against his leg ceased so quickly that he was startled. He had had no chance to take a bite of biscuit. He struck the fingers repeatedly and returned them to the mitten, baring the other hand for the purpose of eating. He tried to take a mouthful, but the ice muzzle prevented. He had forgotten to build a fire and thaw out. He chuckled at his foolishness, and as he chuckled he noted the numbness creeping into the exposed fingers. Also he noted that the stinging which had first come to his toes when he sat down was already passing away. He wondered whether the toes were warm or numb. He moved them inside the moccasins and decided that they were numb.

He pulled the mitten on hurriedly and stood up. He was a bit frightened. He stamped up and down until the stinging returned into the feet. It certainly was cold, was his thought. That man from Sulfur Creek had spoken the truth when telling how cold it sometimes got in the country. And he had laughed at him at the time! That showed one must not be too sure of things. There was no mistake about it, it *was* cold. He strode up and down, stamping his feet and threshing his arms, until reassured by the returning warmth. Then he got out matches and proceeded to make a fire. From the undergrowth, where high water of the previous spring had lodged a supply of seasoned twigs, he got his firewood. Working carefully from a small beginning, he soon had a roaring fire, over which he thawed the ice from his face and in the protection of which he ate his biscuits. For the moment the cold of space was outwitted. The dog took satisfaction in the fire, stretching out close enough for warmth and far enough away to escape being singed.

When the man had finished, he filled his pipe and took his comfortable time over a smoke. Then he pulled on his mittens, settled the ear flaps of his cap firmly about his ears, and took the creek trail up the left fork. The dog was disappointed and yearned back toward the fire. This man did not know cold. Possibly all the generations of his ancestry had been ignorant of cold, of real cold, of cold one hundred and seven degrees below freezing point. But the dog knew; all its ancestry knew, and it had inherited the knowledge. And it knew that it was not good to walk abroad in such fearful cold. It was the time to lie snug in a hole in the snow and wait for a curtain of cloud to be drawn across the face of outer space whence this cold came. On the other hand, there was no keen intimacy between the dog and the man. The one was the toil-slave of the other, and the only caresses it had ever received were the caresses of the whiplash and of harsh and menacing throat sounds that threatened the whiplash. So the dog made no effort to communicate its apprehension to the man. It was not concerned in the welfare of the man; it was for its own sake that it yearned back toward the fire. But the man whistled, and spoke to it with the sound of whiplashes, and the dog swung in at the man's heels and followed after.

The man took a chew of tobacco and proceeded to start a new amber beard. Also, his moist breath quickly powdered with white his mustache, eyebrows, and lashes. There did not seem to be so many springs on the left fork of the Henderson, and for half an hour the man saw no signs of any. And then it happened. At a place where there were no signs, where the soft, unbroken snow seemed to advertise solidity beneath, the man broke through. It was not deep. He wet himself halfway to the knees before he floundered out to the firm crust.

He was angry, and cursed his luck aloud. He had hoped to get into camp with the boys at six o'clock, and this would delay him an hour, for he would have to build a fire and dry out his footgear. This was imperative at that low temperature — he knew that much; and he turned aside to the bank, which he climbed. On top, tangled in the underbrush about the trunks of several small spruce trees, was a high-water deposit of dry firewood — sticks and twigs, principally, but also larger portions of seasoned branches and fine, dry, last year's grasses. He threw down several large pieces on top of the snow. This served for a foundation and prevented the young flame from drowning itself in the snow it otherwise would melt. The flame he got by touching a match to a small shred of birch bark that he took from his pocket. This burned even more readily than paper. Placing it on the foundation, he fed the young flame with wisps of dry grass and with the tiniest dry twigs.

He worked slowly and carefully, keenly aware of his danger. Gradually, as the flame grew stronger, he increased the size of the twigs with which he fed it. He squatted in the snow, pulling the twigs out from their entanglement in the brush and feeding directly to the flame. He knew there must be no failure. When it is seventy-five below zero a man must not fail in his first attempt to build a fire — that is, if his feet are wet. If his feet are dry, and he fails, he can run along the trail for half a mile and restore his circulation. But the circulation of wet and freezing feet cannot be restored by running when it is seventy-five below. No matter how fast he runs, the wet feet will freeze the harder.

All this the man knew. The old-timer on Sulfur Creek had told him about it the previous fall, and now he was appreciating the advice. Already all sensation had gone out of his feet. To build the fire, he had been forced to remove his mittens, and the fingers had quickly gone numb. His pace of four miles an hour had kept his heart pumping blood to the surface of his body and to all the extremities. But the instant he stopped, the action of the pump eased down. The cold of space smote the unprotected tip of the planet, and he, being on that unprotected tip, received the full force of the blow. The blood of his body recoiled before it. The blood was alive, like the dog, and like the dog it wanted to hide away and cover itself up from the fearful cold. So long as he walked four miles an hour, he pumped that blood, willy-nilly, to the surface; but now it ebbed away and sank down into the recesses of his body. The extremities were the first to feel its absence. His wet feet froze the faster, and his exposed fingers numbed the faster, though they had not yet begun to freeze. Nose and cheeks were already freezing, while the skin of all his body chilled as it lost its blood.

But he was safe. Toes and nose and cheeks would be only touched by the frost, for the fire was beginning to burn with strength. He was feeding it with twigs the size of his finger. In another minute he would be able to feed it with branches the size of his wrist, and then he could remove his wet footgear, and, while it dried, he could keep his naked feet warm by the fire, rubbing them at first, of course, with snow. The fire was a success. He was safe. He remembered the advice of the old-timer on Sulfur Creek, and smiled. The old-timer had been very serious in laying down the law that no man must travel alone in the Klondike after fifty below. Well, here he was; he had had the accident; he was alone; and he had saved himself. Those old-timers were rather womanish, some of them, he thought. All a man had to do was to keep his head, and he was all right. Any man who was a man could travel alone. But it was surprising the rapidity with which his cheeks and nose were freezing. And he had not thought his fingers could go lifeless in so short a time. Lifeless they were, for he could scarcely make them move together to grip a twig, and they seemed remote from his body and from him. When he touched a twig he had to look and see whether or not he had hold of it. The wires were pretty well down between him and his finger ends.

All of which counted for little. There was the fire, snapping and crackling and promising life with every dancing flame. He started to untie his moccasins. They were coated with ice; the thick German socks were like sheaths of iron halfway to the knees; and the moccasin strings were like rods of steel all twisted and knotted as by some conflagration. For a moment he tugged with his numb fingers, then, realizing the folly of it, he drew his sheath knife.

But before he could cut the strings it happened. It was his own fault, or, rather, his mistake. He should not have built the fire under the spruce tree. He should have built it in the open. But it had been easier to pull the twigs from the bush and drop them directly on the fire. Now the tree under which he had done this carried a weight of snow on its boughs. No wind had blown for weeks, and each bough was fully freighted. Each time he had pulled a twig he had communicated a slight agitation to the tree — an imperceptible agitation, so far as he was concerned, but an agitation sufficient to bring about the disaster. High up in the tree one bough capsized its load of snow.

This fell on the boughs beneath, capsizing them. This process continued, spreading out and involving the whole tree. It grew like an avalanche, and it descended without warning upon the man and the fire, and the fire was blotted out! Where it had burned was a mantle of fresh and disordered snow.

The man was shocked. It was as though he had just heard his own sentence of death. For a moment he sat and stared at the spot where the fire had been. Then he grew very calm. Perhaps the old-timer on Sulfur Creek was right. If he had only had a trailmate he would have been in no danger now. The trailmate could have built the fire. Well, it was up to him to build the fire over again, and this second time there must be no failure. Even if he succeeded, he would most likely lose some toes. His feet must be badly frozen by now, and there would be some time before the second fire was ready.

Such were his thoughts, but he did not sit and think them. He was busy all the time they were passing through his mind. He made a new foundation for a fire, this time in the open, where no treacherous tree could blot it out. Next he gathered dry grasses and tiny twigs from the high-water flotsam. He could not bring his fingers together to pull them out, but he was able to gather them by the handful. In this way he got many rotten twigs and bits of green moss that were undesirable, but it was the best he could do. He worked methodically, even collecting an armful of the larger branches to be used later when the fire gathered strength. And all the while the dog sat and watched him, a certain yearning wistfulness in its eyes, for it looked upon him as the fire provider, and the fire was slow in coming.

When all was ready, the man reached in his pocket for a second piece of birch bark. He knew the bark was there, and, though he could not feel it with his fingers, he could hear its crisp rustling as he fumbled for it. Try as he would, he could not clutch hold of it. And all the time, in his consciousness, was the knowledge that each instant his feet were freezing. This thought tended to put him in a panic, but he fought against it and kept calm. He pulled on his mittens with his teeth, and threshed his arms back and forth, beating his hands with all his might against his sides. He did this sitting down, and he stood up to do it; and all the while the dog sat in the snow, its wolf brush of a tail curled around warmly over its forefeet, its sharp wolf ears pricked forward intently as it watched the man. And the man, as he beat and threshed with his arms and hands, felt a great surge of envy as he regarded the creature that was warm and secure in its natural covering.

After a time he was aware of the first faraway signals of sensation in his beaten fingers. The faint tingling grew stronger till it evolved into a stinging ache that was excruciating, but which the man hailed with satisfaction. He stripped the mitten from his right hand and fetched forth the birch bark. The exposed fingers were quickly going numb again. Next he brought out his bunch of sulfur matches. But the tremendous cold had already driven the life out of his fingers. In his effort to separate one match from the others, the whole bunch fell in the snow. He tried to pick it out of the snow, but failed. The dead fingers could neither touch nor clutch. He was very careful. He drove the thought of his freezing feet, and nose, and cheeks, out of his mind, devoting his whole soul to the matches. He watched, using the sense of vision in place of that of touch, and when he saw his fingers on each side of the bunch, he closed them — that is, he willed to close them, for the wires were down, and the fingers did not obey. He pulled the mitten on the right hand, and beat it fiercely against his knee. Then, with both mittened hands, he scooped the bunch of matches, along with much snow, into his lap. Yet he was no better off.

After some manipulation he managed to get the bunch between the heels of his mittened hands. In this fashion he carried it to his mouth. The ice crackled and snapped when by a violent effort he opened his mouth. He drew the lower jaw in, curled the upper lip out of the way, and scraped the bunch with his upper teeth in order to separate a match. He succeeded in getting one, which he dropped on his lap. He was no better off. He could not pick it up. Then he devised a way. He picked it up in his teeth and scratched it on his leg. Twenty times he scratched before he succeeded in lighting it. As it flamed he held it with his teeth to the birch bark. But the burning brimstone went up his nostrils and into his lungs, causing him to cough spasmodically. The match fell into the snow and went out.

The old-timer on Sulfur Creek was right, he thought in the moment of controlled despair that ensued: after fifty below, a man should travel with a partner. He beat his hands, but failed in exciting any sensation. Suddenly he bared both hands, removing the mittens with his teeth. He caught the whole bunch between the heels of his hands. His arm muscles, not being frozen, enabled him to press the hand heels tightly against the matches. Then he scratched the bunch along his leg. It flared into flame, seventy sulfur matches at once! There was no wind to blow them out. He kept his head to one side to escape the strangling fumes, and held the blazing bunch to the birch bark. As he so held it, he became aware of sensation in his hand. His flesh was burning. He could smell it. Deep down below the surface he could feel it. The sensation developed into pain that grew acute. And still he endured it, holding the flame of the matches clumsily to the bark that would not light readily because his own burning hands were in the way, absorbing most of the flame.

At last, when he could endure no more, he jerked his hands apart. The blazing matches fell sizzling into the snow, but the birch bark was alight. He began laying dry grasses and the tiniest twigs on the flame. He could not pick and choose, for he had to lift the fuel between the heels of his hands. Small pieces of rotten wood and green moss clung to the twigs, and he bit them off as well as he could with his teeth. He cherished the flame carefully and awkwardly. It meant life, and it must not perish. The withdrawal of blood from the surface of his body now made him begin to shiver, and he grew more awkward. A large piece of green moss fell squarely on the little fire. He tried to poke it out with his fingers, but his shivering frame made him poke too far, and he disrupted the nucleus of the little fire, the burning grasses and tiny twigs separating and scattering. He tried to poke them together again, but, in spite of the tenseness of the effort, his shivering got away with him, and the twigs were hopelessly scattered. Each twig gushed a puff of smoke and went out. The fire provider had failed. As he looked apathetically about him, his eyes chanced on the dog, sitting across the ruins of the fire from him, in the snow, making restless, hunching movements, slightly lifting one forefoot and then the other, shifting its weight back and forth on them with wistful eagerness.

The sight of the dog put a wild idea into his head. He remembered the tale of the man, caught in a blizzard, who killed a steer and crawled inside the carcass, and so was saved. He would kill the dog and bury his hands in the warm body until the numbness went out of them. Then he could build another fire. He spoke to the dog, calling it to him; but in his voice was a strange note of fear that frightened the animal, who had never known the man to speak in such way before. Something was the matter, and its suspicious nature sensed danger — it knew not what danger, but somewhere, somehow, in its brain arose an apprehension of the man. It flattened its ears down at the sound of the man's voice, and its restless, hunching movements and the liftings and shiftings of its forefeet became more pronounced; but it would not come to the man. He got on his hands and knees and crawled toward the dog. This unusual posture again excited suspicion, and the animal sidled mincingly away.

The man sat up in the snow for a moment and struggled for calmness. Then he pulled on his mittens, by means of his teeth, and got upon his feet. He glanced down at first in order to assure himself that he was really standing up, for the absence of sensation in his feet left him unrelated to the earth. His erect position in itself started to drive the webs of suspicion from the dog's mind; and when he spoke peremptorily with the sound of whiplashes in his voice, the dog rendered its customary allegiance and came to him. As it came within reaching distance, the man lost his control. His arms flashed out to the dog, and he experienced genuine surprise when he discovered that his hands could not clutch, that there was neither bend nor feeling in the fingers. He had forgotten for the moment that they were frozen and that they were freezing more and more. All this happened quickly, and before the animal could get away, he encircled its body with his arms. He sat down in the snow, and in this fashion held the dog, while it snarled and whined and struggled.

But it was all he could do, hold its body encircled in his arms and sit there. He realized that he could not kill the dog. There was no way to do it. With his helpless hands he could neither draw nor hold his sheath knife nor throttle the animal. He released it, and it plunged wildly away, with tail between its legs, and still snarling. It halted forty feet away and surveyed him curiously, with ears sharply pricked forward. The man looked down at his hands in order to locate them, and found them hanging on the ends of his arms. It struck him as curious that one should have to use his eyes in order to find out where his hands were. He began threshing his arms back and forth, beating the mittened hands against his sides. He did this for five minutes, violently, and his heart pumped enough blood up to the surface to put a stop to his shivering. But no sensation was aroused in the hands. He had an impression that they hung like weights on the ends of his arms, but when he tried to run the impression down, he could not find it.

A certain fear of death, dull and oppressive, came to him. This fear quickly became poignant as he realized that it was no longer a mere matter of freezing his fingers and toes, or of losing his hands and feet, but that it was a matter of life and death, with the chances against him. This threw him into a panic, and he turned and ran up the creek bed along the old dim trail. The dog joined in behind and kept up with him. He ran blindly, without intention, in fear such as he had never known in his life. Slowly, as he plowed and floundered through the snow, he began to see things again — the banks of the creek, the old timber jams, the leafless aspens, and the sky. The running made him feel better. He did not shiver. Maybe, if he ran on, his feet would thaw out; and, anyway, if he ran far enough, he would reach the camp and the boys. Without doubt he would lose some fingers and toes and some of his face; but the boys would take care of him, and save the rest of him when he got there. And at the same time there was another thought in his mind that said he would never get to the camp and the boys; that it was too many miles away, that the freezing had too great a start on him, and that he would soon be stiff and dead. This thought he kept in the background and refused to consider. Sometimes it pushed itself forward and demanded to be heard, but he thrust it back and strove to think of other things.

It struck him as curious that he could run at all on feet so frozen that he could not feel them when they struck the earth and took the weight of his body. He seemed to himself to skim along above the surface, and to have no connection with the earth. Somewhere he had once seen a winged Mercury, and he wondered if Mercury felt as he felt when skimming over the earth.

His theory of running until he reached camp and the boys had one flaw in it: he lacked the endurance. Several times he stumbled, and finally he tottered, crumpled up, and fell. When he tried to rise, he failed. He must sit and rest, he decided, and next time he would merely walk and keep on going. As he sat and regained his breath, he noted that he was feeling quite warm and comfortable. He was not shivering, and it even seemed that a warm glow had come to his chest and trunk. And yet, when he touched his nose or cheeks, there was no sensation. Running would not thaw them out. Nor would it thaw out his hands and feet. Then the thought came to him that the frozen portions of his body must be extending. He tried to keep this thought down, to forget it, to think of something else; he was aware of the panicky feeling that it caused, and he was afraid of the panic. But the thought asserted itself, and persisted, until it produced a vision of his body totally frozen. This was too much, and he made another wild run along the trail. Once he slowed down to a walk, but the thought of the freezing extending itself made him run again.

And all the time the dog ran with him, at his heels. When he fell down a second time, it curled its tail over its forefeet and sat in front of him, facing him, curiously eager and intent. The warmth and security of the animal angered him, and he cursed it till it flattened down its ears appeasingly. This time the shivering came more quickly upon the man. He was losing in his battle with the frost. It was creeping into his body from all sides. The thought of it drove him on, but he ran no more than a hundred feet, when he staggered and pitched headlong. It was his last panic. When he had recovered his breath and control he sat up and entertained in his mind the conception of meeting death with dignity. However, the conception did not come to him in such terms. His idea of it was that he had been making a fool of himself, running around like a chicken with its head cut off — such was the simile that occurred to him. Well, he was bound to freeze anyway, and he might as well take it decently. With this newfound peace of mind came the first glimmerings of drowsiness. A good idea, he thought, to sleep off to death. It was like taking an anesthetic. Freezing was not so bad as people thought. There were lots worse ways to die.

He pictured the boys finding his body next day. Suddenly he found himself with them, coming along the trail and looking for himself. And, still with them, he came around a turn in the trail and found himself lying in the snow. He did not belong with himself any more, for even then he was out of himself standing with the boys and looking at himself in the snow. It certainly was cold, was his thought. When he got back to the States, he could tell the folks what real cold was. He drifted on from this to a vision of the old-timer on Sulfur Creek. He could see him quite clearly, warm and comfortable, and smoking a pipe.

"You were right, old hoss; you were right," the man mumbled to the old-timer of Sulfur Creek.

Then the man drowsed off into what seemed to him the most comfortable and satisfying sleep he had ever known. The dog sat facing him and waiting. The brief day drew to a close in a long, slow twilight. There were no signs of a fire to be made, and, besides, never in the dog's experience had it known a man to sit like that in the snow and make no fire. As the twilight drew on its eager yearning for the fire mastered it, and with a great lifting and shifting of forefeet, it whined softly, then flattened its ears down in anticipation of being chidden by the man. But the man remained silent. Later, the

dog whined loudly. And still later it crept close to the man and caught the scent of death. This made the animal bristle and back away. A little longer it delayed, howling under the stars that leaped and danced and shone brightly in the cold sky. Then it turned and trotted up the trail in the direction of the camp it knew, where were the other food providers and fire providers.

Assignment: see teacher's manual - page 20 (bottom) - one about the story's ending.

Read: 4/22/87, 4/28/88, 3/2/98

Read: 4/29/86

Due: 2-4-85

SOPHIS-TICATION

SHERWOOD ANDERSON

Sophisticated — not simple or naive; worldly-wise or knowledgeable.

Good descriptive writing . . . many sensory impressions!

IT was early evening of a day in the late fall and the Winesburg County Fair had brought crowds of country people into town. The day had been clear and the night came on warm and pleasant. On the Trunion Pike, where the road after it left town stretched away between berry fields now covered with dry brown leaves, the dust from passing wagons arose in clouds. Children, curled into little balls, slept on the straw scattered on wagon beds. Their hair was full of dust and their fingers black and sticky. The dust rolled away over the fields and the departing sun set it ablaze with colors.

In the main street of Winesburg crowds filled the stores and the sidewalks. Night came on, horses whinnied, the clerks in the stores ran madly about, children became lost and cried lustily, an American town worked terribly at the task of amusing itself.

Pushing his way through the crowds in Main Street, young George Willard concealed himself in the stairway leading to Doctor Reefy's office and looked at the people. With feverish eyes he watched the faces drifting past under the store lights. Thoughts kept coming into his head and he did not want to think. He stamped impatiently on the wooden steps and looked sharply about. "Well, is she going to stay with him all day? Have I done all this waiting for nothing?" he muttered.

George Willard, the Ohio village boy, was fast growing into manhood and new thoughts had been coming into his mind. All that day, amid the jam of people at the Fair, he had gone about feeling lonely. He was about to leave Winesburg to go away to some city where he hoped to get work on a city newspaper and he felt grown up. The mood that had taken possession of him was a thing known to men and unknown to boys. He felt old and a little tired. Memories awoke in him. To his mind his new sense of maturity set him apart, made of him a half-tragic figure. He wanted someone to understand the feeling that had taken possession of him after his mother's death.

There is a time in the life of every boy when he for the first time takes the backward view of life. Perhaps that is the moment when he crosses the line into manhood. The boy is walking through the street of his town. He is thinking of the future and of the figure he will cut in the world. Ambitions and regrets awake within him. Suddenly something happens; he stops under a tree and waits as for a voice calling his name. Ghosts of old things creep into his consciousness; the voices outside of himself whisper a message concerning the limitations of life. From being quite sure of himself and his future he becomes not at all sure. If he be an imaginative boy a door is torn open and for the first time he looks out upon the world, seeing, as though they marched in procession before him, the countless figures of men who before his time have come out of nothingness into the world, lived their lives and again disappeared into nothingness. The sadness of sophistication has come to the boy. With a little gasp he sees himself as merely a leaf blown by the wind through the streets of his village. He knows that in spite of all the stout talk of his fellows he must live and die in uncertainty, a thing blown by the winds, a thing destined like corn to wilt in the sun. He shivers and looks eagerly about. The eighteen years he has lived seem but a moment, a breathing space in the long march of humanity. Already he hears death calling. With all his heart he wants to come close to some other human, touch someone with his hands, be touched by the hand of another. If he prefers that the other be a woman, that is because he believes that a woman will be gentle, that she will understand. He wants, most of all, understanding.

When the moment of sophistication came to George Willard his mind turned to Helen White, the Winesburg banker's daughter. Always he had been conscious of the girl growing into womanhood as he grew into manhood. Once on a summer night when he was eighteen, he had walked with her on a country road and in her presence had given way to an impulse to boast, to make himself appear big and significant in her eyes. Now he wanted to see her for another purpose. He wanted to tell her of the new impulses that had come to him. He had tried to make her think of him as a man when he knew nothing of manhood and now he wanted to be with her and to try to make her feel the change he believed had taken place in his nature.

As for Helen White, she also had come to a period of change. What George felt, she in her young woman's way felt also. She was no longer a girl and hungered to reach into the grace and beauty of womanhood. She had come home from Cleveland, where she was attending college, to spend a day at the Fair. She also had begun to have memories. During the day she sat in the grand-stand with a young man, one of the instructors from the college, who was a guest of her mother's. The young man was of a pedantic turn of mind and she felt at once he would not do for her purpose. At the Fair she was glad to be seen in his company as he was well dressed and a stranger. She knew that the fact of his presence would create an impression. During the day she was happy, but when night came on she began to grow restless. She wanted to drive the instructor away, to get out of his presence. While they sat together in the grand-stand and while the eyes of former schoolmates were upon them, she paid so much attention to her escort that he grew interested. "A scholar needs money. I should marry a woman with money," he mused.

Helen White was thinking of George Willard even as he wandered gloomily through the crowds thinking of her. She remembered the summer evening when they had walked together and wanted to walk with him again. She thought that the months she had spent in the city, the going to theaters and the seeing of great crowds wandering in lighted thoroughfares, had changed her profoundly. She wanted him to feel and be conscious of the change in her nature.

The summer evening together that had left its mark on the memory of both the young man and woman had, when looked at quite sensibly, been rather stupidly spent. They had walked out of town along a country road. Then they had stopped by a fence near a field of young corn and George had taken off his coat and let it hang on his arm. "Well, I've stayed here in Winesburg — yes — I've not yet gone away but I'm growing up," he had said. "I've been reading books and I've been thinking. I'm going to try to amount to something in life.

"Well," he explained, "that isn't the point. Perhaps I'd better quit talking."

The confused boy put his hand on the girl's arm. His voice trembled. The two started to walk back along the road toward town. In his desperation George boasted, "I'm going to be a big man, the biggest that ever lived here in Winesburg," he declared. "I want you to do something, I don't know what. Perhaps it is none of my business. I want you to try to be different from other women. You see the point. It's none of my business I tell you. I want you to be a beautiful woman. You see what I want."

The boy's voice failed and in silence the two came back into town and went along the street to Helen White's house. At the gate he tried to say something impressive. Speeches he had thought out came into his head, but they seemed utterly pointless. "I thought — I used to think — I had it in my mind you would marry Seth Richmond. Now I know you won't," was all he could find to say as she went through the gate and toward the door of her house.

On the warm fall evening as he stood in the stairway and looked at the crowd drifting through Main Street, George thought of the talk beside the field of young corn and was ashamed of the figure he had made of himself. In the street the people surged up and down like cattle confined in a pen. Buggies and wagons almost filled the narrow thoroughfare. A band played and small boys raced along the sidewalk, diving between the legs of men. Young men with shining red faces walked awkwardly about with girls on their arms. In a room above one of the stores, where a dance was to be held, the fiddlers tuned their instruments. The broken sounds floated down through an open window and out across the murmur of voices and the loud blare of the horns of the band. The medley of sounds got on young Willard's nerves. Everywhere, on all sides, the sense of crowding, moving life closed in about him. He wanted to run away by himself and think. "If she wants to stay with that fellow she may. Why should I care? What difference does it make to me?" he growled and went along Main Street and through Hern's Grocery into a side street.

George felt so utterly lonely and dejected that he wanted to weep but pride made him walk rapidly along, swinging his arms. He came to Wesley Moyer's livery barn and stopped in the shadows to listen to a group of men who talked of a race Wesley's stallion, Tony Tip, had won at the Fair during the afternoon. A crowd had gathered in front of the barn and before the crowd walked Wesley, prancing up and down and boasting. He held a whip in his hand and kept tapping the gound. Little puffs of dust arose in the lamplight. " . . ., quit your talking," Wesley exclaimed. "I wasn't afraid, I knew I had 'em beat all the time. I wasn't afraid."

Ordinarily George Willard would have been intensely interested in the boasting of Moyer, the horseman. Now it made him angry. He turned and hurried away along the street. "Old windbag," he sputtered. "Why does he want to be bragging? Why don't he shut up?"

George went into a vacant lot and, as he hurried along, fell over a pile of rubbish. A nail protruding from an empty barrel tore his trousers. He sat down on the ground and swore. With a pin he mended the torn place and then arose and went on. "I'll go to Helen White's house, that's what I'll do. I'll walk right in. I'll say that I want to see her. I'll walk right in and sit down, that's what I'll do," he declared, climbing over a fence and beginning to run.

On the veranda of Banker White's house Helen was restless and distraught. The instructor sat between the mother and daughter. His talk wearied the girl. Although he had also been raised in an Ohio town, the instructor began to put on the airs of the city. He wanted to appear cosmopolitan. "I like the chance you have given me to study the background out of which most of our girls come," he declared. "It was good of you, Mrs. White, to have me down for the day." He turned to Helen and laughed. "Your life is still bound up with the life of this town?" he asked. "There are people here in whom you are interested?" To the girl his voice sounded pompous and heavy.

Helen arose and went into the house. At the door leading to a garden at the back she stopped and stood listening. Her mother began to talk. "There is no one here fit to associate with a girl of Helen's breeding," she said.

Helen ran down a flight of stairs at the back of the house and into the garden. In the darkness she stopped and stood trembling. It seemed to her that the world was full of meaningless people saying words. Afire with eagerness she ran through a garden gate and, turning a corner by the banker's barn, went into a little side street. "George! Where are you, George?" she cried, filled with nervous excitement. She stopped running, and leaned against a tree to laugh hysterically. Along the dark little street came George Willard, still saying words. "I'm going to walk right into her house. I'll go right in and sit down," he declared as he came up to her. He stopped and stared stupidly. "Come on," he said and took hold of her hand. With hanging heads they walked away along the street under the trees. Dry leaves rustled under foot. Now that he had found her George wondered what he had better do and say.

At the upper end of the Fair Ground, in Winesburg, there is a half decayed old grand-stand. It has never been painted and the boards are all warped out of shape. The Fair Ground stands on top of a low hill rising out of the valley of Wine Creek and from the grand-stand one can see at night, over a cornfield, the lights of the town reflected against the sky.

George and Helen climbed the hill to the Fair Ground, coming by the path past Waterworks Pond. The feeling of loneliness and isolation that had come to the young man in the crowded streets of his town was both broken and intensified by the presence of Helen. What he felt was reflected in her.

In youth there are always two forces fighting in people. The warm unthinking little animal struggles against the thing that reflects and remembers, and the older, the more sophisticated thing had possession of George Willard. Sensing his mood, Helen walked beside him filled with respect. When they got to the grand-stand they climbed up under the roof and sat down on one of the long bench-like seats.

There is something memorable in the experience to be had by going into a fair ground that stands at the edge of a Middle Western town on a night after the annual fair has been held. The sensation is one never to be forgotten. On all sides are ghosts, not of the dead, but of living people. Here, during the day just passed, have come the people pouring in from the town and the country around. Farmers with their wives and children and all the people from the hundreds of little frame houses have gathered within these board walls. Young girls have laughed and men with beards have talked of the affairs of their lives. The place has been filled to overflowing with life. It has itched and squirmed with life and now it is night and the life has all gone away. The silence is almost terrifying. One conceals oneself standing silently beside the trunk of a tree and what there is of a reflective tendency in his nature is intensified. One shudders at the thought of the meaninglessness of life while at the same instant, and if the people of the town are his people, one loves life so intensely that tears come into the eyes.

In the darkness under the roof of the grand-stand, George Willard sat beside Helen White and felt very keenly his own insignificance in the scheme of existence. Now that he had come out of town where the presence of the people stirring about, busy with a multitude of affairs, had been so irritating, the irritation was all gone. The presence of Helen renewed and refreshed him. It was as though her woman's hand was assisting him to make some minute readjustment of the machinery of his life. He began to think of the people in the town where he had always lived with something like reverence. He had reverence for Helen. He wanted to love and to be loved by her, but he did not want at the moment to be confused by her womanhood. In the darkness he took hold of her hand and when she crept close put a hand on her shoulder. A wind began to blow and he shivered. With all his strength he tried to hold and to understand the mood that had come upon him. In that high place in the darkness the two oddly sensitive human atoms held each other tightly and waited. In the mind of each was the same thought. "I have come to this lonely place and here is this other," was the substance of the thing felt.

In Winesburg the crowded day had run itself out into the long night of the late fall. Farm horses jogged away along lonely country roads pulling their portion of weary people. Clerks began to bring samples of goods in off the sidewalks and lock the doors of stores. In the Opera House a crowd had gathered to see a show and further down Main Street the fiddlers, their instruments tuned, sweated and worked to keep the feet of youth flying over a dance floor.

In the darkness in the grand-stand Helen White and George Willard remained silent. Now and then the spell that held them was broken and they turned and tried in the dim light to see into each other's eyes. They kissed but that impulse did not last. At the upper end of the Fair Ground a half dozen men worked over horses that had raced during the afternoon. The men had built a fire and were heating kettles of water. Only their legs could be seen as they passed back and forth in the light. When the wind blew the little flames of the fire danced crazily about.

George and Helen arose and walked away into the darkness. They went along a path past a field of corn that had not yet been cut. The wind whispered among the dry corn blades. For a moment during the walk back into town the spell that held them was broken. When they had come to the crest of Waterworks Hill they stopped by a tree and George again put his hands on the girl's shoulders. She embraced him eagerly and then again they drew quickly back from that impulse. They stopped kissing and stood a little apart. Mutual respect grew big in them. They were both embarrassed and to relieve their embarrassment dropped into the animalism of youth. They laughed and began to pull and haul at each other. In some way chastened and purified by the mood they had been in, they became, not man and woman, not boy and girl, but excited little animals.

It was so they went down the hill. In the darkness they played like two splendid young things in a young world. Once, running swiftly forward, Helen tripped George and he fell. He squirmed and shouted. Shaking with laughter, he rolled down the hill. Helen ran after him. For just a moment she stopped in the darkness. There is no way of knowing what woman's thoughts went through her mind but, when the bottom of the hill was reached and she came up to the boy, she took his arm and walked beside him in dignified silence. For some reason they could not have explained they had both got from their silent evening together the thing needed. Man or boy, woman or girl, they had for a moment taken hold of the thing that makes the mature life of men and women in the modern world possible.

Assignment: see teacher's manual – pages 21 & 22 – form own questions that students will respond to (from questions suggested on these pages).

(1.) Is there any truth in this story? If so, describe it.
(2.) Write a brief description of the future for George & Helen.
(3.) Go through the story & find details of the setting that provide good pictorial representations of the town.

Answer 2 of the 3

ROPE

KATHERINE ANNE PORTER

ON the third day after they moved to the country he came walking back from the village carrying a basket of groceries and a twenty-four-yard coil of rope. She came out to meet him, wiping her hands on her green smock. Her hair was tumbled, her nose was scarlet with sunburn; he told her that already she looked like a born country woman. His gray flannel shirt stuck to him, his heavy shoes were dusty. She assured him he looked like a rural character in a play.

Had he brought the coffee? She had been waiting all day long for coffee. They had forgot it when they ordered at the store the first day.

Gosh, no, he hadn't. Lord, now he'd have to go back. Yes, he would if it killed him. He thought, though, he had everything else. She reminded him it was only because he didn't drink coffee himself. If he did he would remember it quick enough. Suppose they ran out of cigarettes? Then she saw the rope. What was that for? Well, he thought it might do to hang clothes on, or something. Naturally she asked him if he thought they were going to run a laundry? They already had a fifty-foot line hanging right before his eyes? Why, hadn't he noticed it, really? It was a blot on the landscape to her.

He thought there were a lot of things a rope might come in handy for. She wanted to know what, for instance. He thought a few seconds, but nothing occurred. They could wait and see, couldn't they? You need all sorts of strange odds and ends around a place in the country. She said, yes, that was so; but she thought just at that time when every penny counted, it seemed funny to buy more rope. That was all. She hadn't meant anything else. She hadn't just seen, not at first, why he felt it was necessary.

Well, thunder, he had bought it because he wanted to, and that was all there was to it. She thought that was reason enough, and couldn't understand why he hadn't said so, at first. Undoubtedly it would be useful, twenty-four yards of rope, there were hundreds of things, she couldn't think of any at the moment, but it would come in. Of course. As he had said, things always did in the country.

But she was a little disappointed about the coffee, and oh, look, look, look at the eggs! Oh, my, they're all running! What had he put on top of them? Hadn't he known eggs musn't be squeezed? Squeezed, who had squeezed them, he wanted to know. What a silly thing to say. He had simply brought them along in the basket with the other things. If they got broke it was the grocer's fault. He should know better than to put heavy things on top of eggs.

She believed it was the rope. That was the heaviest thing in the pack, she saw him plainly when he came in from the road, the rope was a big package on top of everything. He desired the whole wide world to witness that this was not a fact. He had carried the rope in one hand and the basket in the other, and what was the use of her having eyes if that was the best they could do for her?

Well, anyhow, she could see one thing plain: no eggs for breakfast. They'd have to scramble them now, for supper. It was too . . . bad. She had planned to have steak for supper. No ice, meat wouldn't keep. He wanted to know why she couldn't finish breaking the eggs in a bowl and set them in a cool place.

Cool place! if he could find one for her, she'd be glad to set them there. Well, then, it seemed to him they might very well cook the meat at the same time they cooked the eggs and then warm up the meat for tomorrow. The idea simply choked her. Warmed-over meat, when they might as well have had it fresh. Second best and scraps and makeshifts, even to the meat! He rubbed her shoulder a little. It doesn't really matter so much, does it, darling? Sometimes when they were playful, he would rub her shoulder and she would arch and purr. This time she hissed and almost clawed. He was getting ready to say that they could surely manage somehow when she turned on him and said, if he told her they could manage somehow she would certainly slap his face.

He swallowed the words red hot, his face burned. He picked up the rope and started to put it on the top shelf. She would not have it on the top shelf, the jars and tins belonged there; positively she would not have the top shelf cluttered up with a lot of rope. She had borne all the clutter she meant to bear in the flat in town, there was space here at least and she meant to keep things in order.

Well, in that case, he wanted to know what the hammer and nails were doing up there? And why had she put them there when she knew very well he needed that hammer and those nails upstairs to fix the window sashes? She simply slowed down everything and made double work on the place with her insane habit of changing things around and hiding them.

She was sure she begged his pardon, and if she had had any reason to believe he was going to fix the sashes this summer she would have left the hammer and nails right where he put them; in the middle of the bedroom floor where they could step on them in the dark. And now if he didn't clear the whole mess out of there she would throw them down the well.

Oh, all right, all right — could he put them in the closet? Naturally not, there were brooms and mops and dustpans in the closet, and why couldn't he find a place for his rope outside her kitchen? Had he stopped to consider there were seven God-forsaken rooms in the house, and only one kitchen?

He wanted to know what of it? And did she realize she was making a complete fool of herself? And what did she take him for, a three-year-old idiot? The whole trouble with her was she needed something weaker than she was to heckle and tyrannize over. He wished . . . now they had a couple of children she could take it out on. Maybe he'd get some rest.

Her face changed at this, she reminded him he had forgot the coffee and had bought a worthless piece of rope. And when she thought of all the things they actually needed to make the place even decently fit to live in, well, she could cry, that was all. She looked so forlorn, so lost and despairing he couldn't believe it was only a piece of rope that was causing all the racket. What *was* the matter . . . ?

Oh, would he please hush and go away, and *stay* away, if he could, for five minutes? By all means, yes, he would. He'd stay away indefinitely if she wished. Lord, yes, there was nothing he'd like better than to clear out and never come back. She couldn't for the life of her see what was holding him, then. It was a swell time. Here she was, stuck, miles from a railroad, with a half-empty house on her hands, and not a penny in her pocket, and everything on earth to do; it seemed the God-sent moment for him to get out from under. She was surprised he hadn't stayed in town as it was until she had come out and done the work and got things straightened out. It was his usual trick.

It appeared to him that this was going a little far. Just a touch out of bounds, if she didn't mind his saying so. Why . . . had he stayed in town the summer before? To do a half-dozen extra jobs to get the money he had sent her. That was it. She knew perfectly well they couldn't have done it otherwise. She had agreed with him at the time. And that was the only time so help him he had ever left her to do anything by herself.

Oh, he could tell that to his great-grandmother. She had her notion of what had kept him in town. Considerably more than a notion, if he wanted to know. So, she was going to bring all that up again, was she? Well, she could just think what she pleased. He was tired of explaining. It may have looked funny but he simply got hooked in, and what could he do? It was impossible to believe that she was going to take it seriously. Yes, yes, she knew how it was with a man: if he was left by himself a minute, some woman was certain to kidnap him. And naturally he couldn't hurt her feelings by refusing!

Well, what was she raving about? Did she forget she had told him those two weeks alone in the country were the happiest she had known for four years? And how long had they been married when she said that? All right, shut up! If she thought that hadn't stuck in his craw.

She hadn't meant she was happy because she was away from him. She meant she was happy getting the devilish house nice and ready for him. That was what she had meant, and now look! Bringing up something she had said a year ago simply to justify himself for forgetting her coffee and breaking the eggs and buying a wretched piece of rope they couldn't afford. She really thought it was time to drop the subject, and now she wanted only two things in the world. She wanted him to get that rope from underfoot, and go back to the village and get her coffee, and if he could remember it, he might bring a metal mitt for the skillets, and two more curtain rods, and if there were any rubber gloves in the village, her hands were simply raw, and a bottle of milk of magnesia from the drugstore.

He looked out at the dark blue afternoon sweltering on the slopes, and mopped his forehead and sighed heavily and said, if only she could wait a minute for *anything*, he was going back. He had said so, hadn't he, the very instant they found he had overlooked it?

Oh, yes, well . . . run along. She was going to wash windows. The country was so beautiful! She doubted they'd have a moment to enjoy it. He meant to go, but he could not until he had said that if she wasn't such a hopeless melancholiac she might see that this was only for a few days. Couldn't she remember anything pleasant about the other summers? Hadn't they ever had any fun? She hadn't time to talk about it, and now would he please not leave that rope lying around for her to trip on? He picked it up, somehow it had toppled off the table, and walked out with it under his arm.

Was he going this minute? He certainly was. She thought so. Sometimes it seemed to her he had second sight about the precisely perfect moment to leave her ditched. She had meant to put the mattresses out to sun, if they put them out this minute they would get at least three hours, he must have heard her say that morning she meant to put them out. So of course he would walk off and leave her to it. She supposed he thought the exercise would do her good.

Well, he was merely going to get her coffee. A four-mile walk for two pounds of coffee was ridiculous, but he was perfectly willing to do it. The habit was making a wreck of her, but if she wanted to wreck herself there was nothing he could do about it. If he thought it was coffee that was making a wreck of her, she congratulated him: he must have a . . . easy conscience.

Conscience or no conscience, he didn't see why the mattresses couldn't very well wait until tomorrow. And anyhow . . . were they living *in* the house, or were they going to let the house ride them to death? She paled at this, her face grew livid about the mouth, she looked quite dangerous, and reminded him that housekeeping was no more her work than it was his: she had other work to do as well, and when did he think she was going to find time to do it at this rate?

Was she going to start on that again? She knew as well as he did that his work brought in the regular money, hers was only occasional, if they depended on what *she* made — and she might as well get straight on this question once for all!

That was positively not the point. The question was, when both of them were working on their own time, was there going to be a division of the housework, or wasn't there? She merely wanted to know, she had to make her plans. Why, he thought that was all arranged. It was understood that he was to help. Hadn't he always, in summers?

Hadn't he, though? Oh, just hadn't he? And when, and where, and doing what? Lord, what an uproarious joke!

It was such a very uproarious joke that her face turned slightly purple, and she screamed with laughter. She laughed so hard she had to sit down, and finally a rush of tears spurted from her eyes and poured down into the lifted corners of her mouth. He dashed towards her and dragged her up to her feet and tried to pour water on her head. The dipper hung by a string on a nail and he broke it loose. Then he tried to pump water with one hand while she struggled in the other. So he gave it up and shook her instead.

She wrenched away, crying out for him to take his rope and go to . . ., she had simply given him up: and ran. He heard her high-heeled bedroom slippers clattering and stumbling on the stairs.

He went out around the house and into the lane; he suddenly realized he had a blister on his heel and his shirt felt as if it were on fire. Things broke so suddenly you didn't know where you were. She could work herself into a fury about simply nothing. She was terrible, . . . : not an ounce of reason. You might as well talk to a sieve as that woman when she got going. . . . if he'd spend his life humoring her! Well, what to do now? He would take back the rope and exchange it for something else. Things accumulated, things were mountainous, you couldn't move them or sort them out or get rid of them. They just lay and rotted around. He'd take it back. . . . , why should he? He wanted it. What was it anyhow? A piece of rope. Imagine anybody caring more about a piece of rope than about a man's feelings. What earthly right had she to say a word about it? He remembered all the useless, meaningless things she bought for herself: Why? because I wanted it, that's why! He stopped and selected a large stone by the road. He would put the rope behind it. He would put it in the tool-box when he got back. He'd heard enough about it to last him a life-time.

When he came back she was leaning against the post box beside the road waiting. It was pretty late, the smell of broiled steak floated nose high in the cooling air. Her face was young and smooth and fresh-looking. Her unmanageable funny black hair was all on end. She waved to him from a distance, and he speeded up. She called out that supper was ready and waiting, was he starved?

You bet he was starved. Here was the coffee. He waved it at her. She looked at his other hand. What was that he had there?

Well, it was the rope again. He stopped short. He had meant to exchange it but forgot. She wanted to know why he should exchange it, if it was something he really wanted. Wasn't the air sweet now, and wasn't it fine to be here?

She walked beside him with one hand hooked into his leather belt. She pulled and jostled him a little as he walked, and leaned against him. He put his arms clear around her and patted her stomach. They exchanged wary smiles. Coffee, coffee for the Ootsum-Wootsums! He felt as if he were bringing her a beautiful present.

He was a love, she firmly believed, and if she had had her coffee in the morning, she wouldn't have behaved so funny . . . There was a whippoorwill still coming back, imagine, clear out of season, sitting in the crab-apple tree calling all by himself. Maybe his girl stood him up. Maybe she did. She hoped to hear him once more, she loved whippoorwills . . . He knew how she was, didn't he?

Sure, he knew how she was.

Answer 1 of the 2 questions

(1.) Do you consider the marriage in this story a typical one? Write a paper telling why you do or do not feel that it is. Include your own ideas about the qualities a good marriage should have.

OR

(2.) Discuss, in writing, the author's use of irony in the story. Show how she uses both irony of expression and irony of situation, using concrete examples from the story.

Read: 4/23/87, 4/29/88, 3/4/98

Read: 4/29/86

a festival (dance, party, etc.) of ancient times honoring the devil; held on April 30, at night.

Due: 2-19-85

THE WALTZ

DOROTHY PARKER

Mazurka - a Polish dance.

WHY, *thank you so much. I'd adore to.*

I don't want to dance with him. I don't want to dance with anybody. And even if I did, it wouldn't be him. He'd be well down among the last ten. I've seen the way he dances; it looks like something you do on St. Walpurgis Night. Just think, not a quarter of an hour ago, here I was sitting, feeling so sorry for the poor girl he was dancing with. And now *I'm* going to be the poor girl. Well, well. Isn't it a small world?

And a peach of a world, too. A true little corker. Its events are so fascinatingly unpredictable, are not they? Here I was, minding my own business, not doing a stitch of harm to any living soul. And then he comes into my life, all smiles and city manners, to sue me for the favor of one memorable mazurka. Why, he scarcely knows my name, let alone what it stands for. It stands for Despair, Bewilderment, Futility, Degradation, and Premeditated Murder, but little does he wot. I don't wot his name, either; I haven't any idea what it is. Jukes, would be my guess from the look in his eyes. How do you do, Mr. Jukes? And how is that dear little brother of yours, with the two heads?

Ah, now why did he have to come around me, with his low requests? Why can't he let me lead my own life? I ask so little — just to be left alone in my quiet corner of the table, to do my evening brooding over all my sorrows. And he must come, with his bows and his scrapes and his may-I-have-this-ones. And I had to go and tell him that I'd adore to dance with him. I cannot understand why I wasn't struck right down dead. Yes, and being struck dead would look like a day in the country, compared to struggling out a dance with this boy. But what could I do? Everyone else at the table had got up to dance, except him and me. There I was, trapped. Trapped like a trap in a trap.

What can you say, when a man asks you to dance with him? I most certainly will *not* dance with you, I'll see you in hell first. Oh, yes, *do* let's dance together — it's so nice to meet a man who isn't a scaredy-cat about catching my beri-beri. No. There was nothing for me to do, but say I'd adore to. Well, we might as well get it over with. All right, Cannonball, let's run out on the field. You won the toss; you can lead.

Why, I think it's more of a waltz, really. Isn't it? We might just listen to the music a second. Shall we? Oh, yes, it's a waltz. Mind? Why, I'm simply thrilled. I'd love to waltz with you.

I'd love to waltz with you. I'd love to waltz with you, I'd love to have my tonsils out, I'd love to be in a midnight fire at sea. Well, it's too late now. We're getting under way. *Oh.* Oh, dear. Oh, dear, dear, dear. Oh, this is even worse than I thought it would be. I suppose that's the one dependable law of life — everything is always worse than you thought it was going to be. Oh, if I had had any real grasp of what this dance would be like, I'd have held out for sitting it out. Well, it will probably amount to the same thing in the end. We'll be sitting it out on the floor in a minute, if he keeps this up.

I'm so glad I brought it to his attention that this is a waltz they're playing. Heaven knows what might have happened, if he had thought it was something fast; we'd have blown the sides right out of the building. Why does he always want to be somewhere that he isn't? Why can't we stay in one place just long enough to get acclimated? It's this constant rush, rush, rush, that's the curse of American life. That's the reason that we're all of us so — *Ow*! Don't *kick*, you idiot; this is only second down. Oh, my shin. My poor, poor shin, that I've had ever since I was a little girl!

Oh, no, no, no. Goodness, no. It didn't hurt the least little bit. And anyway it was my fault. Really it was. Truly. Well, you're just being sweet, to say that. It really was all my fault.

I wonder what I'd better do — kill him this instant, with my naked hands, or wait and let him drop in his traces. Maybe it's best not to make a scene. I guess I'll just lie low, and watch the pace get him. He can't keep this up indefinitely — he's only flesh and blood. Die he must, and die he shall, for what he did to me. I don't want to be of the over-sensitive type, but you can't tell me that kick was unpremeditated. Freud says there are no accidents. I've led no cloistered life, I've known dancing partners who have spoiled my slippers and torn my dress; but when it comes to kicking, I am Outraged Womanhood. When you kick me in the shin, *smile.*

Maybe he didn't do it maliciously. Maybe it's just his way of showing his high spirits. I suppose I ought to be glad that one of us is having such a good time. I suppose I ought to think myself lucky if he brings me back alive. Maybe it's captious to demand of a practically strange man that he leave your shins as he found them. After all, the poor boy's doing the best he can. Probably he grew up in the hill country, and never had no larnin'. I bet they had to throw him on his back to get shoes on him.

Yes, it's lovely, isn't it? It's simply lovely. It's the loveliest waltz. Isn't it? Oh, I think it's lovely, too.

Why, I'm getting positively drawn to the Triple Threat here. He's my hero. He has the heart of a lion, and the sinews of a buffalo. Look at him — never a thought of the consequences, never afraid of his face, hurling himself into every scrimmage, eyes shining, cheeks ablaze. And shall it be said that I hung back? No, a thousand times no. What's it to me if I have to spend the next couple of years in a plaster cast? Come on, Butch, right through them! Who wants to live forever?

Oh. Oh, dear. Oh, he's all right, thank goodness. For a while I thought they'd have to carry him off the field. Ah, I couldn't bear to have anything happen to him. I love him. I love him better than anybody in the world. Look at the spirit he gets into a dreary, commonplace waltz; how effete the other dancers seem, beside him. He is youth and vigor and courage, he is strength and gayety and — *Ow!* Get off my instep, you hulking peasant! What do you think I am, anyway — a gangplank? *Ow!*

No, of course it didn't hurt. Why, it didn't a bit. Honestly. And it was all my fault. You see, that little step of yours — well, it's perfectly lovely, but it's just a tiny bit tricky to follow at first. Oh, did you work it up yourself? You really did? Well, aren't you amazing! Oh, now I think I've got it. Oh, I think it's lovely. I was watching you do it when you were dancing before. It's awfully effective when you look at it.

It's awfully effective when you look at it. I bet I'm awfully effective when you look at me. My hair is hanging along my cheeks, my skirt is swaddled about me, I can feel the cold damp of my brow. I must look like something out of the Fall of the House of Usher. This sort of thing takes a fearful toll of a woman my age. And he worked up his little step himself, he with his degenerate cunning. And it was just a tiny bit tricky at first, but now I think I've got it. Two stumbles, slip, and a twenty-yard dash; yes, I've got it. I've got several other things, too, including a split shin and a bitter heart. I hate this creature I'm chained to. I hated him the moment I saw his leering, bestial face. And here I've been locked in his noxious embrace for the thirty-five years this waltz has lasted. Is that orchestra never going to stop playing? Or must this obscene travesty of a dance go on until hell burns out?

Oh, they're going to play another encore. Oh, goody. Oh, that's lovely. Tired? I should say I'm not tired. I'd like to go on like this forever.

I should say I'm not tired. I'm dead, that's all I am. Dead, and in what a cause! And the music is never going to stop playing, and we're going on like this, Double-Time Charlie and I, throughout eternity. I suppose I won't care any more, after the first hundred thousand years. I suppose nothing will matter then, not heat nor pain nor broken heart nor cruel, aching weariness. Well. It can't come too soon for me.

I wonder why I didn't tell him I was tired. I wonder why I didn't suggest going back to the table. I could have said let's just listen to the music. Yes, and if he would, that would be the first bit of attention he has given it all evening. George Jean

Nathan said that the lovely rhythms of the waltz should be listened to in stillness and not be accompanied by strange gyrations of the human body. I think that's what he said. I think it was George Jean Nathan. Anyhow, whatever he said and whoever he was and whatever he's doing now, he's better off than I am. That's safe. Anybody who isn't waltzing with this Mrs. O'Leary's cow I've got here is having a good time.

Still, if we were back at the table, I'd probably have to talk to him. Look at him — what could you say to a thing like that! Did you go to the circus this year, what's your favorite kind of ice cream, how do you spell cat? I guess I'm as well off here. As well off as if I were in a cement mixer in full action.

I'm past all feeling now. The only way I can tell when he steps on me is that I can hear the splintering of bones. And all the events of my life are passing before my eyes. There was the time I was in a hurricane in the West Indies, there was the day I got my head cut open in the taxi smash, there was the night the drunken lady threw a bronze ashtray at her own true love and got me instead, there was that summer that the sailboat kept capsizing. Ah, what an easy, peaceful time was mine, until I fell in with Swifty, here. I didn't know what trouble was, before I got drawn into this *danse macabre*. I think my mind is beginning to wander. It almost seems to me as if the orchestra were stopping. It couldn't be, of course; it could never, never be. And yet in my ears there is a silence like the sound of angel voices. . . .

Oh, they've stopped, the mean things. They're not going to play any more. Oh, darn. Oh, do you think they would? Do you really think so, if you gave them fifty dollars? Oh, that would be lovely. And look, do tell them to play this same thing. I'd simply adore to go on waltzing.

Assignment: None . . . in written form. We read this story aloud & then discussed modern day lines (both rejection & pick-ups) at dances.

Read: 4/23/87, 5/2/88

Read: 5/4/86

Read: 5/8/85

WINTER DREAMS

F. SCOTT FITZGERALD

SOME of the caddies were poor as sin and lived in one-room houses with a neurasthenic cow in the front yard, but Dexter Green's father owned the second best grocery-store in Black Bear — the best one was "The Hub," patronized by the wealthy people from Sherry Island — and Dexter caddied only for pocket-money.

In the fall when the days became crisp and gray, and the long Minnesota winter shut down like the white lid of a box, Dexter's skis moved over the snow that hid the fairways of the golf course. At these times the country gave him a feeling of profound melancholy — it offended him that the links should lie in enforced fallowness, haunted by ragged sparrows for the long season. It was dreary, too, that on the tees where the gay colors fluttered in summer there were now only the desolate sandboxes knee-deep in crusted ice. When he crossed the hills the wind blew cold as misery, and if the sun was out he tramped with his eyes squinted up against the hard dimensionless glare.

In April the winter ceased abruptly. The snow ran down into Black Bear Lake scarcely tarrying for the early golfers to brave the season with red and black balls. Without elation, without an interval of moist glory, the cold was gone.

Dexter knew that there was something dismal about this Northern spring, just as he knew there was something gorgeous about the fall. Fall made him clinch his hands and tremble and repeat idiotic sentences to himself, and make brisk abrupt gestures of command to imaginary audiences and armies.

October filled him with hope which November raised to a sort of ecstatic triumph, and in this mood the fleeting brilliant impressions of the summer at Sherry Island were ready grist to his mill. He became a golf champion and defeated Mr. T. A. Hedrick in a marvellous match played a hundred times over the fairways of his imagination, a match each detail of which he changed about untiringly — sometimes he won with almost laughable ease, sometimes he came up magnificently from behind. Again, stepping from a Pierce-Arrow automobile, like Mr. Mortimer Jones, he strolled frigidly into the lounge of the Sherry Island Golf Club — or perhaps, surrounded by an admiring crowd, he gave an exhibition of fancy diving from the spring-board of the club raft. . . . Among those who watched him in open-mouthed wonder was Mr. Mortimer Jones.

And one day it came to pass that Mr. Jones — himself and not his ghost — came up to Dexter with tears in his eyes and said that Dexter was the —— best caddy in the club, and wouldn't he decide not to quit if Mr. Jones made it worth his while, because every other —— caddy in the club lost one ball a hole for him — regularly ——

"No, sir," said Dexter decisively, "I don't want to caddy any more." Then, after a pause: "I'm too old."

"You're not more than fourteen. Why the devil did you decide just this morning that you wanted to quit? You promised that next week you'd go over to the State tournament with me."

"I decided I was too old."

Dexter handed in his "A Class" badge, collected what money was due him from the caddy master, and walked home to Black Bear Village.

"The best —— caddy I ever saw," shouted Mr. Mortimer Jones over a drink that afternoon. "Never lost a ball! Willing! Intelligent! Quiet! Honest! Grateful!"

The little girl who had done this was eleven — beautifully ugly as little girls are apt to be who are destined after a few years to be inexpressibly lovely and bring no end of misery to a great number of men. The spark, however, was perceptible. There was a general ungodliness in the way her lips twisted down at the corners when she smiled, and in the — Heaven help us! — in the almost passionate quality of her eyes. Vitality is born in such women. It was utterly in evidence now, shining through her thin frame in a sort of glow.

She had come eagerly out on to the course at nine o'clock with a white linen nurse and five small new golf-clubs in a white canvas bag which the nurse was carrying. When Dexter first saw her she was standing by the caddy house, rather ill at ease and trying to conceal the fact by engaging her nurse in an obviously unnatural conversation graced by startling and irrelevant grimaces from herself.

"Well, it's certainly a nice day, Hilda," Dexter heard her say. She drew down the corners of her mouth, smiled, and glanced furtively around, her eyes in transit falling for an instant on Dexter.

Then to the nurse:

"Well, I guess there aren't very many people out here this morning, are there?"

The smile again — radiant, blatantly artificial — convincing.

"I don't know what we're supposed to do now," said the nurse, looking nowhere in particular.

"Oh, that's all right. I'll fix it up."

Dexter stood perfectly still, his mouth slightly ajar. He knew that if he moved forward a step his stare would be in her line of vision — if he moved backward he would lose his full view of her face. For a moment he had not realized how young she was. Now he remembered having seen her several times the year before — in bloomers.

Suddenly, involuntarily, he laughed, a short abrupt laugh — then, startled by himself, he turned and began to walk quickly away.

"Boy!"

Dexter stopped.

"Boy ——"

Beyond question he was addressed. Not only that, but he was treated to that absurd smile, that preposterous smile —

the memory of which at least a dozen men were to carry into middle age.

"Boy, do you know where the golf teacher is?"

"He's giving a lesson."

"Well, do you know where the caddy-master is?"

"He isn't here yet this morning."

"Oh." For a moment this baffled her. She stood alternately on her right and left foot.

"We'd like to get a caddy," said the nurse. "Mrs. Mortimer Jones sent us out to play golf, and we don't know how without we get a caddy."

Here she was stopped by an ominous glance from Miss Jones, followed immediately by the smile.

"There aren't any caddies here except me," said Dexter to the nurse, "and I got to stay here in charge until the caddy-master gets here."

"Oh."

Miss Jones and her retinue now withdrew, and at a proper distance from Dexter became involved in a heated conversation, which was concluded by Miss Jones taking one of the clubs and hitting it on the ground with violence. For further emphasis she raised it again and was about to bring it down smartly upon the nurse's bosom, when the nurse seized the club and twisted it from her hands.

"You damn little mean old *thing!*" cried Miss Jones wildly.

Another argument ensued. Realizing that the elements of comedy were implied in the scene, Dexter several times began to laugh, but each time restrained the laugh before it reached audibility. He could not resist the monstrous conviction that the little girl was justified in beating the nurse.

The situation was resolved by the fortuitous appearance of the caddy-master, who was appealed to immediately by the nurse.

"Miss Jones is to have a little caddy, and this one says he can't go."

"Mr. McKenna said I was to wait here till you came," said Dexter quickly.

"Well, he's here now." Miss Jones smiled cheerfully at the

caddy-master. Then she dropped her bag and set off at a haughty mince toward the first tee.

"Well?" The caddy-master turned to Dexter. "What you standing there like a dummy for? Go pick up the young lady's clubs."

"I don't think I'll go out to-day," said Dexter.

"You don't ——"

"I think I'll quit."

The enormity of his decision frightened him. He was a favorite caddy, and the thirty dollars a month he earned through the summer were not to be made elsewhere around the lake. But he had received a strong emotional shock, and his perturbation required a violent and immediate outlet.

It is not so simple as that, either. As so frequently would be the case in the future, Dexter was unconsciously dictated to by his winter dreams.

2

Now, of course, the quality and the seasonability of these winter dreams varied, but the stuff of them remained. They persuaded Dexter several years later to pass up a business course at the State university — his father, prospering now, would have paid his way — for the precarious advantage of attending an older and more famous university in the East, where he was bothered by his scanty funds. But do not get the impression, because his winter dreams happened to be concerned at first with musings on the rich, that there was anything merely snobbish in the boy. He wanted not association with glittering things and glittering people — he wanted the glittering things themselves. Often he reached out for the best without knowing why he wanted it — and sometimes he ran up against the mysterious denials and prohibitions in which life indulges. It is with one of those denials and not with his career as a whole that this story deals.

He made money. It was rather amazing. After college he went to the city from which Black Bear Lake draws its wealthy patrons. When he was only twenty-three and had been there not quite two years, there were already people who liked to say: "Now *there's* a boy —" All about him rich men's sons were peddling bonds precariously, or investing patrimonies precariously, or plodding through the two dozen volumes of the "George Washington Commercial Course," but Dexter borrowed a thousand dollars on his college degree and his confident mouth, and bought a partnership in a laundry.

It was a small laundry when he went into it, but Dexter made a specialty of learning how the English washed fine woolen golf-stockings without shrinking them, and within a year he was catering to the trade that wore knickerbockers. Men were insisting that their Shetland hose and sweaters go to his laundry, just as they had insisted on a caddy who could find golf-balls. A little later he was doing their wives' lingerie as well — and running five branches in different parts of the city. Before he was twenty-seven he owned the largest string of laundries in his section of the country. It was then that he sold out and went to New York. But the part of his story that concerns us goes back to the days when he was making his first big success.

When he was twenty-three Mr. Hart — one of the gray-haired men who liked to say "Now there's a boy" — gave him a guest card to the Sherry Island Golf Club for a week-end. So he signed his name one day on the register, and that afternoon played golf in a foursome with Mr. Hart and Mr. Sandwood and Mr. T. A. Hedrick. He did not consider it necessary to remark that he had once carried Mr. Hart's bag over this same links, and that he knew every trap and gully with his eyes shut — but he found himself glancing at the four caddies who trailed them, trying to catch a gleam or gesture that would remind him of himself, that would lessen the gap which lay between his present and his past.

It was a curious day, slashed abruptly with fleeting, familiar impressions. One minute he had the sense of being a trespasser — in the next he was impressed by the tremendous superiority he felt toward Mr. T. A. Hedrick, who was a bore and not even a good golfer any more.

Then, because of a ball Mr. Hart lost near the fifteenth green, an enormous thing happened. While they were searching the stiff grasses of the rough there was a clear call of "Fore!" from behind a hill in their rear. And as they all turned abruptly from their search a bright new ball sliced abruptly over the hill and caught Mr. T. A. Hedrick in the abdomen.

"By Gad!" cried Mr. T. A. Hedrick, "they ought to put some of these crazy women off the course. It's getting to be outrageous."

A head and a voice came up together over the hill:

"Do you mind if we go through?"

"You hit me in the stomach!" declared Mr. Hedrick wildly.

"Did I?" The girl approached the group of men. "I'm sorry. I yelled 'Fore!' "

Her glance fell casually on each of the men — then scanned the fairway for her ball.

"Did I bounce into the rough?"

It was impossible to determine whether this question was ingenuous or malicious. In a moment, however, she left no doubt, for as her partner came up over the hill she called cheerfully:

"Here I am! I'd have gone on the green except that I hit something."

As she took her stance for a short mashie shot, Dexter looked at her closely. She wore a blue gingham dress, rimmed at throat and shoulders with a white edging that accentuated her tan. The quality of exaggeration, of thinness, which had made her passionate eyes and down-turning mouth absurd at eleven, was gone now. She was arrestingly beautiful. The color in her cheeks was centered like the color in a picture — it was not a "high" color, but a sort of fluctuating and feverish warmth, so shaded that it seemed at any moment it would recede and disappear. This color and the mobility of her mouth gave a continual impression of flux, of intense life, of passionate vitality — balanced only partially by the sad luxury of her eyes.

She swung her mashie impatiently and without interest, pitching the ball into a sand-pit on the other side of the green. With a quick, insincere smile and a careless "Thank you!" she went on after it.

"That Judy Jones!" remarked Mr. Hedrick on the next tee,

as they waited — some moments — for her to play on ahead. "All she needs is to be turned up and spanked for six months and then to be married off to an old-fashioned cavalry captain."

"My God, she's good-looking!" said Mr. Sandwood, who was just over thirty.

"Good-looking!" cried Mr. Hedrick contemptuously. "She always looks as if she wanted to be kissed! Turning those big cow-eyes on every calf in town!"

It was doubtful if Mr. Hedrick intended a reference to the maternal instinct.

"She'd play pretty good golf if she'd try," said Mr. Sandwood.

"She has no form," said Mr. Hedrick solemnly.

"She has a nice figure," said Mr. Sandwood.

"Better thank the Lord she doesn't drive a swifter ball," said Mr. Hart, winking at Dexter.

Later in the afternoon the sun went down with a riotous swirl of gold and varying blues and scarlets, and left the dry, rustling night of Western summer. Dexter watched from the veranda of the Golf Club, watched the even overlap of the waters in the little wind, silver molasses under the harvest-moon. Then the moon held a finger to her lips and the lake became a clear pool, pale and quiet. Dexter put on his bathing-suit and swam out to the farthest raft, where he stretched dripping on the wet canvas of the springboard.

There was a fish jumping and a star shining and the lights around the lake were gleaming. Over on a dark peninsula a piano was playing the songs of last summer and of summers before that — songs from "Chin-Chin" and "The Count of Luxemburg" and "The Chocolate Soldier" — and because the sound of a piano over a stretch of water had always seemed beautiful to Dexter he lay perfectly quiet and listened.

The tune the piano was playing at that moment had been gay and new five years before when Dexter was a sophomore at college. They had played it at a prom once when he could not afford the luxury of proms, and he had stood outside the gymnasium and listened. The sound of the tune precipitated in him a sort of ecstasy and it was with that ecstasy he viewed what happened to him now. It was a mood of intense appreciation, a sense that, for once, he was magnificently attuned to life and that everything about him was radiating a brightness and a glamour he might never know again.

A low, pale oblong detached itself suddenly from the darkness of the Island, spitting forth the reverberated sound of a racing motorboat. Two white streamers of cleft water rolled themselves out behind it and almost immediately the boat was beside him, drowning out the hot tinkle of the piano in the drone of its spray. Dexter raising himself on his arms was aware of a figure standing at the wheel, of two dark eyes regarding him over the lengthening space of water — then the boat had gone by and was sweeping in an immense and purposeless circle of spray round and round in the middle of the lake. With equal eccentricity one of the circles flattened out and headed back toward the raft.

"Who's that?" she called, shutting off her motor. She was so near now that Dexter could see her bathing-suit, which consisted apparently of pink rompers.

The nose of the boat bumped the raft, and as the latter tilted rakishly he was precipitated toward her. With different degrees of interest they recognized each other.

"Aren't you one of those men we played through this afternoon?" she demanded.

He was.

"Well, do you know how to drive a motor-boat? Because if you do I wish you'd drive this one so I can ride on the surfboard behind. My name is Judy Jones" — she favored him with an absurd smirk — rather, what tried to be a smirk, for, twist her mouth as she might, it was not grotesque, it was merely beautiful — "and I live in a house over there on the Island, and in that house there is a man waiting for me. When he drove up at the door I drove out of the dock because he says I'm his ideal."

There was a fish jumping and a star shining and the lights around the lake were gleaming. Dexter sat beside Judy Jones and she explained how her boat was driven. Then she was in the water, swimming to the floating surf-board with a sinuous crawl. Watching her was without effort to the eye, watching a branch waving or a sea-gull flying. Her arms, burned to butternut, moved sinuously among the dull platinum ripples, elbow appearing first, casting the forearm back with a cadence of falling water, then reaching out and down, stabbing a path ahead.

They moved out into the lake; turning. Dexter saw that she was kneeling on the low rear of the now uptilted surf-board.

"Go faster," she called, "fast as it'll go."

Obediently he jammed the lever forward and the white spray mounted at the bow. When he looked around again the girl was standing up on the rushing board, her arms spread wide, her eyes lifted toward the moon.

"It's awful cold," she shouted. "What's your name?"

He told her.

"Well, why don't you come to dinner to-morrow night?"

His heart turned over like the fly-wheel of the boat, and, for the second time, her casual whim gave a new direction to his life.

3

Next evening while he waited for her to come downstairs, Dexter peopled the soft deep summer room and the sun-porch that opened from it with the men who had already loved Judy Jones. He knew the sort of men they were — the men who when he first went to college had entered from the great prep schools with graceful clothes and the deep tan of healthy summers. He had seen that, in one sense, he was better than these men. He was newer and stronger. Yet in acknowledging to himself that he wished his children to be like them he was admitting that he was but the rough, strong stuff from which they eternally sprang.

When the time had come for him to wear good clothes, he had known who were the best tailors in America, and the best tailors in America had made him the suit he wore this evening. He had acquired that particular reserve peculiar to his university, that set it off from other universities. He recognized the value to him of such a mannerism and he had adopted it; he knew that to be careless in dress and manner required more confidence than to be careful. But carelessness was for his children. His mother's name had been Krimplich. She was a Bohemian of the peasant class and she had talked broken English to the end of her days. Her son must keep to the set patterns.

At a little after seven Judy Jones came down-stairs. She wore a blue silk afternoon dress, and he was disappointed at first that she had not put on something more elaborate. This feeling was accentuated when, after a brief greeting, she went to the door of a butler's pantry and pushing it open called: "You can serve dinner, Martha." He had rather expected that a butler would announce dinner, that there would be a cocktail. Then he put these thoughts behind him as they sat down side by side on a lounge and looked at each other.

"Father and mother won't be here," she said thoughtfully.

He remembered the last time he had seen her father, and he was glad the parents were not to be here to-night — they might wonder who he was. He had been born in Keeble, a Minnesota village fifty miles farther north, and he always gave Keeble as his home instead of Black Bear Village. Country towns were well enough to come from if they weren't inconveniently in sight and used as footstools by fashionable lakes.

They talked of his university, which she had visited frequently during the past two years, and of the near-by city which supplied Sherry Island with its patrons, and whither Dexter would return next day to his prospering laundries.

During dinner she slipped into a moody depression which gave Dexter a feeling of uneasiness. Whatever petulance she uttered in her throaty voice worried him. Whatever she smiled at — at him, at a chicken liver, at nothing — it disturbed him that her smile could have no root in mirth, or even in amusement. When the scarlet corners of her lips curved down, it was less a smile than an invitation to a kiss.

Then, after dinner, she led him out on the dark sun-porch and deliberately changed the atmosphere.

"Do you mind if I weep a little?" she said.

"I'm afraid I'm boring you," he responded quickly.

"You're not. I like you. But I've just had a terrible afternoon. There was a man I cared about, and this afternoon he told me out of a clear sky that he was poor as a churchmouse. He'd never even hinted it before. Does this sound horribly mundane?"

"Perhaps he was afraid to tell you."

"Suppose he was," she answered. "He didn't start right. You see, if I'd thought of him as poor — well, I've been mad about loads of poor men, and fully intended to marry them all. But in this case, I hadn't thought of him that way, and my interest in him wasn't strong enough to survive the shock. As if a girl calmly informed her fiancé that she was a widow. He might not object to widows, but ——

"Let's start right," she interrupted herself suddenly. "Who are you, anyhow?"

For a moment Dexter hesitated. Then:

"I'm nobody," he announced. "My career is largely a matter of futures."

"Are you poor?"

"No," he said frankly, "I'm probably making more money than any man my age in the Northwest. I know that's an obnoxious remark, but you advised me to start right."

There was a pause. Then she smiled and the corners of her mouth drooped and an almost imperceptible sway brought her closer to him, looking up into his eyes. A lump rose in Dexter's throat, and he waited breathless for the experiment, facing the unpredictable compound that would form mysteriously from the elements of their lips. Then he saw — she communicated her excitement to him, lavishly, deeply, with kisses that were not a promise but a fulfilment. They aroused in him not hunger demanding renewal but surfeit that would demand more surfeit . . . kisses that were like charity, creating want by holding back nothing at all.

It did not take him many hours to decide that he had

wanted Judy Jones ever since he was a proud, desirous little boy.

4

It began like that — and continued, with varying shades of intensity, on such a note right up to the dénouement. Dexter surrendered a part of himself to the most direct and unprincipled personality with which he had ever come in contact. Whatever Judy wanted, she went after with the full pressure of her charm. There was no divergence of method, no jockeying for position or premeditation of effects — there was a very little mental side to any of her affairs. She simply made men conscious to the highest degree of her physical loveliness. Dexter had no desire to change her. Her deficiencies were knit up with a passionate energy that transcended and justified them.

When, as Judy's head lay against his shoulder that first night, she whispered, "I don't know what's the matter with me. Last night I thought I was in love with a man and to-night I think I'm in love with you ——" — it seemed to him a beautiful and romantic thing to say. It was the exquisite excitability that for the moment he controlled and owned. But a week later he was compelled to view this same quality in a different light. She took him in her roadster to a picnic supper, and after supper she disappeared, likewise in her roadster, with another man. Dexter became enormously upset and was scarcely able to be decently civil to the other people present. When she assured him that she had not kissed the other man, he knew she was lying — yet he was glad that she had taken the trouble to lie to him.

He was, as he found before the summer ended, one of a varying dozen who circulated about her. Each of them had at one time been favored above all others — about half of them still basked in the solace of occasional sentimental revivals. Whenever one showed signs of dropping out through long neglect, she granted him a brief honeyed hour, which encouraged him to tag along for a year or so longer. Judy made these forays upon the helpless and defeated without malice, indeed half unconscious that there was anything mischievous in what she did.

When a new man came to town every one dropped out — dates were automatically cancelled.

The helpless part of trying to do anything about it was that she did it all herself. She was not a girl who could be "won" in the kinetic sense — she was proof against cleverness, she was proof against charm; if any of these assailed her too strongly she would immediately resolve the affair to a physical basis, and under the magic of her physical splendor the strong as well as the brilliant played her game and not their own. She was entertained only by the gratification of her desires and by the direct exercise of her own charm. Perhaps from so much youthful love, so many youthful lovers, she had come, in self-defense, to nourish herself wholly from within.

Succeeding Dexter's first exhilaration came restlessness and dissatisfaction. The helpless ecstasy of losing himself in her was opiate rather than tonic. If was fortunate for his work during the winter that those moments of ecstasy came infrequently. Early in their acquaintance it had seemed for a while that there was a deep and spontaneous mutual attraction — that first August, for example — three days of long evenings on her dusky veranda, of strange wan kisses through the late afternoon, in shadowy alcoves or behind the protecting trellises of the garden arbors, of mornings when she was fresh as a dream and almost shy at meeting him in the clarity of the rising day. There was all the ecstasy of an engagement about it, sharpened by his realization that there was no engagement. It was during those three days that, for the first time, he had asked her to marry him. She said "maybe some day," she said "kiss me," she said "I'd like to marry you," she said "I love you" — she said — nothing.

The three days were interrupted by the arrival of a New York man who visited at her house for half September. To Dexter's agony, rumor engaged them. The man was the son of the president of a great trust company. But at the end of a month it was reported that Judy was yawning. At a dance one night she sat all evening in a motor-boat with a local beau, while the New Yorker searched the club for her frantically. She told the local beau that she was bored with her visitor, and two days later he left. She was seen with him at the station, and it was reported that he looked very mournful indeed.

On this note the summer ended. Dexter was twenty-four, and he found himself increasingly in a position to do as he wished. He joined two clubs in the city and lived at one of them. Though he was by no means an integral part of the stag-lines at these clubs, he managed to be on hand at dances where Judy Jones was likely to appear. He could have gone out socially as much as he liked — he was an eligible young man, now, and popular with down-town fathers. His confessed devotion to Judy Jones had rather solidified his position. But he had no social aspirations and rather despised the dancing men who were always on tap for the Thursday or Saturday parties and who filled in at dinners with the younger married set. Already he was playing with the idea of going East to New York. He wanted to take Judy Jones with him. No disillusion as to the world in which she had grown up could cure his illusion as to her desirability.

Remember that — for only in the light of it can what he did for her be understood.

Eighteen months after he first met Judy Jones he became engaged to another girl. Her name was Irene Scheerer, and her father was one of the men who had always believed in Dexter. Irene was light-haired and sweet and honorable, and a little stout, and she had two suitors whom she pleasantly relinquished when Dexter formally asked her to marry him.

Summer, fall, winter, spring, another summer, another fall — so much he had given of his active life to the incorrigible lips of Judy Jones. She had treated him with interest, with encouragement, with malice, with indifference, with contempt. She had inflicted on him the innumerable little slights and indignities possible in such a case — as if in revenge for having ever cared for him at all. She had beckoned him and yawned at him and beckoned him again and he had responded often with bitterness and narrowed eyes. She had brought him ecstatic happiness and intolerable agony of spirit. She had caused him untold inconvenience and not a little trouble. She had insulted him, and she had ridden over him, and she had played his interest in her against his interest in his work — for fun. She had done everything to him except to criticize him — this she had not done — it seemed to him only because it might have sullied the utter indifference she manifested and sincerely felt toward him.

When autumn had come and gone again it occurred to him that he could not have Judy Jones. He had to beat this into his mind but he convinced himself at last. He lay awake at night for a while and argued it over. He told himself the trouble and the pain she had caused him, he enumerated her glaring deficiencies as a wife. Then he said to himself that he loved her, and after a while he fell asleep. For a week, lest he imagined her husky voice over the telephone or her eyes opposite him at lunch, he worked hard and late, and at night he went to his office and plotted out his years.

At the end of a week he went to a dance and cut in on her once. For almost the first time since they had met he did not ask her to sit out with him or tell her that she was lovely. It hurt him that she did not miss these things — that was all. He was not jealous when he saw that there was a new man to-night. He had been hardened against jealousy long before.

He stayed late at the dance. He sat for an hour with Irene Scheerer and talked about books and about music. He knew very little about either. But he was beginning to be master of his own time now, and he had a rather priggish notion that he — the young and already fabulously successful Dexter Green — should know more about such things.

That was in October, when he was twenty-five. In January, Dexter and Irene became engaged. It was to be announced in June, and they were to be married three months later.

The Minnesota winter prolonged itself interminably, and it was almost May when the winds came soft and the snow ran down into Black Bear Lake at last. For the first time in over a year Dexter was enjoying a certain tranquillity of spirit. Judy Jones had been in Florida, and afterward in Hot Springs, and somewhere she had been engaged, and somewhere she had broken it off. At first, when Dexter had definitely given her up, it had made him sad that people still linked them together and asked for news of her, but when he began to be placed at dinner next to Irene Scheerer people didn't ask him about her any more — they told him about her. He ceased to be an authority on her.

May at last. Dexter walked the streets at night when the darkness was damp as rain, wondering that so soon, with so little done, so much of ecstasy had gone from him. May one year back had been marked by Judy's poignant, unforgivable, yet forgiven turbulence — it had been one of those rare times when he fancied she had grown to care for him. That old penny's worth of happiness he had spent for this bushel of content. He knew that Irene would be no more than a curtain spread behind him, a hand moving among gleaming teacups, a voice calling to children . . . fire and loveliness were gone, the magic of nights and the wonder of the varying hours and seasons . . . slender lips, down-turning, dropping to his lips and bearing him up into a heaven of eyes. . . . The thing was deep in him. He was too strong and alive for it to die lightly.

In the middle of May when the weather balanced for a few days on the thin bridge that led to deep summer he turned in one night at Irene's house. Their engagement was to be announced in a week now — no one would be surprised at it. And to-night they would sit together on the lounge at the University Club and look on for an hour at the dancers. It gave him a sense of solidity to go with her — she was so sturdily popular, so intensely "great."

He mounted the steps of the brownstone house and stepped inside.

"Irene," he called.

Mrs. Scheerer came out of the living-room to meet him.

"Dexter," she said, "Irene's gone up-stairs with a splitting headache. She wanted to go with you but I made her go to bed."

"Nothing serious, I ——"

"Oh, no. She's going to play golf with you in the morning. You can spare her for just one night, can't you, Dexter?"

Her smile was kind. She and Dexter liked each other. In

the living-room he talked for a moment before he said good-night.

Returning to the University Club, where he had rooms, he stood in the doorway for a moment and watched the dancers. He leaned against the door-post, nodded at a man or two — yawned.

"Hello, darling."

The familiar voice at his elbow startled him. Judy Jones had left a man and crossed the room to him — Judy Jones, a slender enameled doll in cloth of gold: gold in a band at her head, gold in two slipper points at her dress's hem. The fragile glow of her face seemed to blossom as she smiled at him. A breeze of warmth and light blew through the room. His hands in the pockets of his dinner-jacket tightened spasmodically. He was filled with a sudden excitement.

"When did you get back?" he asked casually.

"Come here and I'll tell you about it."

She turned and he followed her. She had been away — he could have wept at the wonder of her return. She had passed through enchanted streets, doing things that were like provocative music. All mysterious happenings, all fresh and quickening hopes, had gone away with her, come back with her now.

She turned in the doorway.

"Have you a car here? If you haven't, I have."

"I have a coupé."

In then, with a rustle of golden cloth. He slammed the door. Into so many cars she had stepped — like this — like that — her back against the leather, so — her elbow resting on the door — waiting. She would have been soiled long since had there been anything to soil her — except herself — but this was her own self outpouring.

With an effort he forced himself to start the car and back into the street. This was nothing, he must remember. She had done this before, and he had put her behind him, as he would have crossed a bad account from his books.

He drove slowly down-town and, affecting abstraction, traversed the deserted streets of the business section, peopled here and there where a movie was giving out its crowd or where consumptive or pugilistic youth lounged in front of pool halls. The clink of glasses and the slap of hands on the bars issued from saloons, cloisters of glazed glass and dirty yellow light.

She was watching him closely and the silence was embarrassing, yet in this crisis he could find no casual word with which to profane the hour. At a convenient turning he began to zigzag back toward the University Club.

"Have you missed me?" she asked suddenly.

"Everybody missed you."

He wondered if she knew of Irene Scheerer. She had been back only a day — her absence had been almost contemporaneous with his engagement.

"What a remark!" Judy laughed sadly — without sadness. She looked at him searchingly. He became absorbed in the dashboard.

"You're handsomer than you used to be," she said thoughtfully. "Dexter, you have the most rememberable eyes."

He could have laughed at this, but he did not laugh. It was the sort of thing that was said to sophomores. Yet it stabbed at him.

"I'm awfully tired of everything, darling." She called every one darling, endowing the endearment with careless, individual camaraderie. "I wish you'd marry me."

The directness of this confused him. He should have told her now that he was going to marry another girl, but he could not tell her. He could as easily have sworn that he had never loved her.

"I think we'd get along," she continued, on the same note, "unless probably you've forgotten me and fallen in love with another girl."

Her confidence was obviously enormous. She had said, in effect, that she found such a thing impossible to believe, that if it were true he had merely committed a childish indiscretion — and probably to show off. She would forgive him, because it was not a matter of any moment but rather something to be brushed aside lightly.

"Of course you could never love anybody but me," she continued, "I like the way you love me. Oh, Dexter, have you forgotten last year?"

"No, I haven't forgotten."

"Neither have I!"

Was she sincerely moved — or was she carried along by the wave of her own acting?

"I wish we could be like that again," she said, and he forced himself to answer:

"I don't think we can."

"I suppose not. . . . I hear you're giving Irene Scheerer a violent rush."

There was not the faintest emphasis on the name, yet Dexter was suddenly ashamed.

"Oh, take me home," cried Judy suddenly; "I don't want to go back to that idiotic dance — with those children."

Then, as he turned up the street that led to the residence district, Judy began to cry quietly to herself. He had never seen her cry before.

The dark street lightened, the dwellings of the rich loomed up around them, he stopped his coupé in front of the great white bulk of the Mortimer Joneses' house, somnolent, gorgeous, drenched with the splendor of the damp moonlight. Its solidity startled him. The strong walls, the steel of the girders, the breadth and beam and pomp of it were there only to bring out the contrast with the young beauty beside him. It was sturdy to accentuate her slightness — as if to show what a breeze could be generated by a butterfly's wing.

He sat perfectly quiet, his nerves in wild clamor, afraid that if he moved he would find her irresistibly in his arms. Two tears had rolled down her wet face and trembled on her upper lip.

"I'm more beautiful than anybody else," she said brokenly, "why can't I be happy?" Her moist eyes tore at his stability — her mouth turned slowly downward with an exquisite sadness: "I'd like to marry you if you'll have me, Dexter. I suppose you think I'm not worth having, but I'll be so beautiful for you, Dexter."

A million phrases of anger, pride, passion, hatred, tenderness fought on his lips. Then a perfect wave of emotion washed over him, carrying off with it a sediment of wisdom, of convention, of doubt, of honor. This was his girl who was speaking, his own, his beautiful, his pride.

"Won't you come in?" He heard her draw in her breath sharply.

Waiting.

"All right," his voice was trembling, "I'll come in."

5

It was strange that neither when it was over nor a long time afterward did he regret that night. Looking at it from the perspective of ten years, the fact that Judy's flare for him endured just one month seemed of little importance. Nor did it matter that by his yielding he subjected himself to a deeper agony in the end and and gave serious hurt to Irene Scheerer and to Irene's parents, who had befriended him. There was nothing sufficiently pictorial about Irene's grief to stamp itself on his mind.

Dexter was at bottom hard-minded. The attitude of the city on his action was of no importance to him, not because he was going to leave the city, but because any outside attitude on the situation seemed superficial. He was completely indifferent to popular opinion. Nor, when he had seen that it was no use, that he did not possess in himself the power to move fundamentally or to hold Judy Jones, did he bear any malice toward her. He loved her, and he would love her until the day he was too old for loving — but he could not have her. So he tasted the deep pain that is reserved only for the strong, just as he had tasted for a little while the deep happiness.

Even the ultimate falsity of the grounds upon which Judy terminated the engagement that she did not want to "take him away" from Irene — Judy, who had wanted nothing else — did not revolt him. He was beyond any revulsion or any amusement.

He went East in February with the intention of selling out

his laundries and settling in New York — but the war came to America in March and changed his plans. He returned to the West, handed over the management of the business to his partner, and went into the first officers' training-camp in late April. He was one of those young thousands who greeted the war with a certain amount of relief, welcoming the liberation from webs of tangled emotion.

6

This story is not his biography, remember, although things creep into it which have nothing to do with those dreams he had when he was young. We are almost done with them and with him now. There is only one more incident to be related here, and it happens seven years farther on.

It took place in New York, where he had done well — so well that there were no barriers too high for him. He was thirty-two years old, and, except for one flying trip immediately after the war, he had not been West in seven years. A man named Devlin from Detroit came into his office to see him in a business way, and then and there this incident occurred, and closed out, so to speak, this particular side of his life.

"So you're from the Middle West," said the man Devlin with careless curiosity. "That's funny — I thought men like you were probably born and raised on Wall Street. You know — wife of one of my best friends in Detroit came from your city. I was an usher at the wedding."

Dexter waited with no apprehension of what was coming.

"Judy Simms," said Devlin with no particular interest; "Judy Jones she was once."

"Yes, I knew her." A dull impatience spread over him. He had heard, of course, that she was married — perhaps deliberately he had heard no more.

"Awfully nice girl," brooded Devlin meaninglessly, "I'm sort of sorry for her."

"Why?" Something in Dexter was alert, receptive, at once.

"Oh, Lud Simms has gone to pieces in a way. I don't mean he ill-uses her, but he drinks and runs around ——"

"Doesn't she run around?"

"No. Stays at home with her kids."

"Oh."

"She's a little too old for him," said Devlin.

"Too old!" cried Dexter. "Why, man, she's only twenty-seven."

He was possessed with a wild notion of rushing out into the streets and taking a train to Detroit. He rose to his feet spasmodically.

"I guess you're busy," Devlin apologized quickly. "I didn't realize ——"

"No, I'm not busy," said Dexter, steadying his voice. "I'm not busy at all. Not busy at all. Did you say she was — twenty-seven? No, I said she was twenty-seven."

"Yes, you did," agreed Devlin dryly.

"Go on, then. Go on.

"What do you mean?"

"About Judy Jones."

Devlin looked at him helplessly.

"Well, that's — I told you all there is to it. He treats her like the devil. Oh, they're not going to get divorced or anything. When he's particularly outrageous she forgives him. In fact, I'm inclined to think she loves him. She was a pretty girl when she first came to Detroit."

A pretty girl! The phrase struck Dexter as ludicrous.

"Isn't she — a pretty girl, any more?"

"Oh, she's all right."

"Look here," said Dexter, sitting down suddenly. "I don't understand. You say she was a 'pretty girl' and now you say she's 'all right.' I don't understand what you mean — Judy Jones wasn't a pretty girl, at all. She was a great beauty. Why, I knew her, I knew her. She was ——"

Devlin laughed pleasantly.

"I'm not trying to start a row," he said. "I think Judy's a nice girl and I like her. I can't understand how a man like Lud Simms could fall madly in love with her, but he did." Then he added: "Most of the women like her."

Dexter looked closely at Devlin, thinking wildly that

there must be a reason for this, some insensitivity in the man or some private malice.

"Lots of women fade just like *that,*" Devlin snapped his fingers. "You must have seen it happen. Perhaps I've forgotten how pretty she was at her wedding. I've seen her so much since then, you see. She has nice eyes."

A sort of dullness settled down upon Dexter. For the first time in his life he felt like getting very drunk. He knew that he was laughing loudly at something Devlin had said, but he did not know what it was or why it was funny. When, in a few minutes, Devlin went he lay down on his lounge and looked out the window at the New York sky-line into which the sun was sinking in dull lovely shades of pink and gold.

He had thought that having nothing else to lose he was invulnerable at last — but he knew that he had just lost something more, as surely as if he had married Judy Jones and seen her fade away before his eyes.

The dream was gone. Something had been taken from him. In a sort of panic he pushed the palms of his hands into his eyes and tried to bring up a picture of the waters lapping on Sherry Island and the moonlit veranda, and gingham on the golf-links and the dry sun and the gold color of her neck's soft down. And her mouth damp to his kisses and her eyes plaintive with melancholy and her freshness like new fine linen in the morning. Why, these things were no longer in the world! They had existed and they existed no longer.

For the first time in years the tears were streaming down his face. But they were for himself now. He did not care about mouth and eyes and moving hands. He wanted to care, and he could not care. For he had gone away and he could never go back any more. The gates were closed, the sun was gone down, and there was no beauty but the gray beauty of steel that withstands all time. Even the grief he could have borne was left behind in the country of illusion, of youth, of the richness of life, where his winter dreams had flourished.

"Long ago," he said, "long ago, there was something in me, but now that thing is gone. Now that thing is gone, that thing is gone. I cannot cry. I cannot care. That thing will come back no more."

1922

43-67

Read: 4/24/87, 5/3/88, 6/3/92, 6/22/93, 2/13/98

Read: 5/4/86

Read: 5/16/85

THE TALL MEN

WILLIAM FAULKNER

THEY passed the dark bulk of the cotton gin. Then they saw the lamplit house and the other car, the doctor's coupé, just stopping at the gate, and they could hear the hound baying.

"Here we are," the old deputy marshal said.

"What's that other car?" the younger man said, the stranger, the state draft investigator.

"Doctor Schofield's," the marshal said. "Lee McCallum asked me to send him out when I telephoned we were coming."

"You mean you warned them?" the investigator said. "You telephoned ahead that I was coming out with a warrant for these two evaders? Is this how you carry out the orders of the United States Government?"

The marshal was a lean, clean old man who chewed tobacco, who had been born and lived in the county all his life.

"I understood all you wanted was to arrest these two McCallum boys and bring them back to town," he said.

"It was!" the investigator said. "And now you have warned them, given them a chance to run. Possibly put the Government to the expense of hunting them down with troops. Have you forgotten that you are under a bond yourself?"

"I ain't forgot it," the marshal said. "And ever since we left Jefferson I been trying to tell you something for you not to forget. But I reckon it will take these McCallums to impress that on you. . . . Pull in behind the other car. We'll try to find out first just how sick whoever it is that is sick is."

The investigator drew up behind the

other car and switched off and blacked out his lights. "These people," he said. Then he thought, *But this doddering, tobacco-chewing old man is one of them, too, despite the honor and pride of his office, which should have made him different.* So he didn't speak it aloud, removing the keys and getting out of the car, and then locking the car itself, rolling the windows up first, thinking, *These people who lie about and conceal the ownership of land and property in order to hold relief jobs which they have no intention of performing, standing on their constitutional rights against having to work, who jeopardize the very job itself through petty and transparent subterfuge to acquire a free mattress which they intend to attempt to sell; who would relinquish even the job, if by so doing they could receive free food and a place, any rathole, in town to sleep in; who, as farmers, make false statements to get seed loans which they will later misuse, and then react in loud vituperative outrage and astonishment when caught at it. And then, when at long last a suffering and threatened Government asks one thing of them in return, one thing simply, which is to put their names down on a selective-service list, they refuse to do it.*

The old marshal had gone on. The investigator followed, through a stout paintless gate in a picket fence, up a broad brick walk between two rows of old shabby cedars, toward the rambling and likewise paintless sprawl of the two-story house in the open hall of which the soft lamplight glowed and the lower story of which, as the investigator now perceived, was of logs.

He saw a hall full of soft lamplight beyond a stout paintless gallery running across the log front, from beneath which the same dog which they had heard, a big hound, came booming again, to stand foursquare facing them in the walk, bellowing, until a man's voice spoke to it from the house. He followed the marshal up the steps onto the gallery. Then he saw the man standing in the door, waiting for them to approach — a man of about forty-five, not tall, but blocky, with a brown, still face and horseman's hands, who looked at him once, brief and hard, and then no more, speaking to the marshal, "Howdy, Mr. Gombault. Come in."

"Howdy, Rafe," the marshal said. "Who's sick?"

"Buddy," the other said. "Slipped and caught his leg in the hammer mill this afternoon."

"Is it bad?" the marshal said.

"It looks bad to me," the other said. "That's why we sent for the doctor instead of bringing him in to town. We couldn't get the bleeding stopped."

"I'm sorry to hear that," the marshal said. "This is Mr. Pearson." Once more the investigator found the other looking at him, the brown eyes still, courteous enough in the brown face, the hand he offered hard enough, but the clasp quite limp, quite cold. The marshal was still speaking. "From Jackson. From the draft board." Then he said, and the investigator could discern no change whatever in his tone: "He's got a warrant for the boys."

The investigator could discern no change whatever anywhere. The limp hard hand merely withdrew from his, the still face now looking at the marshall. "You mean we have declared war?"

"No," the marshal said.

"That's not the question, Mr. McCallum," the investigator said. "All required of them was to register. Their numbers might not even be drawn this time; under the law of averages, they probably would not be. But they refused — failed, anyway — to register."

"I see," the other said. He was not looking at the investigator. The investigator couldn't tell certainly if he was even looking at the marshal, although he spoke to him, "You want to see Buddy? The doctor's with him now."

"Wait," the investigator said. "I'm sorry about your brother's accident, but I ——" The marshal glanced back at him for a moment, his shaggy gray brows beetling, with something at once courteous yet a little impatient about the glance, so that during the instant the investigator sensed from the old marshal the same quality which had been in the other's brief look.

The investigator was a man of better than average intelligence; he was already becoming aware of something a little different here from what he had expected. But he had been in relief work in the state several years, dealing almost exclusively with country people, so he still believed he knew them. So he looked at the old marshal, thinking, *Yes. The same sort of people, despite the office, the authority and responsibility which should have changed him.* Thinking again, *These people. These people.* "I intend to take the night train back to Jackson," he said. "My reservation is already made. Serve the warrant and we will ——"

"Come along," the old marshal said. "We are going to have plenty of time."

So he followed — there was nothing else to do — fuming and seething, attempting in the short length of the hall to regain control of himself in order to control the situation, because he realized now that if the situation were controlled, it would devolve upon him to control it; that if their departure with their prisoners were expedited, it must be himself and not the old marshal who would expedite it. He had been right. The doddering old officer was not only at bottom one of these people, he had apparently been corrupted anew to his old, inherent, shiftless sloth and unreliability merely by entering the house. So he followed in turn, down the hall and into a bedroom; whereupon he looked about him not only with amazement but with something very like terror. The room was a big room, with a bare unpainted floor, and besides the bed, it contained only a chair or two and one other piece of old-fashioned furniture. Yet to the investigator it seemed so filled with tremendous men cast in the same mold as the man who had met them that the very walls themselves must bulge. Yet they were not big, not tall, and it was not vitality, exuberance, because they made no sound, merely looking quietly at him where he stood in the door, with faces bearing an almost identical stamp of kinship — a thin, almost frail old man of about seventy, slightly taller than the others; a second one, white-haired, too, but otherwise identical with the man who had met them at the door; a third one about the same age as the man who had met them, but with something delicate in his face and something tragic and dark and wild in the same dark eyes; the two absolutely identical blue-eyed youths; and lastly the blue-eyed man on the bed over which the doctor, who might have been any city doctor, in his neat city suit, leaned — all of them turning to look quietly at him and the marshal as they entered. And he saw, past the doctor, the slit trousers of the man on the bed and the exposed, bloody, mangled leg, and he turned sick, stopping just inside the door under that quiet, steady regard while the marshal went up to the man who lay on the bed, smoking a cob pipe, a big, old-fashioned, wicker-covered demijohn, such as the investigator's grandfather had kept his whisky in, on the table beside him.

"Well, Buddy," the marshal said, "this is bad."

"Ah, it was my own . . . fault," the man on the bed said. "Stuart kept warning me about that frame I was using."

"That's correct," the second old one said.

Still the others said nothing. They just looked steadily and quietly at the investigator until the marshal turned slightly and said, "This is Mr. Pearson. From Jackson. He's got a warrant for the boys."

Then the man on the bed said, "What for?"

"That draft business, Buddy," the marshal said.

"We're not at war now," the man on the bed said.

"No," the marshal said. "It's that new law. They didn't register."

"What are you going to do with them?"

"It's a warrant, Buddy. Swore out."

"That means jail."

"It's a warrant," the old marshal said. Then the investigator saw that the man on the bed was watching him, puffing steadily at the pipe.

"Pour me some whisky, Jackson," he said.

"No," the doctor said. "He's had too much already."

"Pour me some whisky, Jackson," the man on the bed said. He puffed steadily at the pipe, looking at the investigator. "You come from the Government?" he said.

"Yes," the investigator said. "They should have registered. That's all required of them yet. They did not ——" His voice ceased, while the seven pairs of eyes contemplated him, and the man on the bed puffed steadily.

"We would have still been here," the man on the bed said. "We wasn't going to run." He turned his head. The two youths were standing side by side at the foot of the bed. "Anse, Lucius," he said.

To the investigator it sounded as if they answered as one, "Yes, father."

"This gentleman has come all the way from Jackson to say the Government is ready for you. I reckon the quickest place to enlist will be Memphis. Go upstairs and pack."

The investigator started, moved forward. "Wait!" he cried.

But Jackson, the eldest, had forestalled him. He said, "Wait," also, and now they were not looking at the investigator. They were looking at the doctor.

"What about his leg?" Jackson said.

"Look at it," the doctor said. "He almost amputated it himself. It won't wait. And he can't be moved now. I'll need my nurse to help me, and some ether, provided he hasn't had too much whisky to stand the anesthetic too. One of you can drive to town in my car. I'll telephone ——"

"Ether?" the man on the bed said. "What for? You just said yourself it's pretty near off now. I could whet up one of Jackson's butcher knives and finish it myself, with another drink or two. Go on. Finish it."

"You couldn't stand any more shock," the doctor said. "This is whisky talking now."

"Shucks," the other said. "One day in France we was running through a wheat field and I saw the machine gun, coming across the wheat, and I tried to jump it like you would jump a fence rail somebody was swinging at your middle, only I never made it. And I was on the ground then, and along toward dark that begun to hurt, only about that time something went whang on the back of my helmet, like when you hit a anvil, so I never knowed nothing else until I woke up. There was a heap of us racked up along a bank outside a field dressing station, only it took a long time for the doctor to get around to all of us, and by that time it was hurting bad. This here ain't hurt none to speak of since I got a-holt of this johnny-jug. You go on and finish it. If it's help you need, Stuart and Rafe will help you. . . . Pour me a drink, Jackson."

This time the doctor raised the demijohn and examined the level of the liquor. "There's a good quart gone," he said. "If you've drunk a quart of whisky since four o'clock, I doubt if you could stand the anesthetic. Do you think you could stand it if I finished it now?"

"Yes, finish it. I've ruined it; I want to get shut of it."

The doctor looked about at the others, at the still, identical faces watching him. "If I had him in town, in the hospital, with a nurse to watch him, I'd probably wait until he got over this first shock and got the whisky out of his system. But he can't be moved now, and I can't stop the bleeding like this, and even if I had ether or a local anesthetic —"

"Shucks," the man on the bed said. "God never made no better local nor general comfort or anesthetic neither than what's in this johnny-jug. And this ain't Jackson's leg nor Stuart's nor Rafe's nor Lee's. It's mine. I done started it; I reckon I can finish cutting it off any way I want to."

But the doctor was still looking at Jackson. "Well, Mr. McCallum?" he said. "You're the oldest."

But it was Stuart who answered. "Yes," he said. "Finish it. What do you want? Hot water, I reckon."

"Yes," the doctor said. "Some clean sheets. Have you got a big table you can move in here?"

"The kitchen table," the man who had met them at the door said. "Me and the boys —"

"Wait," the man on the bed said. "The boys won't have time to help you." He looked at them again. "Anse, Lucius," he said.

Again it seemed to the investigator that they answered as one, "Yes, father."

"This gentleman yonder is beginning to look impatient. You better start. Come to think of it, you won't need to pack. You will have uniforms in a day or two. Take the truck. There won't be nobody to drive you to Memphis and bring the truck back, so you can leave it at the Gayoso Feed Company until we can send for it. I'd like for you to enlist into the old Sixth Infantry, where I used to be. But I reckon that's too much to hope, and you'll just have to chance where they send you. But it likely won't matter, once you are in. The Government done right by me in my day, and it will do right by you. You just enlist wherever they want to send you, need you, and obey your sergeants and officers until you find out how to be soldiers. Obey them, but remember your name and don't take nothing from no man. You can go now."

"Wait!" the investigator cried again; again he started, moved forward into the center of the room. "I protest this! I'm sorry about Mr. McCallum's accident. I'm sorry about the whole business. But it's out of my hands and out of his hands now. This charge, failure to register according to law, has been made and the warrant issued. It cannot be evaded this way. The course of the action must be completed before any other step can be taken. They should have thought of this when these boys failed to register. If Mr. Gombault refuses to serve this warrant, I will serve it myself and take these men back to Jefferson with me to answer this charge as made. And I must warn Mr. Gombault that he will be cited for contempt!"

The old marshal turned, his shaggy eyebrows beetling again, speaking down to the investigator as if he were a child, "Ain't you found out yet that me or you neither ain't going nowhere for a while?"

"What?" the investigator cried. He looked about at the grave faces once more contemplating him with that remote and speculative regard. "Am I being threatened?" he cried.

"Ain't anybody paying any attention to you at all," the marshal said. "Now you just be quiet for a while, and you will be all right, and after a while we can go back to town."

So he stopped again and stood while the grave, contemplative faces freed him once more of that impersonal and unbearable regard, and saw the two youths approach the bed and bend down in turn and kiss their father on the mouth, and then turn as one and leave the room, passing him without even looking at him. And sitting in the lamplit hall beside the old marshal, the bedroom door closed now, he heard the truck start up and back and turn and go down the road, the sound of it dying away, ceasing, leaving the still, hot night — the Mississippi Indian summer, which had already outlasted half of November — filled with the loud last shrilling of the summer's cicadas, as though they, too, were aware of the imminent season of cold weather and of death.

"I remember old Anse," the marshal said pleasantly, chattily, in that tone in which an adult addresses a strange child. "He's been dead fifteen-sixteen years now. He was about sixteen when the old war broke out, and he walked all the way to Virginia to get into it. He could have enlisted and fought right here at home, but his ma was a Carter, so wouldn't nothing do him but to go all the way back to Virginia to do his fighting, even though he hadn't never seen Virginia before himself; walked all the way back to a land he hadn't never even seen before and enlisted in Stonewall Jackson's army and stayed in it all through the Valley, and right up to Chancellorsville, where them Carolina boys shot Jackson by mistake, and right on up to that morning in 'Sixty-five when Sheridan's cavalry blocked the road from Appomattox to the Valley, where they might have got away again. And he walked back to Mississippi with just about what he had carried away with him when he left, and he got married and built the first story of this house — this here log story we're in right now — and started getting them boys — Jackson and Stuart and Raphael and Lee and Buddy.

"Buddy come along late, late enough to be in the other war, in France in it. You heard him in there. He brought back two medals, an American medal and a French one, and no man knows till yet how he got them, just what he done. I don't believe he even told Jackson and Stuart and them. He hadn't hardly got back home, with them numbers on his uniform and the wound stripes and them two medals, before he had found him a girl, found her right off, and a year later them twin boys was born, the livin', spittin' image of old Anse McCallum. If old Anse had just been about seventy-five years younger, the three of them might have been thriblets. I remember them —

two little critters exactly alike, and wild as spikehorn bucks, running around here day and night both with a pack of coon dogs until they got big enough to help Buddy and Stuart and Lee with the farm and the gin, and Rafe with the horses and mules, when he would breed and raise and train them and take them to Memphis to sell, right on up to three, four years back, when they went to the agricultural college for a year to learn more about whiteface cattle.

"That was after Buddy and them had quit raising cotton. I remember that too. It was when the Government first begun to interfere with how a man farmed his own land, raised his cotton. Stabilizing the price, using up the surplus, they called it, giving a man advice and help, whether he wanted it or not. You may have noticed them boys in yonder tonight; curious folks almost, you might call them. That first year, when county agents was trying to explain the new system to farmers, the agent come out here and tried to explain it to Buddy and Lee and Stuart, explaining how they could cut down the crop, but that the Government would pay farmers the difference, and so they would actually be better off than trying to farm by themselves.

" 'Why, we're much obliged,' Buddy says. 'But we don't need no help. We'll just make the cotton like we always done; if we can't make a crop of it, that will just be our lookout and our loss, and we'll try again.'

"So they wouldn't sign no papers nor no cards nor nothing. They just went on and made the cotton like old Anse had taught them to; it was like they just couldn't believe that the Government aimed to help a man whether he wanted help or not, aimed to interfere with how much of anything he could make by hard work on his own land, making the crop and ginning it right here in their own gin, like they had always done, and hauling it to town to sell, hauling it all the way into Jefferson before they found out they couldn't sell it because, in the first place, they had made too much of it and, in the second place, they never had no card to sell what they would have been allowed. So they hauled it back. The gin wouldn't hold all of it, so they put some of it under Rafe's mule shed and they put the rest of it right here in the hall where we are setting now, where they would have to walk around it all winter and keep themselves reminded to be sho and fill out that card next time.

"Only next year they didn't fill out no papers neither. It was like they still couldn't believe it, still believed in the freedom and liberty to make or break according to a man's fitness and will to work, guaranteed by the Government that old Anse had tried to tear in two once and failed, and admitted in good faith he had failed and taken the consequences, and that had give Buddy a medal and taken care of him when he was far away from home in a strange land and hurt.

"So they made that second crop. And they couldn't sell it to nobody neither because they never had no cards. This time they built a special shed to put it under, and I remember how in that second winter Buddy come to town one day to see Lawyer Gavin Stevens. Not for legal advice how to sue the Government or somebody into buying the cotton, even if they never had no card for it, but just to find out why. 'I was for going ahead and signing up for it,' Buddy says. 'If that's going to be the new rule. But we talked it over, and Jackson ain't no farmer, but he knowed father longer than the rest of us, and he said father would have said no, and I reckon now he would have been right.'

"So they didn't raise any more cotton; they had a plenty of it to last a while — twenty-two bales, I think it was. That was when they went into whiteface cattle, putting old Anse's cotton land into pasture, because that's what he would have wanted them to do if the only way they could raise cotton was by the Government telling them how much they could raise and how much they could sell it for, and where, and when, and then pay them for not doing the work they didn't do. Only even when they didn't raise cotton, every year the county agent's young fellow would come out to measure the pasture crops they planted so he could pay them for that, even if they never had no not-cotton to be paid for. Except that he never measured no crop on this place. 'You're welcome to look at what we are doing,' Buddy says. 'But don't draw it down on your map.'

" 'But you can get money for this,' the young fellow says. 'The Government wants to pay you for planting all this.'

" 'We are aiming to get money for it,' Buddy says. 'When we can't, we will try something else. But not from the Government. Give that to them that want to take it. We can make out.'

"And that's about all. Them twenty-two bales of orphan cotton are down yonder in the gin right now, because there's room for it in the gin now because they ain't using the gin no more. And them boys grew up and went off a year to the agricultural college to learn right about whiteface cattle, and then come back to the rest of them — these here curious folks living off here to themselves, with the rest of the world all full of pretty neon lights burning night and day both, and easy, quick money scattering itself around everywhere for any man to grab a little, and every man with a shiny new automobile already wore out and throwed away and the new one delivered before the first one was even paid for, and everywhere a fine loud grabble and snatch of AAA and WPA and a dozen other three-letter reasons for a man not to work. Then this here draft comes along, and these curious folks ain't got around to signing that neither, and you come all the way up from Jackson with your paper all signed and regular, and we come out here, and after a while we can go back to town. A man gets around, don't he?"

"Yes," the investigator said. "Do you suppose we can go back to town now?"

"No," the marshal told him in that same kindly tone, "not just yet. But we can leave after a while. Of course you will miss your train. But there will be another one tomorrow."

He rose; though the investigator had heard nothing. The investigator watched him go down the hall and open the bedroom door and enter and close it behind him. The investigator sat quietly, listening to the night sounds and looking at the closed door until it opened presently and the marshal came back, carrying something in a bloody sheet, carrying it gingerly.

"Here," he said. "Hold it a minute."

"It's bloody," the investigator said.

"That's all right," the marshal said. "We can wash when we get through." So the investigator took the bundle and stood holding it while he watched the old marshal go back down the hall and on through it and vanish and return presently with a lighted lantern and a shovel. "Come along," he said. "We're pretty near through now."

The investigator followed him out of the house and across the yard, carrying gingerly the bloody, shattered, heavy bundle in which it still seemed to him he could feel some warmth of life, the marshal striding on ahead, the lantern swinging against his leg, the shadow of his striding scissoring and enormous along the earth, his voice still coming back over his shoulder, chatty and cheerful, "Yes, sir. A man gets around and he sees a heap; a heap of folks in a heap of situations. The trouble is, we done got into the habit of confusing the situations with the folks. Take yourself, now," he said in that same kindly tone, chatty and easy; "you mean all right. You just went and got yourself all fogged up with rules and regulations. That's our trouble. We done invented ourselves so many alphabets and rules and recipes that we can't see anything else; if what we see can't be fitted to an alphabet or a rule, we are lost. We have come to be like critters doctor folks might have created in laboratories, that have learned how to slip off their bones and guts and still live, still be kept alive indefinite and forever maybe even without even knowing the bones and the guts are gone. We have slipped our backbone; we have about decided a man don't need a backbone any more; to have one is old-fashioned. But the groove where the backbone used to be is still there, and the backbone has been kept alive, too, and someday we're going to slip back onto it. I don't know just when nor just how much of a wrench it will take to teach us, but someday."

They had left the yard now. They were mounting a slope; ahead of them the investigator could see another clump of cedars, a small clump, somehow shaggily formal against the starred sky. The marshal entered it and stopped and set the lantern down and, following with the bundle, the investigator saw a small rectangle of earth enclosed by a low brick coping. Then he saw the two graves, or the headstones — two plain granite slabs set upright in the earth.

"Old Anse and Mrs. Anse," the marshal said. "Buddy's wife wanted to be buried with her folks. I reckon she would have been right lonesome up here with just McCallums. Now, let's see." He stood for a moment, his chin in his hand; to the investigator he looked exactly like an old lady trying to decide where to set out a shrub. "They was to run from left to right, beginning with Jackson. But after the boys was born, Jackson and Stuart was to come up here by their pa and ma, so Buddy could move up some and make room. So he will be about here." He moved the lantern nearer and took up the shovel. Then he saw the investigator still holding the bundle. "Set it down," he said. "I got to dig first."

"I'll hold it," the investigator said.

"Nonsense, put it down," the marshal said. "Buddy won't mind."

So the investigator put the bundle down on the brick coping and the marshal began to dig, skillfully and rapidly, still talking in that cheerful, interminable voice, "Yes, sir. We done forgot about folks. Life has done got cheap, and life ain't cheap. Life's a pretty durn valuable thing. I don't mean just getting along from one WPA relief check to the next one, but honor and pride and discipline that make a man worth preserving, make him of any value. That's what we got to learn again. Maybe it takes trouble, bad trouble, to teach it back to us; maybe it was the walking to Virginia because that's where his ma come from, and losing a war and then walking back, that taught it to old Anse. Anyway, he seems to learned it, and to learned it good enough to bequeath it to his boys. Did you notice how all Buddy had to do was to tell them boys of his it was time to go, because the Government had sent them word? And how they told him good-by? Growned men kissing one another without hiding and without shame. Maybe that's what I am trying to say. . . . There." he said. "That's big enough."

He moved quickly, easily; before the investigator could stir, he had lifted the bundle into the narrow trench and was covering it, covering it as rapidly as he had dug, smoothing the earth over it with the shovel. Then he stood up and raised the lantern — a tall, lean old man, breathing easily and lightly.

"I reckon we can go back to town now," he said.

Befo

Read: 4/23/87, 5/4/88, 6/3/92, 2/10/98

Read: 5-2-86

Read: 4-16-85

IN ANOTHER COUNTRY

ERNEST HEMINGWAY

IN the fall the war was always there, but we did not go to it any more. It was cold in the fall in Milan and the dark came very early. Then the electric lights came on, and it was pleasant along the streets looking in the windows. There was much game hanging outside the shops, and the snow powdered in the fur of the foxes and the wind blew their tails. The deer hung stiff and heavy and empty, and small birds blew in the wind and the wind turned their feathers. It was a cold fall and the wind came down from the mountains.

We were all at the hospital every afternoon, and there were different ways of walking across the town through the dusk to the hospital. Two of the ways were alongside canals, but they were long. Always, though, you crossed a bridge across a canal to enter the hospital. There was a choice of three bridges. On one of them a woman sold roasted chestnuts. It was warm, standing in front of her charcoal fire, and the chestnuts were warm afterward in your pocket. The hospital was very old and very beautiful, and you entered through a gate and walked across a courtyard and out of a gate on the other side. There were usually funerals starting from the courtyard. Beyond the old hospital were the new brick pavilions, and there we met every afternoon and were all very polite and interested in what was the matter, and sat in the machines that were to make so much difference.

The doctor came up to the machine where I was sitting and said: "What did you like best to do before the war? Did you practice a sport?"

I said: "Yes, football."

"Good," he said. "You will be able to play football again better than ever."

My knee did not bend and the leg dropped straight from the knee to the ankle without a calf, and the machine was to bend the knee and make it move as in riding a tricycle. But it did not bend yet, and instead the machine lurched when it came to the bending part. The doctor said: "That will all pass. You are a fortunate young man. You will play football again like a champion."

In the next machine was a major who had a little hand like a baby's. He winked at me when the doctor examined his hand, which was between two leather straps that bounced up and down and flapped the stiff fingers, and said: "And will I too play football, captain-doctor?" He had been a very great fencer and, before the war, the greatest fencer in Italy.

The doctor went to his office in the back room and brought a photograph which showed a hand that had been withered almost as small as the major's, before it had taken a machine course, and after was a little larger. The major held the photograph with his good hand and looked at it very carefully. "A wound?" he asked.

"An industrial accident," the doctor said.

"Very interesting, very interesting," the major said, and handed it back to the doctor.

"You have confidence?"

"No," said the major.

There were three boys who came each day who were about the same age I was. They were all three from Milan, and one of them was to be a lawyer, and one was to be a painter, and one had intended to be a soldier, and after we were finished with the machines, sometimes we walked back together to the Café Cova, which was next door to the Scala. We walked the short way through the communist quarter because we were four together. The people hated us because we were officers, and from a wine-shop someone would call out, "A basso gli ufficiali!" as we passed. Another boy who walked with us sometimes and made us five wore a black silk handkerchief across his face because he had no nose then and his face was to be rebuilt. He had gone out to the front from the military academy and been wounded within an hour after he had gone into the front line for the first time. They rebuilt his face, but he came from a very old family and they could never get the nose exactly right. He went to South America and worked in a bank. But this was a long time ago, and then we did not any of us know how it was going to be afterward. We only knew then that there was always the war, but that we were not going to it any more.

We all had the same medals, except the boy with the black silk bandage across his face, and he had not been at the front long enough to get any medals. The tall boy with a very pale face who was to be a lawyer had been a lieutenant of Arditi and had three medals of the sort we each had only one of. He had lived a very long time with death and was a little detached. We were all a little detached, and there was nothing that held us together except that we met every afternoon at the hospital. Although, as we walked to the Cova through the tough part of town, walking in the dark, with light and singing coming out of the wine-shops, and sometimes having to walk into the street when the men and women would crowd together on the sidewalk so that we would have had to jostle them to get by, we felt held together by there being something that had happened that they, the people who disliked us, did not understand.

We ourselves all understood the Cova, where it was rich and warm and not too brightly lighted, and noisy and smoky at certain hours, and there were always girls at the tables and the illustrated papers on a rack on the wall. The girls at the Cova were very patriotic, and I found that the most patriotic people in Italy were the café girls — and I believe they are still patriotic.

The boys at first were very polite about my medals and asked me what I had done to get them. I showed them the papers, which were written in very beautiful language and full of *fratellanza* and *abnegazione*, but which really said, with the adjectives removed, that I had been given the medals because I was an American. After that their manner changed a little toward me, although I was their friend against outsiders. I was a friend, but I was never really one of them after they had read the citations, because it had been different with them and they had done very different things to get their medals. I had been wounded, it was true; but we all knew that being wounded, after all, was really an accident. I was never ashamed of the ribbons, though, and sometimes, after the cocktail hour, I would imagine myself having done all the things they had done to get their medals; but walking home at night through the empty streets with the cold wind and all the shops closed, trying to keep near the street lights, I knew that I would never have done such things, and I was very much afraid to die, and often lay in bed at night by myself, afraid to die and wondering how I would be when I went back to the front again.

The three with the medals were like hunting-hawks; and I was not a hawk, although I might seem a hawk to those who had never hunted; they, the three, knew better and so we drifted apart. But I stayed good friends with the boy who had been wounded his first day at the front, because he would never know now how he would have turned out; so he could never be accepted either, and I liked him because I thought perhaps he would not have turned out to be a hawk either.

The major, who had been the great fencer, did not believe in bravery, and spent much time while we sat in the machines correcting my grammar. He had complimented me on how I spoke Italian, and we talked together very easily. One day I had said that Italian seemed such an easy language to me that I could not take a great interest in it; everything was so easy to say. 'Ah, yes,' the major said. 'Why, then, do you not take up the use of grammar?' So we took up the use of grammar, and soon Italian was such a difficult language that I was afraid to talk to him until I had the grammar straight in my mind.

The major came very regularly to the hospital. I do not think he ever missed a day, although I am sure he did not believe in the machines. There was a time when none of us believed in the machines, and one day the major said it was all nonsense. The machines were new then and it was we who were to prove them. It was an idiotic idea, he said, "a theory, like another." I had not learned my grammar, and he said I was a stupid impossible disgrace, and he was a fool to have bothered with me. He was a small man and he sat straight up in his chair with his right hand thrust into the machine and looked straight ahead at the wall while the straps thumped up and down with his fingers in them.

"What will you do when the war is over if it is over?" he asked me. "Speak grammatically!"

"I will go to the States."

"Are you married?"

"No, but I hope to be."

"The more of a fool you are," he said. He seemed very angry. "A man must not marry."

"Why, Signor Maggiore?"

"Don't call me 'Signor Maggiore.' "

"Why must not a man marry?"

"He cannot marry. He cannot marry," he said angrily. "If he is to lose everything, he should not place himself in a position to lose that. He should not place himself in a positon to lose. He should find things he cannot lose."

He spoke very angrily and bitterly, and looked straight ahead while he talked.

"But why should he necessarily lose it?"

"He'll lose it," the major said. He was looking at the wall. Then he looked down at the machine and jerked his little hand out from between the straps and slapped it hard against his thigh. "He'll lose it," he almost shouted. "Don't argue with me!" Then he called to the attendant who ran the machines. "Come and turn this damned thing off."

He went back into the other room for the light treatment and the massage. Then I heard him ask the doctor if he might use his telephone and he shut the door. When he came back into the room, I was sitting in another machine. He was wearing his cape and had his cap on, and he came directly toward my machine and put his arm on my shoulder.

"I am so sorry," he said, and patted me on the shoulder with his good hand. "I would not be rude. My wife has just died. You must forgive me."

"Oh —" I said, feeling sick for him. "I am *so* sorry."

He stood there biting his lower lip. "It is very difficult," he said. "I cannot resign myself."

He looked straight past me and out through the window. Then he began to cry. "I am utterly unable to resign myself," he said and choked. And then crying, his head up, looking at nothing, carrying himself straight and soldierly, with tears on both his cheeks and biting his lips, he walked past the machines and out of the door.

The doctor told me that the major's wife, who was very young and whom he had not married until he was definitely invalided out of the war, had died of pneumonia. She had been sick only a few days. No one expected her to die. The major did not come to the hospital for three days. Then he came at the usual hour, wearing a black band on the sleeve of his uniform. When he came back, there were large framed photographs around the wall of all sorts of wounds before and after they had been cured by the machines. In front of the machine the major used were three photographs of hands like his that were completely restored. I do not know where the doctor got them. I always understood we were the first to use the machines. The photographs did not make much difference to the major because he only looked out of the window.

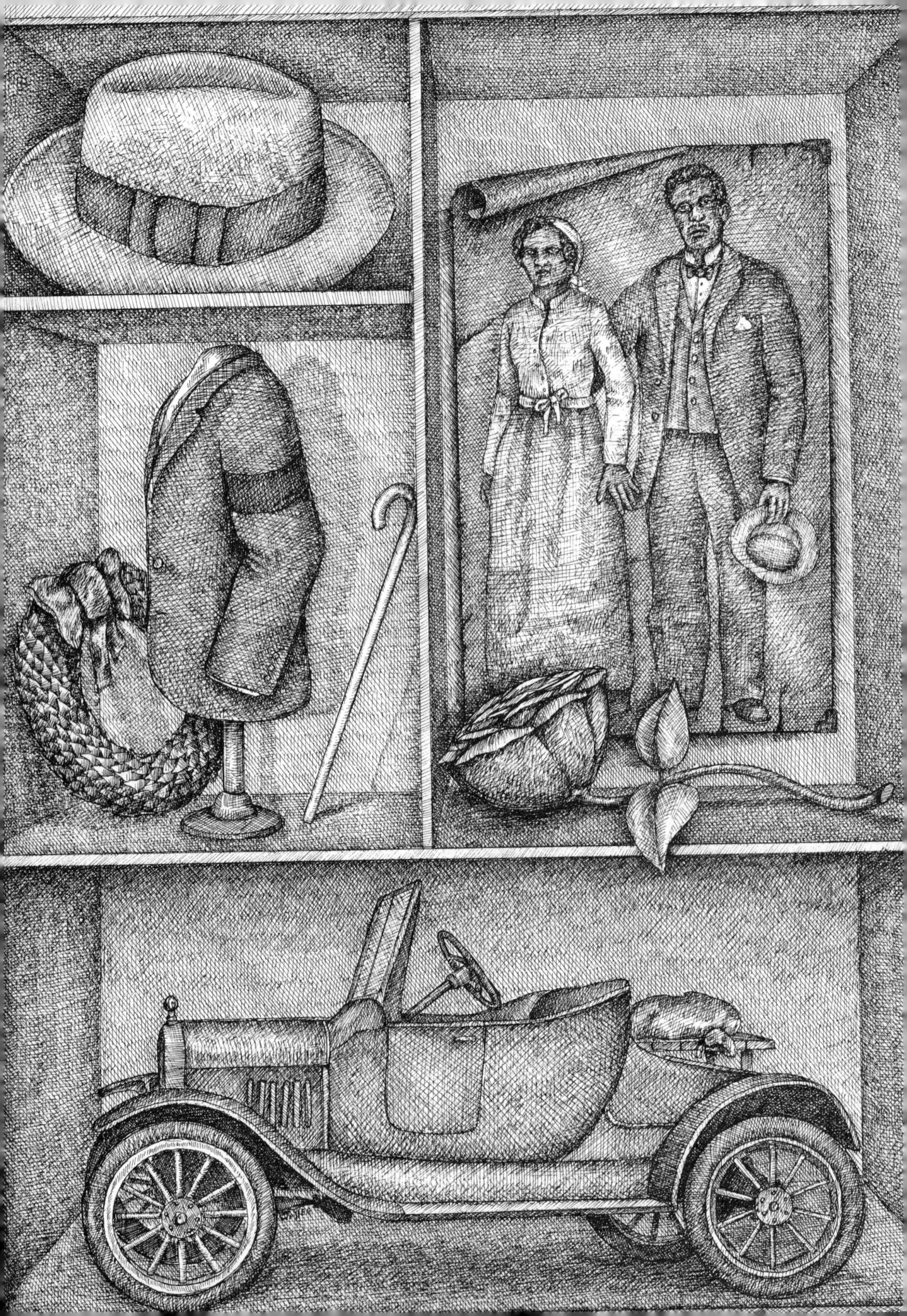

Read: 4/30/87, 5/4/88, 2/6/98

Read: 5/5/86

Read: 5/16/85

A SUMMER TRAGEDY

ARNA BONTEMPS

OLD Jeff Patton, the black share farmer, fumbled with his bow tie. His fingers trembled and the high stiff collar pinched his throat. A fellow loses his hand for such vanities after thirty or forty years of simple life. Once a year, or maybe twice if there's a wedding among his kinfolks, he may spruce up; but generally fancy clothes do nothing but adorn the wall of the big room and feed the moths. That had been Jeff Patton's experience. He had not worn his stiff-bosomed shirt more than a dozen times in all his married life. His swallow-tailed coat lay on the bed beside him, freshly brushed and pressed, but it was as full of holes as the overalls in which he worked on weekdays. The moths had used it badly. Jeff twisted his mouth into a hideous toothless grimace as he contended with the obstinate bow. He stamped his good foot and decided to give up the struggle.

"Jennie," he called.

"What's that, Jeff?" His wife's shrunken voice came out of the adjoining room like an echo. It was hardly bigger than a whisper.

"I reckon you'll have to he'p me wid this heah bow tie, baby," he said meekly. "Dog if I can hitch it up."

Her answer was not strong enough to reach him, but presently the old woman came to the door, feeling her way with a stick. She had a wasted, dead-leaf appearance. Her body, as scrawny and gnarled as a string bean, seemed less than nothing in the ocean of frayed and faded petticoats that surrounded her. These hung an inch or two above the tops of her heavy unlaced shoes and showed little grotesque piles where the stockings had fallen down from her negligible legs.

"You oughta could do a heap mo' wid a thing like that'n me — beingst as you got yo' good sight."

"Looks like I oughta could," he admitted. "But ma fingers is gone democrat on me. I get all mixed up in the looking glass an' can't tell wicha way to twist the devilish thing."

Jennie sat on the side of the bed and old Jeff Patton got down on one knee while she tied the bow knot. It was a slow and painful ordeal for each of them in this position. Jeff's bones cracked, his knee ached, and it was only after a half dozen attempts that Jennie worked a semblance of a bow into the tie.

"I got to dress maself now," the old woman whispered. "These is ma old shoes an' stockings, and I ain't so much as unwrapped ma dress."

"Well, don't worry 'bout me no mo', baby," Jeff said. "That 'bout finishes me. All I gotta do now is slip on that old coat 'n ves' an' I'll be fixed to leave."

Jennie disappeared again through the dim passage into the shed room. Being blind was no handicap to her in that black hole. Jeff heard the cane placed against the wall beside the door and knew that his wife was on easy ground. He put on his coat, took a battered top hat from the bedpost and hobbled to the front door. He was ready to travel. As soon as Jennie could get on her Sunday shoes and her old black silk dress, they would start.

Outside the tiny log house, the day was warm and mellow with sunshine. A host of wasps were humming with busy excitement in the trunk of a dead sycamore. Gray squirrels were searching through the grass for hickory nuts and blue jays were in the trees, hopping from branch to branch. Pine woods stretched away to the left like a black sea. Among them were scattered scores of log houses like Jeff's, houses of black share farmers. Cows and pigs wandered freely among the trees. There was no danger of loss. Each farmer knew his own stock and knew his neighbor's as well as he knew his neighbor's children.

Down the slope to the right were the cultivated acres on which the colored folks worked. They extended to the river, more than two miles away, and they were today green with the unmade cotton crop. A tiny thread of a road, which passed directly in front of Jeff's place, ran through these green fields like a pencil mark.

Jeff, standing outside the door, with his absurd hat in his left hand, surveyed the wide scene tenderly. He had been forty-five years on these acres. He loved them with the unexplained affection that others have for the countries to which they belong.

The sun was hot on his head, his collar still pinched his throat, and the Sunday clothes were intolerably hot. Jeff transferred the hat to his right hand and began fanning with it. Suddenly the whisper that was Jennie's voice came out of the shed room.

"You can bring the car round front whilst you's waitin'," it said feebly. There was a tired pause; then it added, "I'll soon be fixed to go."

"A'right, baby," Jeff answered. "I'll get it in a minute."

But he didn't move. A thought struck him that made his mouth fall open. The mention of the car brought to his mind, with new intensity, the trip he and Jennie were about to take. Fear came into his eyes; excitement took his breath. . . .

"Jeff . . . O Jeff," the old woman's whisper called.

He awakened with a jolt. "Hunh, baby?"

"What you doin'?"

"Nuthin. Jes studyin'. I jes been turnin' things round'n round in ma mind."

"You could be gettin' the car," she said.

"Oh yes, right away, baby."

He started round to the shed, limping heavily on his bad leg. There were three frizzly chickens in the yard. All his other chickens had been killed or stolen recently. But the frizzly chickens had been saved somehow. That was fortunate indeed, for these curious creatures had a way of devouring "Poison" from the yard and in that way protecting against conjure and black luck and spells. But even the frizzly chickens seemed now to be in a stupor. Jeff thought they had some ailment; he expected all three of them to die shortly.

The shed in which the old T-model Ford stood was only a

grass roof held up by four corner poles. It had been built by tremulous hands at a time when the little rattletrap car had been regarded as a peculiar treasure. And, miraculously, despite wind and downpour it still stood.

Jeff adjusted the crank and put his weight upon it. The engine came to life with a sputter and bang that rattled the old car from radiator to taillight. Jeff hopped into the seat and put his foot on the accelerator. The sputtering and banging increased. The rattling became more violent. That was good. It was good banging, good sputtering and rattling, and it meant that the aged car was still in running condition. She could be depended on for this trip.

Again Jeff's thought halted as if paralyzed. The suggestion of the trip fell into the machinery of his mind like a wrench. He felt dazed and weak. He swung the car out into the yard, made a half turn and drove around to the front door. When he took his hands off the wheel, he noticed that he was trembling violently. He cut off the motor and climbed to the ground to wait for Jennie.

A few minutes later she was at the window, her voice rattling against the pane like a broken shutter.

"I'm ready, Jeff."

He did not answer, but limped into the house and took her by the arm. He led her slowly through the big room, down the step and across the yard.

"You reckon I'd oughta lock the do'?" he asked softly.

They stopped and Jennie weighed the question. Finally she shook her head.

"Ne' mind the do'," she said. "I don't see no cause to lock up things."

"You right," Jeff agreed. "No cause to lock up."

Jeff opened the door and helped his wife into the car. A quick shudder passed over him. . . . Again he trembled.

"How come you shaking so?" Jennie whispered.

"I don't know," he said.

"You mus' be scairt, Jeff."

"No, baby, I ain't scairt."

He slammed the door after her and went around to crank up again. The motor started easily. Jeff wished that it had not been so responsive. He would have liked a few more minutes in which to turn things around in his head. As it was, with Jennie chiding him about being afraid, he had to keep going. He swung the car into the little pencil-mark road and started off toward the river, driving very slowly, very cautiously.

Chugging across the green countryside, the small battered Ford seemed tiny indeed. Jeff felt a familiar excitement, a thrill, as they came down the first slope to the immense levels on which the cotton was growing. He could not help reflecting that the crops were good. He knew what that meant, too; he had made forty-five of them with his own hands. It was true that he had worn out nearly a dozen mules, but that was the fault of old man Stevenson, the owner of the land. Major Stevenson had the odd notion that one mule was all a share farmer needed to work a thirty-acre plot. It was an expensive notion, the way it killed mules from overwork, but the old man held to it. Jeff thought it killed a good many share farmers as well as mules, but he had no sympathy for them. He had always been strong, and he had been taught to have no patience with weakness in men. Women or children might be tolerated if they were puny, but a weak man was a curse. Of course, his own children —

Jeff's thought halted there. He and Jennie never mentioned their dead children any more. And naturally he did not wish to dwell upon them in his mind. Before he knew it, some remark would slip out of his mouth and that would make Jennie feel blue. Perhaps she would cry. A woman like Jennie could not easily throw off the grief that comes from losing five grown children within two years. Even Jeff was still staggered by the blow. His memory had not been much good recently. He frequently talked to himself. And, although he had kept it a secret, he knew that his courage had left him. He was terrified by the least unfamiliar sound at night. He was reluctant to venture far from home in the daytime. And that habit of trembling when he felt fearful was now far beyond his control. Sometimes he became afraid and trembled without knowing what had frightened him. The feeling would just come over him like a chill.

The car rattled slowly over the dusty road. Jennie sat erect and silent, with a little absurd hat pinned to her hair. Her useless eyes seemed very large, very white in their deep sockets. Suddenly Jeff heard her voice, and he inclined his head to catch the words.

"Is we passed Delia Moore's house yet?" she asked.

"Not yet," he said.

"You must be drivin' mighty slow, Jeff."

"We might just as well take our time, baby."

There was a pause. A little puff of steam was coming out of the radiator of the car. Heat wavered above the hood. Delia Moore's house was nearly half a mile away. After a moment Jennie spoke again.

"You ain't really scairt, is you, Jeff?"

"Nah, baby, I ain't scairt."

"You know how we agreed — we gotta keep on goin'."

Jewels of perspiration appeared on Jeff's forehead. His eyes rounded, blinked, became fixed on the road.

"I don't know," he said with a shiver. "I reckon it's the only thing to do."

"Hm."

A flock of guinea fowls, pecking in the road, were scattered by the passing car. Some of them took to their wings; others hid under bushes. A blue jay, swaying on a leafy twig, was annoying a roadside squirrel. Jeff held an even speed till he came near Delia's place. Then he slowed down noticeably.

Delia's house was really no house at all, but an abandoned store building converted into a dwelling. It sat near a crossroads, beneath a single black cedar tree. There Delia, a cattish old creature of Jennie's age, lived alone. She had been there more years than anybody could remember, and long ago had won the disfavor of such women as Jennie. For in her young days Delia had been gayer, yellower and saucier than seemed proper in those parts. Her ways with menfolks had been dark and suspicious. And the fact that she had had as many husbands as children did not help her reputation.

"Yonder's old Delia," Jeff said as they passed.

"What she doin'?"

"Jes sittin' in the do," he said.

"She see us?"

"Hm," Jeff said. "Musta did."

That relieved Jennie. It strengthened her to know that her old enemy had seen her pass in her best clothes. That would give the old she-devil something to chew her gums and fret about, Jennie thought. Wouldn't she have a fit if she didn't find out? Old evil Delia! This would be just the thing for her. It would pay her back for being so evil. It would also pay her, Jennie thought, for the way she used to grin at Jeff — long ago when her teeth were good.

The road became smooth and red, and Jeff could tell by the smell of the air that they were nearing the river. He could see the rise where the road turned and ran along parallel to the stream. The car chugged on monotonously. After a long silent spell, Jennie leaned against Jeff and spoke.

"How many bale o' cotton you think we got standin'?" she said.

Jeff wrinkled his forehead as he calculated.

"'Bout twenty-five, I reckon."

"How many you make las' year?"

"Twenty-eight," he said. "How come you ask that?"

"I's jes thinkin'," Jennie said quietly.

"It don't make a speck o' difference though," Jeff reflected. "If we get much or if we get little, we still gonna be in debt to old man Stevenson when he gets through counting up agin us. It's took us a long time to learn that."

Jennie was not listening to these words. She had fallen into a trance-like meditation. Her lips twitched. She chewed her gums and rubbed her gnarled hands nervously. Suddenly she leaned forward, buried her face in the nervous hands and burst into tears. She cried aloud in a dry cracked voice that suggested the rattle of fodder on dead stalks. She cried aloud like a child, for she had never learned to suppress a genuine sob. Her slight old frame shook heavily and seemed hardly able to sustain such violent grief.

"What's the matter, baby?" Jeff asked awkwardly. "Why you cryin' like all that?"

"I's jes thinkin'," she said.

"So you the one what's scairt now, hunh?"

"I ain't scairt, Jeff. I's jes thinkin' 'bout leavin' eve'thing like this — eve'thing we been used to. It's right sad-like."

Jeff did not answer, and presently Jennie buried her face again and cried.

The sun was almost overhead. It beat down furiously on the dusty wagon-path road, on the parched roadside grass and the tiny battered car. Jeff's hands, gripping the wheel, became wet with perspiration; his forehead sparkled. Jeff's lips parted. His mouth shaped a hideous grimace. His face suggested the face of a man being burned. But the torture passed and his expression softened again.

"You mustn't cry, baby," he said to his wife. "We gotta be strong. We can't break down."

Jennie waited a few seconds, then said. "You reckon we oughta do it, Jeff? You reckon we oughta go 'head an' do it, really?"

Jeff's voice choked; his eyes blurred. He was terrified to hear Jennie say the thing that had been in his mind all morning. She had egged him on when he had wanted more than anything in the world to wait, to reconsider, to think things over a little longer. Now she was getting cold feet. Actually there was no need of thinking the question through again. It would only end in making the same painful decision once more. Jeff knew that. There was no need of fooling around longer.

"We jes as well to do like we planned," he said. "They ain't nothin' else for us now — it's the bes' thing."

Jeff thought of the handicaps, the near impossibility, of making another crop with his leg bothering him more and more each week. Then there was always the chance that he would have another stroke, like the one that had made him lame. Another one might kill him. The least it could do would be to leave him helpless. Jeff gasped — . . . He could not bear to think of being helpless, like a baby, on Jennie's hands. Frail, blind Jennie.

The little pounding motor of the car worked harder and harder. The puff of steam from the cracked radiator became larger. Jeff realized that they were climbing a little rise. A moment later the road turned abruptly and he looked down upon the face of the river.

"Jeff."

"Hunh?"

"Is that the water I hear?"

"Hm. Tha's it."

"Well, which way you goin' now?"

"Down this-a way," he said. "The road runs 'long 'side o' the water a lil piece."

She waited a while calmly. Then she said, "Drive faster."

"A'right, baby," Jeff said.

The water roared in the bed of the river. It was fifty or sixty feet below the level of the road. Between the road and the water there was a long smooth slope, sharply inclined. The slope was dry, the clay hardened by prolonged summer heat. The water below, roaring in a narrow channel, was noisy and wild.

"Jeff."

"Hunh?"

"How far you goin'?"

"Jes a lil piece down the road."

"You ain't scairt, is you, Jeff?"

"Nah, baby," he said trembling. "I ain't scairt."

"Remember how we planned it, Jeff. We gotta do it like we said. Brave-like."

"Hm."

Jeff's brain darkened. Things suddenly seemed unreal, like figures in a dream. Thoughts swam in his mind foolishly, hysterically, like little blind fish in a pool within a dense cave. They rushed, crossed one another, jostled, collided, retreated and rushed again. Jeff soon became dizzy. He shuddered violently and turned to his wife.

"Jennie, I can't do it. I can't." His voice broke pitifully.

She did not appear to be listening. All the grief had gone from her face. She sat erect, her unseeing eyes wide open, strained and frightful. Her glossy black skin had become dull. She seemed as thin, as sharp and bony, as a starved bird. Now having suffered and endured the sadness of tearing herself away from beloved things, she showed no anguish. She was absorbed with her own thoughts, and she didn't even hear Jeff's voice shouting in her ear.

Jeff said nothing more. For an instant there was light in his cavernous brain. The great chamber was, for less than a second, peopled by characters he knew and loved. They were simple, healthy creatures, and they behaved in a manner that he could understand. They had quality. But since he had already taken leave of them long ago, the remembrance did not break his heart again. Young Jeff Patton was among them, the Jeff Patton of fifty years ago who went down to New Orleans with a crowd of country boys to the Mardi Gras doings. The gay young crowd, boys with candy-striped shirts and rouged-brown girls in noisy silks, was like a picture in his head. Yet it did not make him sad. On that very trip Slim Burns had killed Joe Beasley — the crowd had been broken up. Since then Jeff Patton's world had been the Greenbriar Plantation. If there had been other Mardi Gras carnivals, he had not heard of them. Since then there had been no time; the years had fallen on him like waves. Now he was old, worn out. Another paralytic stroke (like the one he had already suffered) would put him on his back for keeps. In that condition, with a frail blind woman to look after him, he would be worse off than if he were dead.

Suddenly Jeff's hands became steady. He actually felt brave. He slowed down the motor of the car and carefully pulled off the road. Below, the water of the stream boomed, a soft thunder in the deep channel. Jeff ran the car onto the clay slope, pointed it directly toward the stream and put his foot heavily on the accelerator. The little car leaped furiously down the steep incline toward the water. The movement was nearly as swift and direct as a fall. The two old black folks, sitting quietly side by side, showed no excitement. In another instant the car hit the water and dropped immediately out of sight.

A little later it lodged in the mud of a shallow place. One wheel of the crushed and upturned little Ford became visible above the rushing water.

Read: 5/7/87, 2/19/98

Read: 5/5/86

Read: 5/9/85

FLIGHT

JOHN STEINBECK

ABOUT fifteen miles below Monterey, on the wild coast, the Torres family had their farm, a few sloping acres above a cliff that dropped to the brown reefs and to the hissing white waters of the ocean. Behind the farm the stone mountains stood up against the sky. The farm buildings huddled like little clinging aphids on the mountain skirts, crouched low to the ground as though the wind might blow them into the sea. The little shack, the rattling, rotting barn were grey-bitten with sea salt, beaten by the damp wind until they had taken on the color of the granite hills. Two horses, a red cow and a red calf, half a dozen pigs and a flock of lean, multi-colored chickens stocked the place. A little corn was raised on the sterile slope, and it grew short and thick under the wind, and all the cobs formed on the landward sides of the stalks.

Mama Torres, a lean, dry woman with ancient eyes, had ruled the farm for ten years, ever since her husband tripped over a stone in the field one day and fell full length on a rattlesnake. When one is bitten on the chest there is not much that can be done.

Mama Torres had three children, two undersized black ones of twelve and fourteen, Emilio and Rosy, whom Mama kept fishing on the rocks below the farm when the sea was kind and when the truant officer was in some distant part of Monterey County. And there was Pepé, the tall smiling son of nineteen, a gentle, affectionate boy, but very lazy. Pepé had a tall head, pointed at the top, and from its peak, coarse black hair grew down like a thatch all around. Over his smiling little eyes Mama cut a straight bang so he could see. Pepé had sharp Indian cheek bones and an eagle nose, but his mouth was as sweet and shapely as a girl's mouth, and his chin was fragile and chiseled. He was loose and gangling, all legs and feet and wrists, and he was very lazy. Mama thought him fine and brave, but she never told him so. She said, "Some lazy cow must have got into thy father's family, else how could I have a son like thee." And she said, "When I carried thee, a sneaking lazy coyote came out of the brush and looked at me one day. That must have made thee so."

Pepé smiled sheepishly and stabbed at the ground with his knife to keep the blade sharp and free from rust. It was his inheritance, that knife, his father's knife. The long heavy blade folded back into the black handle. There was a button on the handle. When Pepé pressed the button, the blade leaped out ready for use. The knife was with Pepé always, for it had been his father's knife.

One sunny morning when the sea below the cliff was glinting and blue and the white surf creamed on the reef, when even the stone mountains looked kindly, Mama Torres called out the door of the shack, "Pepé, I have a labor for thee."

There was no answer. Mama listened. From behind the barn she heard a burst of laughter. She lifted her full long skirt and walked in the direction of the noise.

Pepé was sitting on the ground with his back against a box. His white teeth glistened. On either side of him stood the two black ones, tense and expectant. Fifteen feet away a redwood post was set in the ground. Pepé's right hand lay limply in his lap, and in the palm the big black knife rested. The blade was closed back into the handle. Pepé looked smiling at the sky.

Suddenly Emilio cried, "Ya!"

Pepé's wrist flicked like the head of a snake. The blade seemed to fly open in mid-air; and with a thump the point dug into the redwood post, and the black handle quivered. The three burst into excited laughter. Rosy ran to the post and pulled out the knife and brought it back to Pepé. He closed the blade and settled the knife carefully in his listless palm again. He grinned self-consciously at the sky.

"Ya!"

The heavy knife lanced out and sunk into the post again. Mama moved forward like a ship and scattered the play.

"All day you do foolish things with the knife, like a toy-baby," she stormed. "Get up on thy huge feet that eat up shoes. Get up!" She took him by one loose shoulder and hoisted at him. Pepé grinned sheepishly and came half-heartedly to his feet. "Look!" Mama cried. "Big lazy, you must catch the horse and put on him thy father's saddle. You must ride to Monterey. The medicine bottle is empty. There is no salt. Go thou now, Peanut! Catch the horse."

A revolution took place in the relaxed figure of Pepé. "To Monterey, me? Alone? Sí, Mama."

She scowled at him. "Do not think, big sheep, that you will buy candy. No, I will give you only enough for the medicine and the salt."

Pepé smiled. "Mama, you will put the hatband on the hat?"

She relented then. "Yes, Pepé. You may wear the hat-band."

His voice grew insinuating, "And the green handkerchief, Mama?"

"Yes, if you go quickly and return with no trouble, the silk green handkerchief will go. If you make sure to take off the handkerchief when you eat so no spot may fall on it. . . ."

"Sí, Mama. I will be careful. I am a man."

"Thou? A man? Thou art a peanut."

He went into the rickety barn and brought out a rope, and he walked agilely enough up the hill to catch the horse.

When he was ready and mounted before the door, mounted on his father's saddle that was so old that the oaken frame showed through torn leather in many places, then Mama brought out the round black hat with the tooled leather band, and she reached up and knotted the green silk handker-chief about his neck. Pepé's blue denim coat was much darker than his jeans, for it had been washed much less often.

Mama handed up the big medicine bottle and the silver coins. "That for the medicine," she said, "and that for the salt. That for a candle to burn for the papa. That for *dulces* for the little ones. Our friend Mrs. Rodriguez will give you dinner and maybe a bed for the night. When you go to the church say only ten Paternosters and only twenty-five Ave Marias. Oh! I know, big coyote. You would sit there flapping your mouth over Aves all day while you looked at the candles and the holy pictures. That is not good devotion to stare at the pretty things."

The black hat, covering the high pointed head and black thatched hair of Pepé, gave him dignity and age. He sat the rangy horse well. Mama thought how handsome he was, dark and lean and tall. "I would not send thee now alone, thou little one, except for the medicine," she said softly. "It is not good to have no medicine, for who knows when the toothache will come, or the sadness of the stomach. These things are."

"Adios, Mama," Pepé cried. "I will come back soon. You may send me often alone. I am a man."

"Thou art a foolish chicken."

He straightened his shoulders, flipped the reins against the horse's shoulder and rode away. He turned once and saw that they still watched him, Emilio and Rosy and Mama. Pepé grinned with pride and gladness and lifted the tough buckskin horse to a trot.

When he had dropped out of sight over a little dip in the road, Mama turned to the black ones, but she spoke to herself. "He is nearly a man now," she said. "It will be a nice thing to have a man in the house again." Her eyes sharpened on the children. "Go to the rocks now. The tide is going out. There will be abalones to be found." She put the iron hooks into their hands and saw them down the steep trail to the reefs. She brought the smooth stone metate to the doorway and sat grinding her corn to flour and looking occasionally at the road over which Pepé had gone. The noonday came and then the afternoon, when the little ones beat the abalones on a rock to make them tender and Mama patted the tortillas to make them thin. They ate their dinner as the red sun was plunging down toward the ocean. They sat on the doorsteps and watched the big white moon come over the mountain tops.

Mama said, "He is now at the house of our friend Mrs. Rodriguez. She will give him nice things to eat and maybe a present."

Emilio said, "Some day I too will ride to Monterey for medicine. Did Pepé come to be a man today?"

Mama said wisely, "A boy gets to be a man when a man is needed. Remember this thing. I have known boys forty years old because there was no need for a man."

Soon afterwards they retired, Mama in her big oak bed on one side of the room, Emilio and Rosy in their boxes full of straw and sheepskins on the other side of the room.

The moon went over the sky and the surf roared on the rocks. The roosters crowed the first call. The surf subsided to a whispering surge against the reef. The moon dropped toward the sea. The roosters crowed again.

The moon was near down to the water when Pepé rode on a winded horse to his home flat. His dog bounced out and circled the horse yelping with pleasure. Pepé slid off the saddle to the ground. The weathered little shack was silver in the moonlight and the square shadow of it was black to the north and east. Against the east the piling mountains were misty with light; their tops melted into the sky.

Pepé walked wearily up the three steps and into the house. It was dark inside. There was a rustle in the corner.

Mama cried out from her bed. "Who comes? Pepé, is it thou?"

"Sí, Mama."

"Did you get the medicine?"

"Sí, Mama."

"Well, go to sleep, then. I thought you would be sleeping at the house of Mrs. Rodriguez." Pepé stood silently in the dark room. "Why do you stand there, Pepé? Did you drink wine?"

"Sí, Mama."

"Well, go to bed then and sleep out the wine."

His voice was tired and patient, but very firm. "Light the candle, Mama. I must go away into the mountains."

"What is this, Pepé? You are crazy." Mama struck a sulphur match and held the little blue burr until the flame spread up the stick. She set light to the candle on the floor beside her bed. "Now, Pepé, what is this you say?" She looked anxiously into his face.

He was changed. The fragile quality seemed to have gone from his chin. His mouth was less full than it had been, the lines of the lips were straighter, but in his eyes the greatest change had taken place. There was no laughter in them any more, nor any bashfulness. They were sharp and bright and purposeful.

He told her in a tired monotone, told her everything just as it had happened. A few people came into the kitchen of Mrs. Rodriguez. There was wine to drink. Pepé drank wine. The little quarrel — the man started toward Pepé and then the knife — it went almost by itself. It flew, it darted before Pepé knew it. As he talked, Mama's face grew stern, and it seemed to grow more lean. Pepé finished. "I am a man now, Mama. The man said names to me I could not allow."

Mama nodded. "Yes, thou art a man, my poor little Pepé. Thou art a man. I have seen it coming on thee. I have watched you throwing the knife into the post, and I have been afraid." For a moment her face had softened, but now it grew stern again. "Come! We must get you ready. Go. Awaken Emilio and Rosy. Go quickly."

Pepé stepped over to the corner where his brother and sister slept among the sheepskins. He leaned down and shook them gently. "Come, Rosy! Come, Emilio! The mama says you must arise."

The little black ones sat up and rubbed their eyes in the candlelight. Mama was out of bed now, her long black skirt over her nightgown. "Emilio," she cried. "Go up and catch the other horse for Pepé. Quickly, now! Quickly." Emilio put his legs in his overalls and stumbled sleepily out the door.

"You heard no one behind you on the road?" Mama demanded.

"No, Mama. I listened carefully. No one was on the road."

Mama darted like a bird about the room. From a nail on the wall she took a canvas water bag and threw it on the floor. She stripped a blanket from her bed and rolled it into a tight tube and tied the ends with string. From a box beside the stove she lifted a flour sack half full of black stringy jerky. "Your father's black coat, Pepé. Here, put it on."

Pepé stood in the middle of the floor watching her activity. She reached behind the door and brought out the rifle, a long 38–56, worn shiny the whole length of the barrel. Pepé took it from her and held it in the crook of his elbow. Mama brought a little leather bag and counted the cartridges into his hand. "Only ten left," she warned. "You must not waste them."

Emilio put his head in the door. " *'Qui 'st 'l caballo,* Mama."

"Put on the saddle from the other horse. Tie on the blanket. Here, tie the jerky to the saddle horn."

Still Pepé stood silently watching his mother's frantic activity. His chin looked hard, and his sweet mouth was drawn and thin. His little eyes followed Mama about the room almost suspiciously.

Rosy asked softly, "Where goes Pepé?"

Mama's eyes were fierce. "Pepé goes on a journey. Pepé is a man now. He has a man's thing to do."

Pepé straightened his shoulders. His mouth changed until he looked very much like Mama.

At last the preparation was finished. The loaded horse stood outside the door. The water bag dripped a line of moisture down the bay shoulder.

The moonlight was being thinned by the dawn and the big white moon was near down to the sea. The family stood by the shack. Mama confronted Pepé. "Look, my son! Do not stop until it is dark again. Do not sleep even though you are tired. Take care of the horse in order that he may not stop of weariness. Remember to be careful with the bullets — there are only ten. Do not fill thy stomach with jerky or it will make thee sick. Eat a little jerky and fill thy stomach with grass. When thou comest to the high mountains, if thou seest any of the dark watching men, go not near to them nor try to speak to them. And forget not thy prayers." She put her lean hands on Pepé's shoulders, stood on her toes and kissed him formally on both cheeks, and Pepé kissed her on both cheeks. Then he went to Emilio and Rosy and kissed both of their cheeks.

Pepé turned back to Mama. He seemed to look for a little softness, a little weakness in her. His eyes were searching, but

Mama's face remained fierce. "Go now," she said. "Do not wait to be caught like a chicken."

Pepé pulled himself into the saddle. "I am a man," he said.

It was the first dawn when he rode up the hill toward the little canyon which let a trail into the mountains. Moonlight and daylight fought with each other, and the two warring qualities made it difficult to see. Before Pepé had gone a hundred yards, the outlines of his figure were misty; and long before he entered the canyon, he had become a grey, indefinite shadow.

Mama stood stiffly in front of her doorstep, and on either side of her stood Emilio and Rosy. They cast furtive glances at Mama now and then.

When the grey shape of Pepé melted into the hillside and disappeared, Mama relaxed. She began the high, whining keen of the death wail. "Our beautiful — our brave," she cried. "Our protector, our son is gone." Emilio and Rosy moaned beside her. "Our beautiful — our brave, he is gone." It was the formal wail. It rose to a high piercing whine and subsided to a moan. Mama raised it three times and then she turned and went into the house and shut the door.

Emilio and Rosy stood wondering in the dawn. They heard Mama whimpering in the house. They went out to sit on the cliff above the ocean. They touched shoulders. "When did Pepé come to be a man?" Emilio asked.

"Last night," said Rosy. "Last night in Monterey." The ocean clouds turned red with the sun that was behind the mountains.

"We will have no breakfast," said Emilio. "Mama will not want to cook." Rosy did not anwer him. "Where is Pepé gone?" he asked.

Rosy looked around at him. She drew her knowledge from the quiet air. "He has gone on a journey. He will never come back."

"Is he dead? Do you think he is dead?"

Rosy looked back at the ocean again. A little steamer, drawing a line of smoke sat on the edge of the horizon.

"He is not dead," Rosy explained. "Not yet."

Pepé rested the big rifle across the saddle in front of him. He let the horse walk up the hill and he didn't look back. The stony slope took on a coat of short brush so that Pepé found the entrance to a trail and entered it.

When he came to the canyon opening, he swung once in his saddle and looked back, but the houses were swallowed in the misty light. Pepé jerked forward again. The high shoulder of the canyon closed in on him. His horse stretched out its neck and sighed and settled to the trail.

It was a well-worn path, dark soft leaf-mould earth strewn with broken pieces of sandstone. The trail rounded the shoulder of the canyon and dropped steeply into the bed of the stream. In the shallows the water ran smoothly, glinting in the first morning sun. Small round stones on the bottom were as brown as rust with sun moss. In the sand along the edges of the stream the tall, rich wild mint grew, while in the water itself the cress, old and tough, had gone to heavy seed.

The path went into the stream and emerged on the other side. The horse sloshed into the water and stopped. Pepé dropped his bridle and let the beast drink of the running water.

Soon the canyon sides became steep and the first giant sentinel redwoods guarded the trail, great round red trunks bearing foliage as green and lacy as ferns. Once Pepé was among the trees, the sun was lost. A perfumed and purple light lay in the pale green of the underbrush. Gooseberry bushes and blackberries and tall ferns lined the stream, and overhead the branches of the redwoods met and cut off the sky.

Pepé drank from the water bag, and he reached into the flour sack and brought out a black string of jerky. His white teeth gnawed at the string until the tough meat parted. He chewed slowly and drank occasionally from the water bag. His little eyes were slumberous and tired, but the muscles of his face were hard set. The earth of the trail was black now. It gave up a hollow sound under the walking hoofbeats.

The stream fell more sharply. Little waterfalls splashed on the stones. Five-fingered ferns hung over the water and dripped spray from their fingertips. Pepé rode half over in his saddle, dangling one leg loosely. He picked a bay leaf from a tree beside the way and put it into his mouth for a moment to flavor the dry jerky. He held the gun loosely across the pommel.

Suddenly he squared in his saddle, swung the horse from the trail and kicked it hurriedly up behind a big redwood tree. He pulled up the reins tight against the bit to keep the horse from whinnying. His face was intent and his nostrils quivered a little.

A hollow pounding came down the trail, and a horseman rode by, a fat man with red cheeks and a white stubble beard. His horse put down its head and blubbered at the trail when it came to the place where Pepé had turned off. "Hold up!" said the man and he pulled up his horse's head.

When the last sound of the hoofs died away, Pepé came back into the trail again. He did not relax in the saddle any more. He lifted the big rifle and swung the lever to throw a shell into the chamber, and then he let down the hammer to half cock.

The trail grew very steep. Now the redwood trees were smaller and their tops were dead, bitten dead where the wind reached them. The horse plodded on; the sun went slowly overhead and started down toward the afternoon.

Where the stream came out of a side canyon, the trail left it. Pepé dismounted and watered his horse and filled up his water bag. As soon as the trail had parted from the stream, the trees were gone and only the thick brittle sage and manzanita and chaparral edged the trail. And the soft black earth was gone, too, leaving only the light tan broken rock for the trail bed. Lizards scampered away into the brush as the horse rattled over the little stones.

Pepé turned in his saddle and looked back. He was in the open now: he could be seen from a distance. As he ascended the trail the country grew more rough and terrible and dry. The way wound about the bases of great square rocks. Little grey rabbits skittered in the brush. A bird made a monotonous high creaking. Eastward the bare rock mountaintops were pale and powder-dry under the dropping sun. The horse plodded up and up the trail toward a little V in the ridge which was the pass.

Pepé looked suspiciously back every minute or so, and his eyes sought the tops of the ridges ahead. Once, on a white barren spur, he saw a black figure for a moment, but he looked quickly away, for it was one of the dark watchers. No one knew who the watchers were, nor where they lived, but it was better to ignore them and never to show interest in them. They did not bother one who stayed on the trail and minded his own business.

The air was parched and full of light dust blown by the breeze from the eroding mountains. Pepé drank sparingly from his bag and corked it tightly and hung it on the horn again. The trail moved up the dry shale hillside, avoiding rocks, dropping under clefts, climbing in and out of old water scars. When he arrived at the little pass he stopped and looked back for a long time. No dark watchers were to be seen now. The trail behind was empty. Only the high tops of the redwoods indicated where the stream flowed.

Pepé rode on through the pass. His little eyes were nearly closed with weariness, but his face was stern, relentless and manly. The high mountain wind coasted sighing through the pass and whistled on the edges of the big blocks of broken granite. In the air, a red-tailed hawk sailed over close to the ridge and screamed angrily. Pepé went slowly through the broken jagged pass and looked down on the other side.

The trail dropped quickly, staggering among broken rock. At the bottom of the slope there was a dark crease, thick with brush, and on the other side of the crease a little flat, in which a grove of oak trees grew. A scar of green grass cut across the flat. And behind the flat another mountain rose, desolate with dead rocks and starving little black bushes. Pepé drank from the bag again for the air was so dry that it encrusted his nostrils and burned his lips. He put the horse down the trail. The hooves slipped and struggled on the steep way, starting little stones that rolled off into the brush. The sun was gone behind the westward mountain now, but still it glowed brilliantly on the oaks and on the grassy flat. The rocks and the hillsides still sent up waves of the heat they had gathered from the day's sun.

Pepé looked up to the top of the next dry withered ridge. He saw a dark form against the sky, a man's figure standing on top of a rock, and he glanced away quickly not to appear curious. When a moment later he looked up again, the figure was gone.

Downward the trail was quickly covered. Sometimes the horse floundered for footing, sometimes set his feet and slid a little way. They came at last to the bottom where the dark chaparral was higher than Pepé's head. He held up his rifle on one side and his arm on the other to shield his face from the sharp brittle fingers of the brush.

Up and out of the crease he rode, and up a little cliff. The grassy flat was before him, and the round comfortable oaks. For a moment he studied the trail down which he had come, but there was no movement and no sound from it. Finally he rode out over the flat, to the green streak, and at the upper end of the damp he found a little spring welling out of the earth and dropping into a dug basin before it seeped out over the flat.

Pepé filled his bag first, and then he let the thirsty horse drink out of the pool. He led the horse to the clump of oaks, and in the middle of the grove, fairly protected from sight on all sides, he took off the saddle and the bridle and laid them on the ground. The horse stretched his jaws sideways and yawned. Pepé knotted the lead rope about the horse's neck and tied him to a sapling among the oaks, where he could graze in a fairly large circle.

When the horse was gnawing hungrily at the dry grass, Pepé went to the saddle and took a black string of jerky from the sack and strolled to an oak tree on the edge of the grove, from under which he could watch the trail. He sat down in the crisp dry oak leaves and automatically felt for his big black knife to cut the jerky, but he had no knife. He leaned back on his elbow and gnawed at the tough strong meat. His face was blank, but it was a man's face.

The bright evening light washed the eastern ridge, but the valley was darkening. Doves flew down from the hills to the spring, and the quail came running out of the brush and joined them, calling clearly to one another.

Out of the corner of his eye Pepé saw a shadow grow out of the bushy crease. He turned his head slowly. A big spotted wildcat was creeping toward the spring, belly to the ground, moving like thought.

Pepé cocked his rifle and edged the muzzle slowly around. Then he looked apprehensively up the trail and dropped the hammer again. From the ground beside him he picked an oak twig and threw it toward the spring. The quail flew up with a roar and the doves whistled away. The big cat stood up: for a long moment he looked at Pepé with cold yellow eyes, and then fearlessly walked back into the gulch.

The dusk gathered quickly in the deep valley. Pepé muttered his prayers, put his head down on his arm and went instantly to sleep.

The moon came up and filled the valley with cold blue light, and the wind swept rustling down from the peaks. The owls worked up and down the slopes looking for rabbits. Down in the brush of the gulch a coyote gabbled. The oak trees whispered softly in the night breeze.

Pepé started up, listening. His horse had whinnied. The moon was just slipping behind the western ridge, leaving the valley in darkness behind it. Pepé sat tensely gripping his rifle. From far up the trail he heard an answering whinny and the crash of shod hooves on the broken rock. He jumped to his feet, ran to his horse and led it under the trees. He threw on the saddle and cinched it tight for the steep trail, caught the unwilling head and forced the bit into the mouth. He felt the saddle to make sure the water bag and the sack of jerky were there. Then he mounted and turned up the hill.

It was velvet dark. The horse found the entrance to the trail where it left the flat, and started up, stumbling and slipping on the rocks. Pepé's hand rose up to his head. His hat was gone. He had left it under the oak tree.

The horse had struggled far up the trail when the first change of dawn came into the air, a steel greyness as light mixed thoroughly with dark. Gradually the sharp snaggled edge of the ridge stood out above them, rotten granite tortured and eaten by the winds of time. Pepé had dropped his reins on the horn, leaving direction to the horse. The brush grabbed at his legs in the dark until one knee of his jeans was ripped.

Gradually the light flowed down over the ridge. The starved brush and rocks stood out in the half light, strange and lonely in high perspective. Then there came warmth into the light. Pepé drew up and looked back, but he could see nothing in the darker valley below. The sky turned blue over the coming sun. In the waste of the mountainside, the poor dry brush grew only three feet high. Here and there, big outcroppings of unrotted granite stood up like mouldering houses. Pepé relaxed a little. He drank from his water bag and bit off a piece of jerky. A single eagle flew over, high in the light.

Without warning Pepé's horse screamed and fell on its side. He was almost down before the rifle crash echoed up from the valley. From a hole behind the struggling shoulder, a stream of bright crimson blood pumped and stopped and pumped and stopped. The hooves threshed on the ground. Pepé lay half stunned beside the horse. He looked slowly down the hill. A piece of sage clipped off beside his head and another crash echoed up from side to side of the canyon. Pepé flung himself frantically behind a bush.

He crawled up the hill on his knees and one hand. His right hand held the rifle up off the ground and pushed it ahead of him. He moved with the instinctive care of an animal. Rapidly he wormed his way toward one of the big outcroppings of granite on the hill above him. Where the brush was high he doubled up and ran, but where the cover was slight he wriggled forward on his stomach, pushing the rifle ahead of him. In the last little distance there was no cover at all. Pepé poised and then he darted across the space and flashed around the corner of the rock.

He leaned panting against the stone. When his breath came easier he moved along behind the big rock until he came to a narrow split that offered a thin section of vision down the hill. Pepé lay on his stomach and pushed the rifle barrel through the slit and waited.

The sun reddened the western ridges now. Already the buzzards were settling down toward the place where the horse lay. A small brown bird scratched in the dead sage leaves directly in front of the rifle muzzle. The coasting eagle flew back toward the rising sun.

Pepé saw a little movement in the brush far below. His grip tightened on the gun. A little brown doe stepped daintily out on the trail and crossed it and disappeared into the brush again. For a long time Pepé waited. Far below he could see the little flat and the oak trees and the slash of green. Suddenly his eyes flashed back at the trail again. A quarter of a mile down there had been a quick movement in the chaparral. The rifle swung over. The front sight nestled in the V of the rear sight. Pepé studied for a moment and then raised the rear sight a notch. The little movement in the brush came again. The sight settled on it. Pepé squeezed the trigger. The explosion crashed down the mountain and up the other side, and came rattling back. The whole side of the slope grew still. No more movement. And then a white streak cut into the granite of the slit and a bullet whined away and a crash sounded up from below. Pepé felt a sharp pain in his right hand. A sliver of granite was sticking out from between his first and second knuckles and the point protruded from his palm. Carefully he pulled out the sliver of stone. The wound bled evenly and gently. No vein nor artery was cut.

Pepé looked into a little dusty cave in the rock and gathered a handful of spider web, and he pressed the mass into the cut, plastering the soft web into the blood. The flow stopped almost at once.

The rifle was on the ground. Pepé picked it up, levered a new shell into the chamber. And then he slid into the brush on his stomach. Far to the right he crawled, and then up the hill, moving slowly and carefully, crawling to cover and resting and then crawling again.

In the mountains the sun is high in its arc before it penetrates the gorges. The hot face looked over the hill and brought instant heat with it. The white light beat on the rocks and reflected from them and rose up quivering from the earth again, and the rocks and bushes seemed to quiver behind the air.

Pepé crawled in the general direction of the ridge peak, zig-zagging for cover. The deep cut between his knuckles began to throb. He crawled close to a rattlesnake before he saw it, and when it raised its dry head and made a soft beginning whirr, he backed up and took another way. The quick grey lizards flashed in front of him, raising a tiny line of dust. He found another mass of spider web and pressed it against his throbbing hand.

Pepé was pushing the rifle with his left hand now. Little drops of sweat ran to the ends of his coarse black hair and rolled down his cheeks. His lips and tongue were growing thick and heavy. His lips writhed to draw saliva into his mouth. His little dark eyes were uneasy and suspicious. Once when a grey lizard paused in front of him on the parched ground and turned its head sideways he crushed it flat with a stone.

When the sun slid past noon he had not gone a mile. He crawled exhaustedly a last hundred yards to a patch of high sharp manzanita, crawled desperately, and when the patch was reached he wriggled in among the tough gnarly trunks and dropped his head on his left arm. There was little shade in the meager brush, but there was cover and safety. Pepé went to sleep as he lay and the sun beat on his back. A few little birds hopped close to him and peered and hopped away. Pepé squirmed in his sleep and he raised and dropped his wounded hand again and again.

The sun went down behind the peaks and the cool evening came, and then the dark. A coyote yelled from the hillside, Pepé started awake and looked about with misty eyes. His hand was swollen and heavy; a little thread of pain ran up the inside of his arm and settled in a pocket in his armpit. He peered about and then stood up, for the mountains were black and the moon had not yet risen. Pepé stood up in the dark. The coat of his father pressed on his arm. His tongue was swollen until it nearly filled his mouth. He wriggled out of the coat and dropped it in the brush, and then he struggled up the hill, falling over rocks and tearing his way through the brush. The rifle knocked against stones as he went. Little dry avalanches of gravel and shattered stone went whispering down the hill behind him.

After a while the old moon came up and showed the jagged ridge top ahead of him. By moonlight Pepé traveled more easily. He bent forward so that his throbbing arm hung away from his body. The journey uphill was made in dashes and rests, a frantic rush up a few yards and then a rest. The wind coasted down the slope rattling the dry stems of the bushes.

The moon was at meridian when Pepé came at last to the sharp backbone of the ridge top. On the last hundred yards of the rise no soil had clung under the wearing winds. The way was on solid rock. He clambered to the top and looked down on the other side. There was a draw like the last below him, misty with moonlight, brushed with dry struggling sage and chaparral. On the other side the hill rose up sharply and at the top the jagged rotten teeth of the mountain showed against the sky. At the bottom of the cut the brush was thick and dark.

Pepé stumbled down the hill. His throat was almost closed with thirst. At first he tried to run, but immediately he fell and rolled. After that he went more carefully. The moon was just disappearing behind the mountains when he came to the bottom. He crawled into the heavy brush feeling with his fingers for water. There was no water in the bed of the stream, only damp earth. Pepé laid his gun down and scooped up a handful of mud and put it in his mouth, and then he spluttered and scraped the earth from his tongue with his finger, for the mud drew at his mouth like a poultice. He dug a hole in the stream bed with his fingers, dug a little basin to catch water; but before it was very deep his head fell forward on the damp ground and he slept.

The dawn came and the heat of the day fell on the earth, and still Pepé slept. Late in the afternoon his head jerked up. He looked slowly around. His eyes were slits of wariness. Twenty feet away in the heavy brush a big tawny mountain lion stood looking at him. Its long thick tail waved gracefully, its ears were erect with interest, not laid back dangerously. The lion squatted down on its stomach and watched him.

Pepé looked at the hole he had dug in the earth. A half

inch of muddy water had collected in the bottom. He tore the sleeve from his hurt arm, with his teeth ripped out a little square, soaked it in the water and put it in his mouth. Over and over he filled the cloth and sucked it.

Still the lion sat and watched him. The evening came down but there was no movement on the hills. No birds visited the dry bottom of the cut. Pepé looked occasionally at the lion. The eyes of the yellow beast drooped as though he were about to sleep. He yawned and his long thin red tongue curled out. Suddenly his head jerked around and his nostrils quivered. His big tail lashed. He stood up and slunk like a tawny shadow into the thick brush.

A moment later Pepé heard the sound, the faint far crash of horses' hooves on gravel. And he heard something else, a high whining yelp of a dog.

Pepé took his rifle in his left hand and he glided into the brush almost as quietly as the lion had. In the darkening evening he crouched up the hill toward the next ridge. Only when the dark came did he stand up. His energy was short. Once it was dark he fell over the rocks and slipped to his knees on the steep slope, but he moved on and on up the hill, climbing and scrabbling over the broken hillside.

When he was far up toward the top, he lay down and slept for a little while. The withered moon, shining on his face, awakened him. He stood up and moved up the hill. Fifty yards away he stopped and turned back, for he had forgotten his rifle. He walked heavily down and poked about in the brush, but he could not find his gun. At last he lay down to rest. The pocket of pain in his armpit had grown more sharp. His arm seemed to swell out and fall with every heartbeat. There was no position lying down where the heavy arm did not press against his armpit.

With the effort of a hurt beast, Pepé got up and moved again toward the top of the ridge. He held his swollen arm away from his body with his left hand. Up the steep hill he dragged himself, a few steps and a rest, and a few more steps. At last he was nearing the top. The moon showed the uneven sharp back of it against the sky.

Pepé's brain spun in a big spiral up and away from him. He slumped to the ground and lay still. The rock ridge top was only a hundred feet above him.

The moon moved over the sky. Pepé half turned on his back. His tongue tried to make words, but only a thick hissing came from between his lips.

When the dawn came, Pepé pulled himself up. His eyes were sane again. He drew his great puffed arm in front of him and looked at the angry wound. The black line ran up from his wrist to his armpit. Automatically he reached in his pocket for the big black knife, but it was not there. His eyes searched the ground. He picked up a sharp blade of stone and scraped at the wound, sawed at the proud flesh and then squeezed the green juice out in big drops. Instantly he threw back his head and whined like a dog. His whole right side shuddered at the pain, but the pain cleared his head.

In the grey light he struggled up the last slope to the ridge and crawled over and lay down behind a line of rocks. Below him lay a deep canyon exactly like the last, waterless and desolate. There was no flat, no oak trees, not even heavy brush in the bottom of it. And on the other side a sharp ridge stood up, thinly brushed with starving sage, littered with broken granite. Strewn over the hill there were giant outcroppings, and on the top the granite teeth stood out against the sky.

The new day was light now. The flame of the sun came over the ridge and fell on Pepé where he lay on the ground. His coarse black hair was littered with twigs and bits of spider web. His eyes had retreated back into his head. Between his lips the tip of his black tongue showed.

He sat up and dragged his great arm into his lap and nursed it, rocking his body and moaning in his throat. He threw back his head and looked up into the pale sky. A big black bird circled nearly out of sight, and far to the left another was sailing near.

He lifted his head to listen, for a familiar sound had come to him from the valley he had climbed out of; it was the crying yelp of hounds, excited and feverish, on a trail.

Pepé bowed his head quickly. He tried to speak rapid

words but only a thick hiss came from his lips. He drew a shaky cross on his breast with his left hand. It was a long struggle to get to his feet. He crawled slowly and mechanically to the top of a big rock on the ridge peak. Once there, he arose slowly, swaying to his feet, and stood erect. Far below he could see the dark brush where he had slept. He braced his feet and stood there, black against the morning sky.

There came a ripping sound at his feet. A piece of stone flew up and a bullet droned off into the next gorge. The hollow crash echoed up from below. Pepé looked down for a moment and then pulled himself straight again.

His body jarred back. His left hand fluttered helplessly toward his breast. The second crash sounded from below. Pepé swung forward and toppled from the rock. His body struck and rolled over and over, starting a little avalanche. And when at last he stopped against a bush, the avalanche slid slowly down and covered up his head.

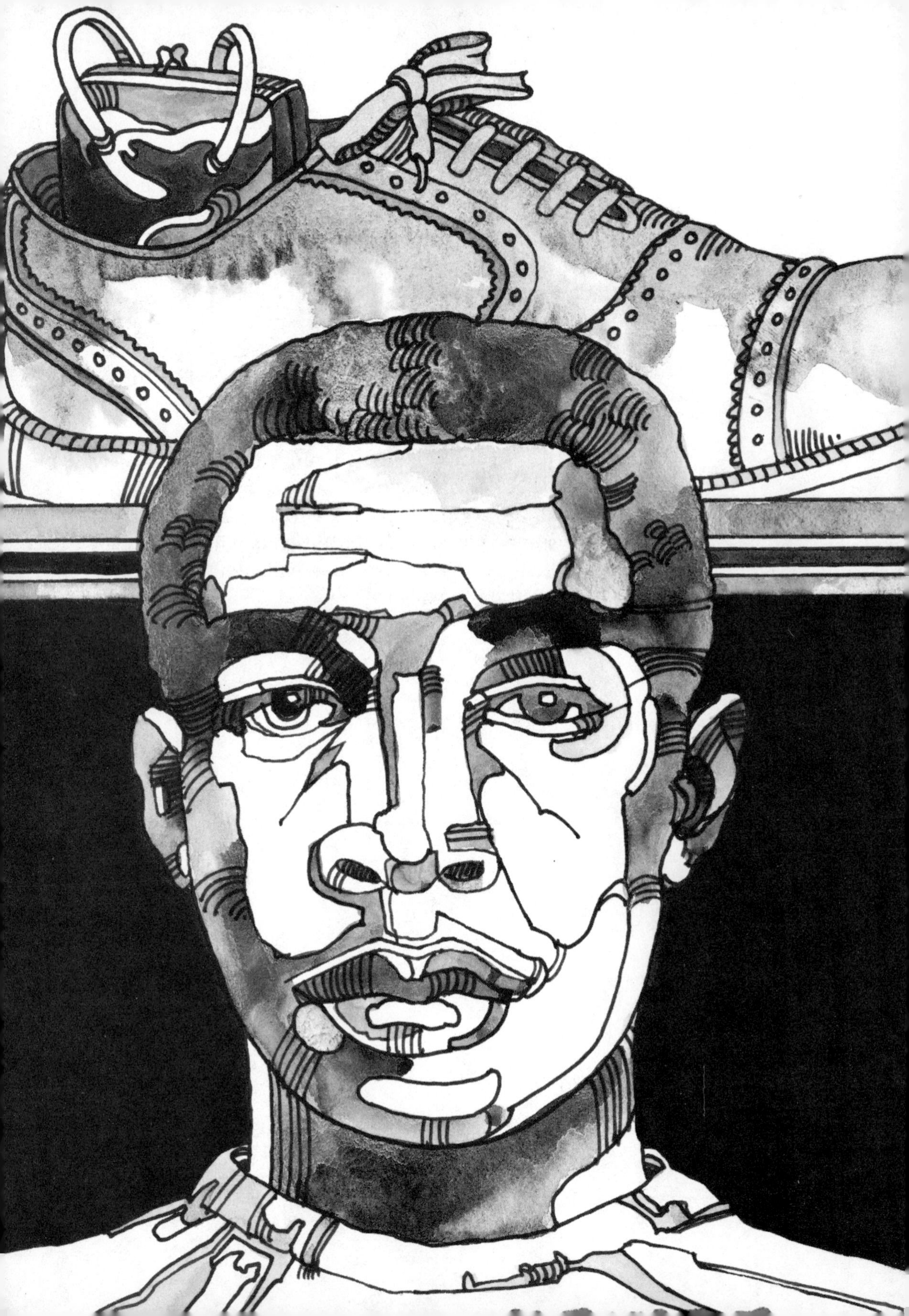

Read: 4/30/87, 5/5/88, 3/11/98

Read: 5/9/86

Read: 4/16/85

THANK YOU, M'AM

LANGSTON HUGHES

SHE was a large woman with a large purse that had everything in it but a hammer and nails. It had a long strap, and she carried it slung across her shoulder. It was about eleven o'clock at night, dark, and she was walking alone, when a boy ran up behind her and tried to snatch her purse. The strap broke with the sudden single tug the boy gave it from behind. But the boy's weight and the weight of the purse combined caused him to lose his balance. Instead of taking off full blast as he had hoped, the boy fell on his back on the sidewalk and his legs flew up. The large woman simply turned around and kicked him right square in his blue-jeaned sitter. Then she reached down, picked the boy up by his shirt front, and shook him until his teeth rattled.

After that the woman said, "Pick up my pocketbook, boy, and give it here."

She still held him tightly. But she bent down enough to permit him to stoop and pick up her purse. Then she said, "Now ain't you ashamed of yourself?"

Firmly gripped by his shirt front, the boy said, "Yes'm."

The woman said, "What did you want to do it for?"

The boy said, "I didn't aim to."

She said, "You a lie!"

By that time two or three people passed, stopped, turned to look, and some stood watching.

"If I turn you loose, will you run?" asked the woman.

"Yes'm," said the boy.

"Then I won't turn you loose," said the woman. She did not release him.

"Lady, I'm sorry," whispered the boy.

"Um-hum! Your face is dirty. I got a great mind to wash your face for you. Ain't you got nobody home to tell you to wash your face?"

"No'm," said the boy.

"Then it will get washed this evening," said the large woman, starting up the street, dragging the frightened boy behind her.

He looked as if he were fourteen or fifteen, frail and willow-wild, in tennis shoes and blue jeans.

The woman said, "You ought to be my son. I would teach you right from wrong. Least I can do right now is to wash your face. Are you hungry?"

"No'm," said the being-dragged boy. "I just want you to turn me loose."

"Was I bothering *you* when I turned that corner?" asked the woman.

"No'm."

"But you put yourself in contact with *me*," said the woman. "If you think that that contact is not going to last awhile, you got another thought coming. When I get through with you, sir, you are going to remember Mrs. Luella Bates Washington Jones."

Sweat popped out on the boy's face and he began to struggle. Mrs. Jones stopped, jerked him around in front of her, put a half nelson about his neck, and continued to drag him up the street. When she got to her door, she dragged the boy inside, down a hall, and into a large kitchenette-furnished room at the rear of the house. She switched on the light and left the door open. The boy could hear other roomers laughing and talking in the large house. Some of their doors were open, too, so he knew he and the woman were not alone. The woman still had him by the neck in the middle of her room.

She said, "What is your name?"

"Roger," answered the boy.

"Then, Roger, you go to that sink and wash your face," said the woman, whereupon she turned him loose — at last. Roger looked at the door — looked at the woman — looked at the door — *and went to the sink.*

"Let the water run until it gets warm," she said. "Here's a clean towel."

"You gonna take me to jail?" asked the boy, bending over the sink.

"Not with that face, I would not take you nowhere," said the woman. "Here I am trying to get home to cook me a bite to eat, and you snatch my pocketbook! Maybe you ain't been to your supper either, late as it be. Have you?"

"There's nobody home at my house," said the boy.

"Then we'll eat," said the woman. "I believe you're hungry — or been hungry — to try to snatch my pocketbook!"

"I want a pair of blue suede shoes," said the boy.

"Well, you didn't have to snatch *my* pocketbook to get some suede shoes," said Mrs. Luella Bates Washington Jones. "You could of asked me."

"M'am?"

The water dripping from his face, the boy looked at her. There was a long pause. A very long pause. After he had dried his face, and not knowing what else to do, dried it again, the boy turned around, wondering what next. The door was open. He could make a dash for it down the hall. He could run, run, run, *run!*

The woman was sitting on the daybed. After a while she said, "I were young once and I wanted things I could not get."

There was another long pause. The boy's mouth opened. Then he frowned, not knowing he frowned.

The woman said, "Um-hum! You thought I was going to say *but*, didn't you? You thought I was going to say, *but I didn't snatch people's pocketbooks*. Well, I wasn't going to say that." Pause. Silence. "I have done things, too, which I would not tell you, son — neither tell God, if He didn't already know. Everybody's got something in common. So you set down while I fix us something to eat. You might run that comb through your hair so you will look presentable."

In another corner of the room behind a screen was a gas plate and an icebox. Mrs. Jones got up and went behind the screen. The woman did not watch the boy to see if he was going to run now, nor did she watch her purse, which she left behind her on the daybed. But the boy took care to sit on the far side of the room, away from the purse, where he thought she could easily see him out of the corner of her eye if she wanted to. He did not trust the woman *not* to trust him. And he did not want to be mistrusted now.

"Do you need somebody to go to the store," asked the boy, "maybe to get some milk or something?"

"Don't believe I do," said the woman, "unless you just want sweet milk yourself. I was going to make cocoa out of this canned milk I got here."

"That will be fine," said the boy.

She heated some lima beans and ham she had in the icebox, made the cocoa, and set the table. The woman did not ask the boy anything about where he lived, or his folks, or anything else that would embarrass him. Instead, as they ate, she told him about her job in a hotel beauty shop that stayed open late, what the work was like, and how all kinds of women came in and out, blondes, redheads, and Spanish. Then she cut him a half of her ten-cent cake.

"Eat some more, son," she said.

When they were finished eating, she got up and said, "Now here, take this ten dollars and buy yourself some blue suede shoes. And next time, do not make the mistake of latching onto *my* pocketbook *nor nobody else's* — because shoes got by devilish ways will burn your feet. I got to get my rest now. But from here on in, son, I hope you will behave yourself."

She led him down the hall to the front door and opened it. "Good night! Behave yourself, boy!" she said, looking out into the street as he went down the steps.

The boy wanted to say something other than, "Thank you, m'am," to Mrs. Luella Bates Washington Jones, but although his lips moved, he couldn't even say that as he turned at the foot of the barren stoop and looked up at the large woman in the door. Then she shut the door.

Blue Plate Special
BEEF STEW
FISH FILET, FRENCH FRIES
Side Orders
HARD BOILED EGG
FRENCH FRIED POTATOES
ONION RINGS
SOUP BOWL
Salads
CHEF'S SALAD
Beverages
COCA COLA · ROOT BEER ·
APPLE BEER (MUG)
LEMONADE, ORANEADE
ICED TEA
MUFFINS · DONUTS · PASTRIES ·
BEEF OR SLICED HAM PILED HIGH
WITH ONIONS
CHEESE
Burgers

Read: 5/7/87, 5/5/88, 6/8/92, 6/15/93, 2/9/98

Read: 5/13/86

Read: 4/16/85

LAND OF OUR ENEMIES

JESSE STUART

PAP will never ride another log raft down this river," Pa said, as he looked from the train window at the Big Sandy River. "I've gone down this river to Gate City with 'im many a time when I was a little shaver. I've seen a big poplar log break loose from the raft and I've seen Pap jump from the raft onto it and the spikes in his boot heels wouldn't ketch and the log would dump 'im in the icy water. Pap would come up a-spittin' water and a-cussin'. But he'd get his log back to the raft. It makes a body have a funny feelin' to remember all of these things."

Our train was lumberin' and creakin' around the curves farther up the twisting Big Sandy. The sun had gone down and twilight was settling over the deep valley. Here and there we could see a light in a shack beside the railroad tracks. Soon the thin-leafed mountain slopes faded into twilight and gradually into darkness, until we could no longer see the outlines of the mountains and the white streams of water. We were riding into darkness, a darkness so thick that it looked like from the train window one could reach out and slice it into black ribbons with a pocketknife.

"Lindsay, Lindsay," the conductor said as he entered our coach. "All out for Lindsay!"

"Do you reckon anybody will be at the station to meet us?" I asked Pa.

"Somebody'll be here," he said. "Somebody'll be at this station to meet every train. Powderjays will be a-comin' back here on every train."

"When will they bury Grandpa?" I asked Pa.

"Shhh! Not so loud," he whispered, as he glanced over his shoulder.

I looked around to see two beardy-faced men with mean-lookin' eyes listening to what we said.

"You never know whether you're a-talkin' before a friend 'r an enemy here," Pa whispered to me.

The two beardy-faced men got up from their seats and followed us from the train.

"Air ye a-goin' to Cousin Mick Powderjay's funeral?" one of the men asked Pa soon as we had stepped off the train.

"That's where we're a-goin'," Pa said. "Is he akin to you?"

"We're brother's children," the man said. "I'm Zack Powderjay. And this is my brother, Dave Powderjay! We're Zack Powderjay's boys."

"I'm Mick Powderjay," Pa told them. "Pap's eleventh child by his first wife!"

"We've heard of ye," Zack Powderjay said. "See, we had to leave the Big Sandy a long time ago."

"When did you leave?" Pa asked.

"In President Hayes's administration," Dave Powderjay said.

"I left in Grover Cleveland's second administration," Pa said.

"Why did you leave?" Dave Powderjay asked Pa.

"Trouble with the Hornbuckles," he said.

"Trouble with th' Hornbuckles and Dangerfields caused us to leave," Dave said.

"Did Cousin Mick die a natural death?" Zack Powderjay asked Pa.

"I ain't heard yet but I know Pap didn't die a natural death," Pa said. "He had more enemies than he had ailments of the body."

"Ye're right, brother," a husky voice sounded in the darkness now that the train had gone. "I'm Keith Powderjay, son of Jimmie Powderjay, oldest son of Mick Powderjay. I've come to meet this train to direct any and all Powderjays and their bloodkin to the right spot."

"Then Pap was killed?" Pa asked Keith Powderjay, who had come close enough for Pa to recognize him.

Keith was a mountain of a man towering above us.

"He was beaten to death with a club," Keith told us. "Wait until you see 'im."

"Who kilt Cousin Mick?" Dave Powderjay asked.

"We know but we ain't a-sayin' now," Keith said. "Two men done it. And we got men out atter 'em tonight. Ye may hear of two deaths before mornin'."

"It makes my blood bile," Pa said. "But I've been expectin' somethin' to happen to Pap fer many years. He's been a-fightin' a long war."

"We're all riled a-plenty," Keith said. "We'd better git goin'."

"Do you have a lantern?" Pa asked. "I can't see well in the dark."

"But ye can't have a lantern, Uncle Mick," Keith said. "Lanterns air good targets at night."

"I've been away a long time," Pa said. "I jist fergot. Hit's all a-comin' back to me now."

And as we followed Keith Powderjay through the darkness, Pa's words came back to me. I remembered when we used to sit around the fire on winter nights at home how Pa would tell about going to the railroad station or to church and how he would walk in the darkness because he was afraid to carry a lantern. He would tell us how men had waited for him because he was a son of old Mick Powderjay and how he had been shot at many times. Once a bullet came so close he felt the wind from it on the tip of his nose.

"No talkin' here," Cousin Keith told us. "Quiet until I tell ye when to talk."

Everybody got quiet and we had to walk hand in hand with Cousin Keith leadin' us. But he had been over this path so many times, he could feel the path with his feet.

I'm glad Grandpa Powderjay moved to the Little Sandy River in Cleveland's administration, I thought. I'm glad Pa didn't go back with Grandpa when he got homesick for the Big Sandy and moved back to fight with his enemies. I'm glad Pa stayed on the Little Sandy and I was born there.

Grandpa had been a soldier; he had fought in Pennsylvania, Maryland, and Virginia. Gettysburg was a name to him that he would never forget; Antietam, Bull Run, Cold Harbor, Fredericksburg, Richmond were names that I had heard him talk about since I could remember. He had fought through the war from beginning to end and the only scars he had were around his wrists where he had been hanged by the arms to the joist of an old house. Captured twice and hanged once, he had come out of the war a living man.

But this was not the war that got Grandpa into trouble. When he came home he fought a long war. It was a war that never ended. He waged war on the guerrilla bands, who had captured, killed, and plundered while he and other mountain men were away fighting in Northern and Southern armies. These guerrilla bands didn't belong to either army. Grandpa had fought them since eighteen sixty-five, all but the three years he had lived on the Little Sandy. Now they had gotten 'im in the end as they said they would.

"We're a-past the dangerous places," Cousin Keith said. "We're a-past the Hornbuckles and Dangerfields."

"How much fudder do we haf to go?" Dave Powderjay asked.

"About three miles," Cousin Keith said.

"When will they bury Pap?" Pa asked.

"Two o'clock in the mornin'," Cousin Keith said.

"It's too bad to haf to bury Pap at night," Pa sighed.

"But this is a land of our enemies," Cousin Keith said. "Grandpa died a-fightin' his enemies. He told me two days before he's kilt that if all his bloodkin had stayed with 'im he'd a-winned this war in the end."

"But brother Zack and I were glad to get out'n it," Dave Powderjay said. "Glad to get into the mountains of West Virginia. We left soon as Pap and brother Tom were kilt, and we have lived in West Virginia and raised our famblies in peace."

I had never heard of a funeral at night but I had read in my history book in school where General Braddock was buried at night so the Indians wouldn't find his grave. I guess the reason that we buried Grandpa at night wasn't that his enemies would bother his grave but that his enemies would bother his bloodkin that had gathered to see him buried. I knew if we couldn't walk from the railroad to the shack where Grandpa lived and carry a light we couldn't have a funeral in the daytime. I knew that we were among our enemies. Though we had killed many of their people, there wasn't a family among us but Pa's where one, two, or three men had not fallen from the ambush shots of our enemies.

Why are we such hated people? I thought.

"I'll tell you where Pap made his mistake," Pa said. "He made it when he married his second wife, Mattie Henson. She's a first cousin of Anse Dangerfield and Tobbie Hornbuckle! I can't understand what made Pap marry an en'my!"

"That's right, Uncle Mick," Cousin Keith said. "Ye hit the nail on the head. If our men air lucky tonight, ye'll know tomorrow that this is the truth."

I couldn't tell when we reached Grandpa's shack. There wasn't a light from any window. Cousin Keith knocked three times on the door; it was opened by Pa's oldest brother, Uncle Cief. "Come in," he said softly.

And we followed him into the crowd of our people—beardy-faced men, and women with deep-lined faces. There was silence in the room, and everybody's face was clouded.

"Where's Mattie?" Pa asked.

"She's not here anymore," Aunt Arabella said. "Pap and her's been separated fer some time."

And now I saw assembled for the first time Pa's people—my bloodkin from the East Kentucky mountains. They were my bloodkin that I had heard about but didn't know very well; many of the men had scars on their faces and hands and many of them limped. I was glad, after I looked at them, that I had not been through a long guerrilla war.

"Come this way," Cousin Keith said, beckoning to us.

We followed him into the room where Grandpa was in his homemade coffin.

"Look at this, won't ye!"

Cousin Keith pointed to the wide blue marks across Grandpa's battered face where he had been beaten to death. And then he bent over and opened his coat and shirt and showed us the pulp-beats on his chest. I had never seen a man

Romeo + Juliet

beaten as he had been beaten — this mountain of a man who had died in the battle he had been fighting forty-six years. His face was clean shaven and his mustache neatly trimmed and his gray hair parted on the side. His mouth was set firmly. I had seen him in life when his mouth was set as it was now. His mouth was like this in life when he spoke of his enemies.

Pa turned and walked away. He couldn't stand to look at Grandpa. He went back into the room where the old crippled soldiers sat, wearing their tattered uniforms and holding their rifles in their hands. They had fought with Grandpa. Now they had come for his funeral. Pa called them by their names and shook their hands. They were white-haired, white-bearded, and grisly old warriors who had seen their best days and had come to see an old comrade buried. They seemed to have risen from a dim and distant past.

"Your pap wuz as good a soldier as ever lived," one spoke feebly to Pa. "But one war wuz not enough fer 'im. He oughta quit then. No use fightin' all his life."

"He was the best wrestler in Grant's army," another said. "I never saw him rode in all the bouts he had."

There were low whispers among my people in the small, crowded, three-room shack. Heavy quilts were hangin' over the windows so not a ray of light could be seen from the outside. Wind came between the log-cracks, and the flames of oil lamps sputtered and smoked the lamp globes. I remembered while I stood here among my people and these old soldiers in their faded uniforms what Pa had told Mom. He had told her how Grandpa wouldn't sleep in a room unless a lamp was burning. Said he put quilts over the windows so they wouldn't be a target for his enemies shooting with rifles from the thickets on the mountain slopes.

We were quiet enough in the shack to hear the roosters crow for midnight. And as soon as they had finished crowing from their roosts outside the shack, Uncle Jason came into the room.

"It's about time fer us to start," he announced.

Six of my cousins, sons of Pa's older brothers, picked up Grandpa's coffin and stepped out into the darkness. They were tall, beardy men with broad shoulders. The muscles in their forearms bulged as they carried the big coffin and the big warrior in it from his shack out into the darkness. Aunt Emerine blew out the lamps, and the crowd of Powderjays, their in-laws and friends, followed the coffin into the darkness. Cousin Keith led the way up the mountain path and we followed. A moon came from behind a dark breadloaf-shaped mountain where jutted rocks were outlined against the misty sky. There were whispers among us as we walked along slowly. Twice my cousins had to let six more cousins carry the coffin, since it was such a load in the darkness to carry up a mountain slope.

"Not one of Pap's eight young'ins by Mattie air here," Uncle Cief told Pa. "And hit's good they ain't here. Thar's too much en'my blood in 'em to suit us."

I didn't know the part-guerrilla Powderjays from the real Powderjays. But I knew that the real Powderjays didn't have any use for them even if the same blood did flow through their veins. I heard Pa and Uncle Cief talking about them as the crowd moved slowly along. I was with my people and it seemed like a dream. I didn't know there was a world like the one I was in.

Suddenly our stumbling, whispering funeral crowd stopped on a lonely mountaintop. I could see rows of brown sandstones that had been chiseled with pickaxes and broadaxes marking the rows of graves. And I saw men standing by a fresh-dug grave holding their picks, adzes, and long-handled shovels. An owl flew over us on outspread wings we could hear fanning the night wind. And on a distant mountaintop we heard a whippoorwill. But there was not a light nor a sound among us while my cousins placed Grandpa's coffin beside his grave. "Tonight, we're a-buryin' a soldier who has had many fights," an old soldier said after Grandpa's coffin had been placed beside the grave. "He has fit through a long war in the land of his enemies and he has fit well."

From among men and women of our silent funeral crowd two men walked toward the old soldier. As they walked toward him, Uncle Cief put his hand on his pistol until he recognized them. One whispered something to the old soldier in charge of Grandpa's funeral.

"And I'm glad to tell you Mick Powderjay's death has

been avenged," the old soldier announced. "Eif Dangerfield and Battle Henson 've paid fer thar crime!"

That was all that was said for Grandpa. There wasn't a preacher to preach his funeral and there weren't any songs. The old soldiers fired a farewell volley across his grave, and the fire from their rifles was the only light we had seen except the moonlight shining dimly through the sheets of white mist rising from the valley below us. Grandpa's coffin was lowered into his grave with leather checklines on a mountaintop where only Powderjays, their bloodkin, and inlaws were buried — a mountain high enough to overlook the rugged land of our people and our enemies.

Read: 5/8/87, 3/19/98

Read: 5/13/86
Read: 5/8/85

THE VASE

JESSAMYN WEST

JESS, who had planned the day for work, tried to turn it to some use by regarding the rain which had spoiled it. He walked restlessly from the sitting-room window on the left of the front door to the sitting-room window on the right; but there was no difference in the rain. From either place he saw it fall in a great sheet which, the house splitting, set himself, he figured, in the center of a cavern of water, set him like the clapper in the middle of a sounding bell. He silent, the bell itself resounding with the clatter which water, dropped from a great height, makes on a shell of almost empty clapboard (beds, stoves, carpets, a human being or two in no wise filling it).

He sent his hearing out beyond the house, testing his belief that the ear alone can tell winter rain from summer, and had his belief bolstered, for rain falling upon trees in full leaf has a gentle huskiness which the bare and rigid limbs of winter cannot duplicate.

Jess, who was no great hand at hiding the light of his knowledge beneath a bushel of silence, called out to Eliza, and she, her bread set, came in from the kitchen.

"Thee call me, Jess?" she asked, wiping her hands, rosy from the kneading, on her apron.

"Eliza," Jess said, "blindfolded, thee could tell the sound of rain in winter from rain in summer."

"I couldn't," Eliza said flatly.

Jess regarded his wife morosely. Among women Eliza was, he knew, peerless; but all women he sometimes feared were flawed, whether in their making or by a throwing away of their natural heritage, he couldn't say.

"Ain't thee interested in knowing how?" he asked. "Ain't thy curiosity pricked? Don't natural phenomena mean anything to thee?"

Some did, some didn't. The sound rain made was one that didn't. Bread rising, house shining, fire dozing on the hearth, these were phenomena, and natural, too, Eliza supposed, and for the time being quite enough for her. "Jess," she said, "I don't see any point being blindfolded and trying to tell winter rain from summer. Leave it off," she advised with great practicality, "and save the guesswork."

Jess turned away from the windows and the rain. Women were too much for him. Still, never despairing of lightening their dark, he said, "Rain on leaves makes a different sound from rain on bare limbs."

"In a stand of pine," Eliza objected, "thee'd have to take thy blindfold off."

Jess sighed. He walked to the secretary which filled a great part of the wall on the south side of the door to the kitchen. "I wasn't speaking of evergreens," he said.

There on the middle shelf of the secretary, in a small clearing between books, stood other reminders of woman's strangeness. A queer race, Jess thought, gazing at the set-out, related to us by marriage but mighty odd in spite of it. What were these objects Eliza had saved, set forth like rarities in a museum, preserved, while articles of greater use were lost and broken? A fragment of stone from the chimney of the old log house, a circle of shining wood stamped "Holy Land," but having, to Jess, the look of a piece of local butternut, well polished; a dried orange fetched home from New Orleans, a thimble which Eliza believed had been used in sewing a rent in William Penn's breeches, six feathers small and much faded, plucked long ago from some California bird and lodged now in a squat red cup; a thing of glass, which Jess in twenty years of seeing had never been able to fathom, and which he now took from the secretary and turned about in his hands.

"What's thee call this thing, Eliza?"

"A vase," Eliza said.

"It couldn't very well be a vase," Jess told her reasonably. "It's open at both ends."

"A vase," Eliza said, "is what I've come to call it."

Jess held it off. He peered through it. He ran his thumb over the putty swans, set up above the surface of the glass, he traced the fluting at the top which putty had enlarged. "Looks like it started life as a lamp chimney," he said.

"It did," said Eliza.

"A broken one at that."

"Yes," said Eliza, "it was broken."

She took the vase from Jess and curved her white, plump fingers about it, the fingers which at the time of the vase's making had been neither white nor plump, but pink and thin like bird's legs, and as quick in their movements as bird's legs, too.

"Thee's made a neat thing of it," Jess admitted. "Ornamental." But he had, in all truth, to add, "Useless though. Painted over so's it won't do for a chimney. Open at both ends so's it won't serve as a vase. When'd thee make it?"

"Thee saw it the morning I started it."

"I took no notice."

"No," Eliza said, remembering, "thee didn't."

"What's thee aim," Jess asked, "making it?" Knowledge of his suppleness, turning in two minutes and with good grace from a scientific contemplation of rain's varying sounds to an examination of a misnamed dido, filled him with content.

Eliza, who had been facing the fire, which lay on the hearth like a red eye, angry with the sight of so much water falling, turned to face her husband. She touched the vase, scalloped top and swelling sides. What was her aim? There were more aims in it, maybe, than she knew, and even if she knew them all, could name and number them for Jess, would he understand? He, who had seen her when the first swan, buoyant upon its painted ripples, was still wet from the brush — and not noted — would he understand now, so many years later? When the colors on the vase were beginning to fade?

There was one purpose clear enough for her to see and say certainly.

"I aimed to make a pretty thing, Jess."

Yes, that was true. That in the beginning had been her whole aim. A spattering of water dashed against the hot lamp chimney had snapped a circle from it, but she had not thrown it away; she had set the chimney on the pantry shelf, remembering a neighbor's saying that such a broken thing could be so painted and decorated as to be an ornament to any parlor. It had stayed there a long time, waiting an hour when, work slackening, she could set a picture onto its glassy bareness. And as the days passed it gave her pleasure, stepping in and out of the pantry to see it waiting. Between all the necessary thoughts of cooking a design to set upon the chimney began to work itself out in her mind, a plan which in the midst of kitchen traffic opened a place of quiet and aloneness for her.

Jess, watching her turn the vase about in her hands, said nothing, so she repeated her words. "I planned it to be an ornament, Jess. A pretty thing for our parlor."

Could Jess understand that? Prettiness outside, Jess understood, she knew. Many a time he'd roused her, just fallen asleep, to look at the stars, had carried many a flower inside to her, had called out to her to look at a cloud, a sky at sundown, a bird, a curious stone, even. But prettiness inside? Did pillow shams thick with satin stitch and French knots give him a smidgin more pleasure than unbleached muslin bare as when it came from the looms? Did it matter to him whether there were peacock feathers over the grate and gilded cat-tails in the corner? She thought not.

But a woman lived in a house, not outdoors. A sunset didn't come inside, light the wall behind the kitchen range so's she could see it while cooking supper; clouds taking this shape or that didn't settle down on the mantelpiece to keep her company while mending. The prettiness a woman saw, she had to make, she had to build it up from odds and ends. Did Jess ever note her handiwork? The articles embroidered, painted, stenciled, gilded, dyed? The combcases, footstools, doilies, tidies, fire screens, rugs, penwipers, lambrequins? Did he see how the bareness of timber and stone had been hidden and softened, until the room, to her eye, showed itself as prettier than any cloud, and not to be outdone, even, by a rose.

Jess thrust out a finger, touched one of the swans. "An ornament for our sitting room," he said. "Time on end."

Eliza noted he didn't say pretty. Well, that didn't matter. It had come to mean more to her than prettiness, anyway.

"Jess," she said, "I don't know but what in case of fire this'd be the first thing I'd save."

Jess looked anew at the object she held. "Before the family Bible?" he asked. "The letters? The deeds?"

"For those," Eliza said, "I could count on thee."

"But for some things, not?"

Eliza said nothing.

Jess' big nose wrinkled at the bridge. The lines that ran downward from cheekbone to jaw deepened. His large, well-muscled mouth moved a little as if he were savoring beforehand the words he was about to say.

"There are those," he said, "who say I carry thee around on a chip, Eliza. Figger me a poor apron-tied old fellow, married to a female preacher and not able to call his soul his own."

Eliza knew this to be true; still, for all they said, there were things Jess was not to be counted on for. Or maybe, not Jess. Maybe man, any man.

Jess remembered temperatures: ten below or 102° in the shade. He remembered the dimensions of snow-drifts and the number of inches that had fallen in a single cloudburst. Eliza remembered how she felt and from this determined season and weather.

She had started her vase on a summer morning, she knew, for she could remember how warm she had felt standing in her nightdress by the bed. In the half-light Jess was only a shadowy mound beneath the covers, stirring a little as he settled toward deeper sleep. It was before sunup and outside, birds, rousing, sang their short easy songs, the ones which could be performed while half awake.

It was earlier than rising time, but she had no sleep left in her and was too happy to lie still any longer. In a moment's musing, she then seventeen, there had come to her such bliss in a sudden picturing of what her life and Jess' might be, that she felt she must be out of bed, and advancing toward it; moving forward into the opening years, toward the children, toward the May mornings and snowy evenings, toward the fine housewifery and lovingkindness, toward the old age when she and Jess, sleepless through the long nights as old people are, would say, Remember, remember, as they lay listening to wind or rain. It all came to her that summer morning on waking and she had to be up out of bed and hastening to meet it.

She carried her clothes downstairs, walking silently with bare feet across floor-boards still warm with yesterday's heat. She washed in soft cistern-water and dressed in the kitchen. She wished that Jess might have been hungry for seven breakfasts in one so that she could have cooked every dish she'd ever heard him say he fancied: buckwheat cakes, soda biscuits, sausage gravy, tenderloin, ham with its taste of salt and hickory smoke.

The fire caught and blazed. The fruity, summer air had to take the column of autumn smelling smoke with what grace it could. Biscuits cut and dolloped with cream waited the oven. Her nightdress was folded as precisely as if measured. The best cups were on the table. Psalm 101 had been read and meditated. But it was not enough. Bliss was not yet served. It was then she remembered her vase.

She brought chimney, putty and paints from the pantry and sitting at the kitchen table, the design, known to her mind a long time, became now a separate thing, began now to live outside herself, and there, seemed able in its expression of her happiness to hasten her advance into the life she had imagined.

Her fingers, remembering flowers, enlarged with putty the meager crimping at the chimney's top to petal-sized scallops. Over the break, mended with putty, she molded a plumed swan, a great bird with arched breast and flaunting tail. About the swan she painted blue water and green reeds and the swan itself she made a dazzling white. Overhead was the sky of summer across which long thin clouds like frayed pencils drifted, and the frayings, all raveling out toward the same direction, made it seem as if a wind, light but persistent, blew across the picture.

There were to be two swans, finally, but now Eliza rested. She rose and walked from the table, set the biscuits to baking and moved the skillets to the front of the stove. Still, it was not they, not the laid table nor cooking food, which seemed nearest to what she had seen, or dreamed, lying upstairs by Jess' side: it was the vase, the swan, the reeds, the summer sky.

"Thee looked it over," Eliza told Jess, "the morning I started it. Came downstairs and rocked on thy toes in front of it."

"What'd I say," Jess asked, "rocking there? I reckon I wasn't speechless."

"No, Jess," said Eliza, "thee wasn't speechless."

"What'd I say?" he persisted.

"Thee said," Eliza told him, "and well I remember, 'What's for breakfast? I'm hungry enough to eat a biled owl.' "

Jess rocked a little on his toes now. "Well," he said, "that was something. Better'n saying I could eat a biled swan, I reckon."

That was something and she had not been unhappy, setting the praised breakfast on the table, speaking with Jess of what fruits he would bring in for canning, saying the day would be another scorcher, lifting the pretty cup, which in itself, set their eating apart from ordinary meals. But when breakfast was over the vase had taken on a paltry look and some of her happiness had ebbed away: it was nothing, she saw, but a mended lamp chimney; the great swan, putty and paint. The wind didn't really blow — that was only a trick of her painting, a thing anybody'd see through. She set the vase away in the pantry again. She looked up at it there on the top shelf and wondered how it could have been for a half-hour, not only a place of stillness for her, beautiful and far away, but a setting forth somehow of all the bliss and eagerness she had felt before sunup, listening to the beginning bird songs and seeing the children's faces.

It was a long time before she touched it again. The children's faces she had seen upstairs were real faces, and their voices and needs were real, not only May mornings and winter evenings, but all the hours between. The house, she trimmed and softened as she had planned that morning, so that now she would rise from her chair, open a door, and surprise herself anew with a room which waited her, as far from bareness as a grafted tree in full bearing is from a seedling.

She often thought of the vase, but there had never come another moment like that of the first summer morning — and time, for her, was always short. Still, she planned to finish it, set the second swan in place beside the first. There were days when its incompletion troubled her mind, gave her the feeling that she had turned away from something more than a painted lamp chimney . . . that all the children, Jess, the house, her church even, were not reason enough for having neglected it . . . that it was more to her than she understood.

In spite of this, the vase waited, unfinished, for years. Then in November, after little Sarah's death, she had taken it from its shelf late one afternoon and with chair pushed close to the sitting-room fire had set about painting the second swan, a companion for the first. It was a miserable day; there had been rain in the morning, but after dinner the air had sharpened and snow had begun to fall, not briskly, so that her thoughts were of sleigh rides or the boys fighting snow battles, but listlessly so that her mind turned toward the year's end and little Sarah's grave. She had passed from the first period of grief when her arms had known the loss of her child as sharply as if a portion of her own flesh had been cut away, and she was able to say God's will be done; still she was left with a great heaviness and it was strange, even to her, that this had seemed the hour to finish the vase.

If little Sarah had been alive she would have stood by her side, watching her brush strokes, saying, "Is thee making a bird, mother?", and outlining the curving breast of the second swan she thought, I can never lose her. She remembered the morning she had started her work, all that joy and vision of joy, as if the whole of life would be nothing but delight, nothing but smoothness with never a setback. How different this was, no vision, never misdoubting that there were sorrows ahead, but somehow a tranquil satisfaction in seeing the second swan, the companion for which the first had waited so many years, take shape, and in believing, once again, that it was a real wind which moved the frayed clouds across the summer sky.

The second swan was never finished, though. It remained a shadow, an outline. As she had begun to touch it with whiteness, Jess, bareheaded, hands and hair wet with melting snow, came in.

"Eliza," he cried, "it is more than I can bear."

She had set her brush aside and said, "What is it, Jess?", though she knew.

"Sarah's grave," Jess said. "Under the snow. She loved the snow, so. Thee knows how she loved it, Eliza."

Then he did a thing he had never done — before or since — he dropped on his knees and laying his head, the red hair darkened with melting snow, on to her lap, had cried, not quietly, for Jess was not a quiet man.

"Eliza," he asked, "has thee forgotten that the first words Sarah ever spoke were about the snow?" He lifted his head from her lap and looked toward the windows. "There she stood," he said, "clapping her little hands and crying, 'Pretty flowers, pretty flowers.' "

Eliza had not forgotten. The words had been in her mind all afternoon, "No, Jess," she said. "I haven't forgotten."

"How can thee be playing then?" Jess cried. "Playing with thy paints? And Sarah's grave there under the snow?"

Eliza smoothed the damp hair. "I haven't forgotten God, either, Jess," she said.

After a time Jess had grown calm, had warmed himself at the fire and gone out to finish his evening's feeding. Then Eliza had set the vase, unfinished as it was, one swan but the dream of a swan, gray and shadowy, and without plumage, on the

shelf of the secretary. Let it stand there, she thought. It was, perhaps, the best she would ever be able to do, and she was content that it should have its place among the other things she treasured — reminding her of so much, the dream before sunup, and much beside, that, never dreamed of, had come since that morning.

The rain was still pelting down and Jess had forgotten the vase. "Eliza," he said, going back to his old idea, "not only seasons, but places, I'll venture, could be told from the sound of the rain. The jungle," he said, fired with the thought of so much rain and so much geography, "how'd it sound there? Or on a mountain peak, how'd it sound falling on bare rocks? Or on the sea? Water spanking down on water? Well, here we are," he subsided. "Stuck. We'll never know."

Eliza didn't feel stuck. She felt at home.

Jess peered out the window. He reconciled himself to rain in Indiana. "Got to make a run for it," he said. "Cows bawling their heads off."

He clasped Eliza to him before he went out, as warmly as if bound, as in his mind no doubt he was, on a journey, and Eliza felt between his clasping arms and herself, the vase, which she still held, separating them. And yet, she supposed, seen in another way, it was a link. After he left she set it back in the secretary, but she could still feel the pressure of its fluted rim against her breast as she moved about the kitchen busy with her evening work.

The New York Times

Read: 5/8/87, 3/1/98

Read: 5/13/86

Read: 5/13/85

A SUMMER'S READING

BERNARD MALAMUD

GEORGE Stoyonovich was a neighborhood boy who had quit high school on an impulse when he was sixteen, run out of patience, and though he was ashamed everytime he went looking for a job, when people asked him if he had finished and he had to say no, he never went back to school. This summer was a hard time for jobs and he had none. Having so much time on his hands, George thought of going to summer school, but the kids in his classes would be too young. He also considered registering in a night high school, only he didn't like the idea of the teachers always telling him what to do. He felt they had not respected him. The result was he stayed off the streets and in his room most of the day. He was close to twenty and had needs with the neighborhood girls, but no money to spend, and he couldn't get more than an occasional few cents because his father was poor, and his sister Sophie, who resembled George, a tall bony girl of twenty-three, earned very little and what she had she kept for herself. Their mother was dead, and Sophie had to take care of the house.

Very early in the morning George's father got up to go to work in a fish market. Sophie left at about eight for her long ride in the subway to a cafeteria in the Bronx. George had his coffee by himself, then hung around in the house. When the house, a five-room railroad flat above a butcher store, got on his nerves he cleaned it up — mopped the floors with a wet mop and put things away. But most of the time he sat in his room. In the afternoons he listened to the ball game. Otherwise he had a couple of old copies of the *World Almanac* he had bought long ago, and he liked to read in them and also the magazines and newspapers that Sophie brought home, that had been left on the tables in the cafeteria. They were mostly picture magazines about movie stars and sports figures, also usually the *News* and *Mirror*. Sophie herself read whatever fell into her hands, although she sometimes read good books.

She once asked George what he did in his room all day and he said he read a lot too.

"Of what besides what I bring home? Do you ever read any worthwhile books?"

"Some," George answered, although he really didn't. He had tried to read a book or two that Sophie had in the house but found he was in no mood for them. Lately he couldn't stand made-up stories, they got on his nerves. He wished he had some hobby to work at — as a kid he was good in carpentry, but where could he work at it? Sometimes during the day he went for walks, but mostly he did his walking after the hot sun had gone down and it was cooler in the streets.

In the evening after supper George left the house and wandered in the neighborhood. During the sultry days some of the storekeepers and their wives sat in chairs on the thick, broken sidewalks in front of their shops, fanning themselves, and George walked past them and the guys hanging out on the candy store corner. A couple of them he had known his whole life, but nobody recognized each other. He had no place special to go, but generally, saving it till the last, he left the neighborhood and walked for blocks till he came to a darkly lit little park with benches and trees and an iron railing, giving it a feeling of privacy. He sat on a bench here, watching the leafy trees and the flowers blooming on the inside of the railing, thinking of a better life for himself. He thought of the jobs he had had since he had quit school — delivery boy, stock clerk, runner, lately working in a factory — and he was dissatisfied with all of them. He felt he would someday like to have a good job and live in a private house with a porch, on a street with trees. He wanted to have some dough in his pocket to buy things with, and a girl to go with, so as not to be so lonely, especially on Saturday nights. He wanted people to like and respect him. He thought about these things often but mostly when he was alone at night. Around midnight he got up and drifted back to his hot and stony neighborhood.

One time while on his walk George met Mr. Cattanzara coming home very late from work. He wondered if he was drunk but then could tell he wasn't. Mr. Cattanzara, a stocky, bald-headed man who worked in a change booth on an IRT station, lived on the next block after George's, above a shoe repair store. Nights, during the hot weather, he sat on his stoop in an undershirt, reading the *New York Times* in the light of the shoemaker's window. He read it from the first page to the last, then went up to sleep. And all the time he was reading the paper, his wife, a fat woman with a white face, leaned out of the window, gazing into the street, her thick white arms folded under her loose breast, on the window ledge.

Once in a while Mr. Cattanzara came home drunk, but it was a quiet drunk. He never made any trouble, only walked stiffly up the street and slowly climbed the stairs into the hall. Though drunk, he looked the same as always, except for his tight walk, the quietness, and that his eyes were wet. George liked Mr. Cattanzara because he remembered him giving him nickels to buy lemon ice with when he was a squirt. Mr. Cattanzara was a different type than those in the neighborhood. He asked different questions than the others when he met you, and he seemed to know what went on in all the newspapers. He read them, as his fat sick wife watched from the window.

"What are you doing with yourself this summer, George?" Mr. Cattanzara asked. "I see you walkin' around at nights."

George felt embarrassed. "I like to walk."

"What are you doin' in the day now?

"Nothing much just right now. I'm waiting for a job." Since it shamed him to admit he wasn't working, George said, "I'm staying home — but I'm reading a lot to pick up my education."

Mr. Cattanzara looked interested. He mopped his hot face with a red handkerchief.

"What are you readin'?"

George hesitated, then said, "I got a list of books in the library once, and now I'm gonna read them this summer." He felt strange and a little unhappy saying this, but he wanted Mr. Cattanzara to respect him.

"How many books are there on it?"

"I never counted them. Maybe around a hundred."

Mr. Cattanzara whistled through his teeth.

"I figure if I did that," George went on earnestly, "it would help me in my education. I don't mean the kind they give you in high school. I want to know different things than they learn there, if you know what I mean."

The change maker nodded. "Still and all, one hundred books is a pretty big load for one summer."

"It might take longer."

"After you're finished with some, maybe you and I can shoot the breeze about them?" said Mr. Cattanzara.

"When I'm finished," George answered.

Mr. Cattanzara went home and George continued on his walk. After that, though he had the urge to, George did nothing different from usual. He still took his walks at night, ending up in the little park. But one evening the shoemaker on the next block stopped George to say he was a good boy, and George figured that Mr. Cattanzara had told him all about the books he was reading. From the shoemaker it must have gone down the street, because George saw a couple of people smiling kindly at him, though nobody spoke to him personally. He felt a little better around the neighborhood and liked it more, though not so much he would want to live in it forever. He had never exactly disliked the people in it, yet he had never liked them very much either. It was the fault of the neighborhood. To his surprise, George found out that his father and Sophie knew about his reading too. His father was too shy to say anything about it — he was never much of a talker in his whole life — but Sophie was softer to George, and she showed him in other ways she was proud of him.

As the summer went on George felt in a good mood about things. He cleaned the house every day, as a favor to Sophie, and he enjoyed the ball games more. Sophie gave him a buck a week allowance, and though it still wasn't enough and he had to use it carefully, it was a helluva lot better than just having two bits now and then. What he bought with the money — cigarettes mostly, an occasional beer or movie ticket — he got a big kick out of. Life wasn't so bad if you knew how to appreciate it. Occasionally he bought a paperback book from the newsstand, but he never got around to reading it, though he was glad to have a couple of books in his room. But he read thoroughly Sophie's magazines and newspapers. And at night was the most enjoyable time, because when he passed the storekeepers sitting outside their stores, he could tell they regarded him highly. He walked erect, and though he did not say much to them, or they to him, he could feel approval on all sides. A couple of nights he felt so good that he skipped the park at the end of the evening. He just wandered in the neighborhood, where people had known him from the time he was a kid playing punchball whenever there was a game of it going; he wandered there, then came home and got undressed for bed, feeling fine.

For a few weeks, he had talked only once with Mr. Cattanzara, and though the change maker had said nothing more about the books, asked no questions, his silence made George a little uneasy. For a while George didn't pass in front of Mr. Cattanzara's house anymore, until one night, forgetting himself, he approached it from a different direction than he usually did when he did. It was already past midnight. The street, except for one or two people, was deserted, and George was surprised when he saw Mr. Cattanzara still reading his newspaper by the light of the street lamp overhead. His impulse was to stop at the stoop and talk to him. He wasn't sure what he wanted to say, though he felt the words would come when he began to talk; but the more he thought about it, the more the idea scared him, and he decided he'd better not. He even considered beating it home by another street, but he was too near Mr. Cattanzara, and the change maker might see him as he ran, and get annoyed. So George unobtrusively crossed the street, trying to make it seem as if he had to look in a store window on the other side, which he did, and then went on, uncomfortable at what he was doing. He feared Mr. Cattanzara would glance up from his paper and call him a dirty rat for walking on the other side of the street, but all he did was sit there, sweating through his undershirt, his bald head shining in the dim light as he read his *Times*, and upstairs his fat wife leaned out of the window, seeming to read the paper along with him. George thought she would spy him and yell out to Mr. Cattanzara, but she never moved her eyes off her husband.

George made up his mind to stay away from the change maker until he had got some of his softback books read, but when he started them and saw they were mostly story books, he lost his interest and didn't bother to finish them. He lost his interest in reading other things too. Sophie's magazines and newspapers went unread. She saw them piling up on a chair in his room and asked why he was no longer looking at them, and George told her it was because of all the other reading he had to do. Sophie said she had guessed that was it. So for most of the day, George had the radio on, turning to music when he was sick of the human voice. He kept the house fairly neat, and Sophie said nothing on the days when he neglected it. She was still kind and gave him his extra buck, though things weren't so good for him as they had been before.

But they were good enough, considering. Also his night walks invariably picked him up, no matter how bad the day was. Then one night George saw Mr. Cattanzara coming down the street toward him. George was about to turn and run but he recognized from Mr. Cattanzara's walk that he was drunk, and if so, probably he would not even bother to notice him. So George kept on walking straight ahead until he came abreast of Mr. Cattanzara and though he felt wound up enough to pop into the sky, he was not surprised when Mr. Cattanzara passed him without a word, walking slowly, his face and body stiff. George drew a breath in relief at his narrow escape, when he heard his name called, and there stood Mr. Cattanzara at his elbow, smelling like the inside of a beer barrel. His eyes were sad as he gazed at George, and George felt so intensely uncomfortable he was tempted to shove the drunk aside and continue on his walk.

But he couldn't act that way to him, and, besides, Mr. Cattanzara took a nickel out of his pants pocket and handed it to him.

"Go buy yourself a lemon ice, Georgie."

"It's not that time anymore, Mr. Cattanzara," George said, "I'm a big guy now."

"No, you ain't," said Mr. Cattanzara, to which George made no reply he could think of.

"How are all your books comin' along now?" Mr. Cattanzara asked. Though he tried to stand steady, he swayed a little.

"Fine, I guess," said George, feeling the red crawling up his face.

"You ain't sure?" The change maker smiled slyly, a way George had never seen him smile.

"Sure I'm sure. They're fine."

Though his head swayed in little arcs, Mr. Cattanzara's eyes were steady. He had small blue eyes which could hurt if you looked at them too long.

"George," he said, "name me one book on that list that you read this summer, and I will drink to your health."

"I don't want anybody drinking to me."

"Name me one so I can ask you a question on it. Who can tell, if it's a good book maybe I might wanna read it myself."

George knew he looked passable on the outside, but inside he was crumbling apart.

Unable to reply, he shut his eyes, but when — years later — he opened them, he saw that Mr. Cattanzara had, out of pity, gone away, but in his ears he still heard the words he had said when he left: "George, don't do what I did."

The next night he was afraid to leave his room, and though Sophie argued with him he wouldn't open the door.

"What are you doing in there?" she asked.

"Nothing."

"Aren't you reading?"

"No."

She was silent a minute, then asked, "Where do you keep the books you read? I never see any in your room outside of a few cheap trashy ones."

He wouldn't tell her.

"In that case you're not worth a buck of my hard-earned money. Why should I break my back for you? Go on out, you bum, and get a job."

He stayed in his room for almost a week, except to sneak into the kitchen when nobody was home. Sophie railed at him, then begged him to come out, and his old father wept, but George wouldn't budge, though the weather was terrible and his small room stifling. He found it very hard to breathe, each breath was like drawing a flame into his lungs.

One night, unable to stand the heat anymore, he burst into the street at one A.M., a shadow of himself. He hoped to sneak to the park without being seen, but there were people all over the block, wilted and listless, waiting for a breeze. George lowered his eyes and walked, in disgrace, away from them, but before long he discovered they were still friendly to him. He figured Mr. Cattanzara hadn't told on him. Maybe when he woke up out of his drunk the next morning, he had forgotten all about meeting George. George felt his confidence slowly come back to him.

That same night a man on a street corner asked him if it was true that he had finished reading so many books, and George admitted he had. The man said it was a wonderful thing for a boy his age to read so much.

"Yeah," George said, but he felt relieved. He hoped nobody would mention the books anymore, and when, after a couple of days, he accidentally met Mr. Cattanzara again, *he* didn't, though George had the idea he was the one who had started the rumor that he had finished all the books.

One evening in the fall, George ran out of his house to the library, where he hadn't been in years. There were books all over the place, wherever he looked, and though he was struggling to control an inward trembling, he easily counted off a hundred, then sat down at a table to read.

Read: 4/30/87, 5/5/88, 6/29/92, 3/11/98

Read: 5/13/86

Read: 5/13/85

CHARLES

SHIRLEY JACKSON

THE day my son Laurie started kindergarten he renounced corduroy overalls with bibs and began wearing blue jeans with a belt; I watched him go off the first morning with the older girl next door, seeing clearly that an era of my life was ended, my sweet-voiced, nursery-school tot replaced by a long-trousered, swaggering character who forgot to stop at the corner and wave good-by to me.

He came home the same way, the front door slamming open, his cap on the floor, and the voice suddenly become raucous shouting, "Isn't anybody *here?*"

At lunch he spoke insolently to his father, spilled his baby sister's milk, and remarked that his teacher said we were not to take the name of the Lord in vain.

"How *was* school today?" I asked, elaborately casual.

"All right," he said.

"Did you learn anything?" his father asked.

Laurie regarded his father coldly. "I didn't learn nothing," he said.

"Anything," I said. "Didn't learn anything."

"The teacher spanked a boy, though," Laurie said, addressing his bread and butter. "For being fresh," he added, with his mouth full.

"What did he do?" I asked. "Who was it?"

Laurie thought. "It was Charles," he said. "He was fresh. The teacher spanked him and made him stand in a corner. He was awfully fresh."

"What did he do?" I asked again, but

Laurie slid off his chair, took a cookie, and left, while his father was still saying, "See here, young man."

The next day Laurie remarked at lunch, as soon as he sat down, "Well, Charles was bad again today." He grinned enormously and said, "Today Charles hit the teacher."

"Good heavens," I said, mindful of the Lord's name, "I suppose he got spanked again?"

"He sure did," Laurie said. "Look up," he said to his father.

"What?" his father said, looking up.

"Look down," Laurie said. "Look at my thumb. Gee, you're dumb." He began to laugh insanely.

"Why did Charles hit the teacher?" I asked quickly.

"Because she tried to make him color with red crayons," Laurie said. "Charles wanted to color with green crayons so he hit the teacher and she spanked him and said nobody play with Charles but everybody did."

The third day — it was Wednesday of the first week — Charles bounced a seesaw on to the head of a little girl and made her bleed, and the teacher made him stay inside all during recess. Thursday Charles had to stand in a corner during storytime because he kept pounding his feet on the floor. Friday Charles was deprived of blackboard privileges because he threw chalk.

On Saturday I remarked to my husband, "Do you think kindergarten is too unsettling for Laurie? All this toughness, and bad grammar, and this Charles boy sounds like such a bad influence."

"It'll be all right," my husband said reassuringly. "Bound to be people like Charles in the world. Might as well meet them now as later."

On Monday Laurie came home late, full of news. "Charles," he shouted as he came up the hill; I was waiting anxiously on the front steps. "Charles," Laurie yelled all the way up the hill, "Charles was bad again."

"Come right in," I said, as soon as he came close enough. "Lunch is waiting."

"You know what Charles did?" he demanded, following me through the door. "Charles yelled so in school they sent a boy in from first grade to tell the teacher she had to make Charles keep quiet, and so Charles had to stay after school. And so all the children stayed to watch him."

"What did he do?" I asked.

"He just sat there," Laurie said, climbing into his chair at the table. "Hi, Pop, y'old dust mop."

"Charles had to stay after school today," I told my husband. "Everyone stayed with him."

"What does this Charles look like?" my husband asked Laurie. "What's his other name?"

"He's bigger than me," Laurie said. "And he doesn't have any rubbers and he doesn't ever wear a jacket."

Monday night was the first Parent-Teachers meeting, and only the fact that the baby had a cold kept me from going; I wanted passionately to meet Charles's mother. On Tuesday Laurie remarked suddenly, "Our teacher had a friend come to see her in school today."

"Charles's mother?" my husband and I asked simultaneously.

"Naaah," Laurie said scornfully. "It was a man who came and made us do exercises, we had to touch our toes. Look." He climbed down from his chair and squatted down and touched his toes. "Like this," he said. He got solemnly back into his chair and said, picking up his fork, "Charles didn't even *do* exercises."

"That's fine," I said heartily. "Didn't Charles want to do exercises?"

"Naaah," Laurie said. "Charles was so fresh to the teacher's friend he wasn't *let* do exercises."

"Fresh again?" I said.

"He kicked the teacher's friend," Laurie said. "The teacher's friend told Charles to touch his toes like I just did and Charles kicked him."

"What are they going to do about Charles, do you suppose?" Laurie's father asked him.

Laurie shrugged elaborately. "Throw him out of school, I guess," he said.

Wednesday and Thursday were routine; Charles yelled

during story hour and hit a boy in the stomach and made him cry. On Friday Charles stayed after school again and so did all the other children.

With the third week of kindergarten Charles was an institution in our family; the baby was being a Charles when she cried all afternoon; Laurie did a Charles when he filled his wagon full of mud and pulled it through the kitchen; even my husband, when he caught his elbow in the telephone cord and pulled telephone, ash tray, and a bowl of flowers off the table, said, after the first minute, "Looks like Charles."

During the third and fourth weeks it looked like a reformation in Charles; Laurie reported grimly at lunch on Thursday of the third week, "Charles was so good today the teacher gave him an apple."

"What?" I said, and my husband added warily, "You mean Charles?"

"Charles," Laurie said. "He gave the crayons around and he picked up the books afterward and the teacher said he was her helper."

"What happened?" I asked incredulously.

"He was her helper, that's all," Laurie said, and shrugged.

"Can this be true, about Charles?" I asked my husband that night. "Can something like this happen?"

"Wait and see," my husband said cynically. "When you've got a Charles to deal with, this may mean he's only plotting."

He seemed to be wrong. For over a week Charles was the teacher's helper; each day he handed things out and he picked things up; no one had to stay after school.

"The P.T.A. meeting's next week again," I told my husband one evening. "I'm going to find Charles's mother there."

"Ask her what happened to Charles," my husband said. "I'd like to know."

"I'd like to know myself," I said.

On Friday of that week things were back to normal. "You know what Charles did today?" Laurie demanded at the lunch table, in a voice slightly awed. "He told a little girl to say a word and she said it and the teacher washed her mouth out with soap and Charles laughed."

"What word?" his father asked unwisely, and Laurie said, "I'll have to whisper it to you, it's so bad." He got down off his chair and went around to his father. His father bent his head down and Laurie whispered joyfully. His father's eyes widened.

"Did Charles tell the little girl to say *that?*" he asked respectfully.

"She said it *twice*," Laurie said. "Charles told her to say it *twice*."

"What happened to Charles?" my husband asked.

"Nothing," Laurie said. "He was passing out the crayons."

Monday morning Charles abandoned the little girl and said the evil word himself three or four times, getting his mouth washed out with soap each time. He also threw chalk.

My husband came to the door with me that evening as I set out for the P.T.A. meeting. "Invite her over for a cup of tea after the meeting," he said. "I want to get a look at her."

"If only she's there," I said prayerfully.

"She'll be there," my husband said. "I don't see how they could hold a P.T.A. meeting without Charles's mother."

At the meeting I sat restlessly, scanning each comfortable matronly face, trying to determine which one hid the secret of Charles. None of them looked to me haggard enough. No one stood up in the meeting and apologized for the way her son had been acting. No one mentioned Charles.

After the meeting I identified and sought out Laurie's kindergarten teacher. She had a plate with a cup of tea and a piece of chocolate cake; I had a plate with a cup of tea and a piece of marshmallow cake. We maneuvered up to one another cautiously, and smiled.

"I've been so anxious to meet you," I said. "I'm Laurie's mother."

"We're all so interested in Laurie," she said.

"Well, he certainly likes kindergarten," I said. "He talks about it all the time."

"We had a little trouble adjusting, the first week or so," she said primly, "but now he's a fine little helper. With occasional lapses, of course."

"Laurie usually adjusts very quickly," I said. "I suppose this time it's Charles's influence."

"Charles?"

"Yes," I said, laughing, "you must have your hands full in that kindergarten, with Charles."

"Charles?" she said. "We don't have any Charles in the kindergarten."

Read: 5/8/87, 3/17/98

Read: 5/15/86

Read: 5/14/85

TOMORROW AND TOMORROW AND TOMORROW

KURT VONNEGUT, JR.

THE year was 2158 A.D., and Lou and Emerald Schwartz were whispering on the balcony outside Lou's family's apartment on the seventy-sixth floor of Building 257 in Alden Village, a New York housing development that covered what had once been known as Southern Connecticut. When Lou and Emerald had married, Em's parents had tearfully described the marriage as being between May and December; but now, with Lou one hundred and twelve and Em ninety-three, Em's parents had to admit that the match had worked out well.

But Em and Lou weren't without their troubles, and they were out in the nippy air of the balcony because of them.

"Sometimes I get so mad, I feel like just up and diluting his anti-gerasone," said Em.

"That'd be against Nature, Em," said Lou, "it'd be murder. Besides, if he caught us tinkering with his anti-gerasone, not only would he disinherit us, he'd bust my neck. Just because he's one hundred and seventy-two doesn't mean Gramps isn't strong as a bull."

"Against Nature," said Em. "Who knows what Nature's like anymore? Ohhhhh — I don't guess I could ever bring myself to dilute his anti-gerasone or anything like that, but, gosh, Lou, a body can't help thinking Gramps is never going to leave if somebody doesn't help him along a little. Golly — we're so crowded a person can hardly turn around, and Verna's dying for a baby, and Melissa's gone thirty years without one." She stamped her feet. "I get so sick of seeing his wrinkled old face, watching him take the only private room and the best chair and the best food, and getting to pick out what to watch on TV, and running everybody's life by changing his will all the time."

"Well, after all," said Lou bleakly, "Gramps *is* head of the family. And he can't help being wrinkled like he is. He was seventy before anti-gerasone was invented. He's going to leave, Em. Just give him time. It's his business. I know he's tough to live with, but be patient. It wouldn't do to do anything that'd rile him. After all, we've got it better'n anybody else, there on the daybed."

"How much longer do you think we'll get to sleep on the daybed before he picks another pet? The world's record's two months, isn't it?"

"Mom and Pop had it that long once, I guess."

"When *is* he going to leave, Lou?" said Emerald.

"Well, he's talking about giving up anti-gerasone right after the five-hundred-mile Speedway Race."

"Yes — and before that it was the Olympics, and before that the World's Series, and before that the Presidential Elections, and before that I-don't-know-what. It's been just one excuse after another for fifty years now. I don't think we're ever going to get a room to ourselves or an egg or anything."

"All right — call me a failure!" said Lou. "What can I do? I work hard and make good money, but the whole thing, practically, is taxed away for defense and old age pensions. And if it wasn't taxed away, where you think we'd find a vacant room to rent? Iowa, maybe? Well, who wants to live on the outskirts of Chicago?"

Em put her arms around his neck. "Lou, hon, I'm not calling you a failure. The Lord knows you're not. You just haven't had a chance to be anything or have anything because Gramps and the rest of his generation won't leave and let somebody else take over."

"Yeah, yeah," said Lou gloomily. "You can't exactly blame 'em, though, can you? I mean, I wonder how quick we'll knock off the anti-gerasone when we get to Gramps' age."

"Sometimes I wish there wasn't any such thing as anti-gerasone!" said Emerald passionately. "Or I wish it was made out of something real expensive and hard-to-get instead of mud and dandelions. Sometimes I wish folks just up and died regular as clockwork, without anything to say about it, instead of deciding themselves how long they're going to stay around. There ought to be a law against selling the stuff to anybody over one hundred and fifty."

"Fat chance of that," said Lou, "with all the money and votes the old people've got." He looked at her closely. "You ready to up and die, Em?"

"Well, for heaven's sake, what a thing to say to your wife. Hon! I'm not even one hundred yet." She ran her hands lightly over her firm, youthful figure, as though for confirmation. "The best years of my life are still ahead of me. But you can bet that when one hundred and fifty rolls around, old Em's going to pour her anti-gerasone down the sink, and quit taking up room, and she'll do it smiling."

"Sure, sure," said Lou, "you bet. That's what they all say. How many you heard of doing it?"

"There was that man in Delaware."

"Aren't you getting kind of tired of talking about him, Em? That was five months ago."

"All right, then — Gramma Winkler, right here in the same building."

"She got smeared by a subway."

"That's just the way she picked to go," said Em.

"Then what was she doing carrying a six-pack of anti-gerasone when she got it?"

Emerald shook her head wearily and covered her eyes. "I dunno, I dunno, I dunno. All I know is, something's just got to be done." She sighed. "Sometimes I wish they'd left a couple of diseases kicking around somewhere, so I could get one and go to bed for a little while. Too many people!" she cried, and her words cackled and gabbled and died in a thousand asphalt-paved, skyscraper-walled courtyards.

Lou laid his hand on her shoulder tenderly. "Aw, hon, I hate to see you down in the dumps like this."

"If we just had a car, like the folks used to in the old days," said Em, "we could go for a drive, and get away from people for a little while. Gee — if *those* weren't the days!"

"Yeah," said Lou, "before they'd used up all the metal."

"We'd hop in, and Pop'd drive up to a filling station and say, 'Fillerup!' "

"That *was* the nuts, wasn't it — before they'd used up all the gasoline."

"And we'd go for a carefree ride in the country."

"Yeah — all seems like a fairyland now, doesn't it, Em? Hard to believe there really used to be all that space between cities."

"And when we got hungry," said Em, "we'd find ourselves a restaurant, and walk in, big as you please, and say, 'I'll have a steak and French-fries, I believe,' or 'How are the pork chops today?' " She licked her lips, and her eyes glistened.

"Yeah man!" growled Lou. "How'd you like a hamburger with the works, Em?"

"Mmmmmmmm."

"If anybody'd offered us processed seaweed in those days, we would have spit right in his eye, huh, Em?"

"Or processed sawdust," said Em.

Doggedly, Lou tried to find the cheery side of the situation.

"Well, anyway, they've got the stuff so it tastes a lot less like seaweed and sawdust than it did at first; and they say it's actually better for us than what we used to eat."

"I felt fine!" said Em fiercely.

Lou shrugged. "Well, you've got to realize, the world wouldn't be able to support twelve billion people if it wasn't for processed seaweed and sawdust. I mean, it's a wonderful thing, really. I guess. That's what they say."

"They say the first thing that pops into their heads," said Em. She closed her eyes. "Golly — remember shopping, Lou? Remember how the stores used to fight to get our folks to buy something? You didn't have to wait for somebody to die to get a bed or chairs or a stove or anything like that. Just went in — bing! — and bought whatever you wanted. Gee whiz, that was nice, before they used up all the raw materials. I was just a little kid then, but I can remember so plain."

Depressed, Lou walked listlessly to the balcony's edge, and looked up at the clean, cold, bright stars against the black velvet of infinity. "Remember when we used to be bugs on science fiction, Em? Flight seventeen, leaving for Mars, launching ramp twelve. 'Board! All non-technical personnel kindly remain in bunkers. Ten seconds . . . nine . . . eight . . . seven . . . six . . . five . . . four . . . three . . . two . . . *one! Main Stage! Barrrrrroooom!*"

"Why worry about what was going on on Earth?" said Em, looking up at the stars with him. "In another few years, we'd all be shooting through space to start life all over again on a new planet."

Lou sighed. "Only it turns out you need something about twice the size of the Empire State Building to get one lousy colonist to Mars. And for another couple of trillion bucks he could take his wife and dog. *That's* the way to lick overpopulation — *emigrate!*"

"Lou — ?"

"Hmmm?"

"When's the Five-Hundred-Mile Speedway Race?"

"Uh — Memorial Day, May thirtieth."

She bit her lip. "Was that awful of me to ask?"

"Not very, I guess. Everybody in the apartment's looked it up to make sure."

"I don't want to be awful," said Em, "But you've just got to talk over these things now and then, and get them out of your system."

"Sure you do. Feel better?"

"Yes — and I'm not going to lose my temper anymore, and I'm going to be just as nice to him as I know how."

"That's my Em."

They squared their shoulders, smiled bravely, and went back inside.

Gramps Schwartz, his chin resting on his hands, his hands on the crook of his cane, was staring irascibly at the five-foot television screen that dominated the room. On the screen, a news commentator was summarizing the day's happenings. Every thirty seconds or so, Gramps would jab the floor with his cane-tip and shout, " . . . ! We did that a hundred years ago!"

Emerald and Lou, coming in from the balcony, were obliged to take seats in the back row, behind Lou's father and mother, brother and sister-in-law, son and daughter-in-law, grandson and wife, granddaughter and husband, great-grandson and wife, nephew and wife, grandnephew and wife, great-grandniece and husband, great-grandnephew and wife, and, of course, Gramps, who was in front of everybody. All, save Gramps, who was somewhat withered and bent, seemed by pre-anti-gerasone standards, to be about the same age — to be somewhere in their late twenties or early thirties.

"*Meanwhile,*" the commentator was saying, "*Council Bluffs, Iowa, was still threatened by stark tragedy. But two hundred weary rescue workers have refused to give up hope, and continue to dig in an effort to save Elbert Haggedorn, one hundred and eighty-three, who has been wedged for two days in a . . .*"

"I wish he'd get something more cheerful," Emerald whispered to Lou.

"Silence!" cried Gramps. "Next one shoots off his big bazoo while the TV's on is gonna find hisself cut off without a dollar" — and here his voice suddenly softened and sweetened — "when they wave that checkered flag at the Indianapolis Speedway, and old Gramps gets ready for the Big Trip Up Yonder." He sniffed sentimentally, while his heirs concentrated desperately on not making the slightest sound. For them, the poignancy of the prospective Big Trip had been dulled somewhat by its having been mentioned by Gramps about once a day for fifty years.

"*Dr. Brainard Keyes Bullard,*" said the commentator, "*President of Wyandotte College, said in an address tonight that most of the world's ills can be traced to the fact that Man's knowledge of himself has not kept pace with his knowledge of the physical world.*"

" . . . !" said Gramps. "We said that a hundred years ago!"

"*In Chicago tonight,*" said the commentator, "*a special celebration is taking place in the Chicago Lying-in Hospital.*

The guest of honor is Lowell W. Hitz, age zero. Hitz, born this morning, is the twenty-five-millionth child to be born in the hospital." The commentator faded, and was replaced on the screen by young Hitz, who squalled furiously.

" . . . ," whispered Lou to Emerald, "we said that a hundred years ago."

"I heard that!" shouted Gramps. He snapped off the television set, and his petrified descendants stared silently at the screen. "You, there, boy — "

"I didn't mean anything by it, sir," said Lou.

"Get me my will. You know where it is. You kids *all* know where it is. Fetch, boy!"

Lou nodded dully, and found himself going down the hall, picking his way over bedding to Gramps's room, the only private room in the Schwartz apartment. The other rooms were the bathroom, the living room, and the wide, windowless hallway, which was originally intended to serve as a dining area, and which had a kitchenette in one end. Six mattresses and four sleeping bags were dispersed in the hallway and living room, and the daybed, in the living room, accommodated the eleventh couple, the favorites of the moment.

On Gramps's bureau was his will, smeared, dog-eared, perforated, and blotched with hundreds of additions, deletions, accusations, conditions, warnings, advice, and homely philosophy. The document was, Lou reflected, a fifty-year diary, all jammed onto two sheets — a garbled, illegible log of day after day of strife. This day, Lou would be disinherited for the eleventh time, and it would take him perhaps six months of impeccable behavior to regain the promise of a share in the estate.

"Boy!" called Gramps.

"Coming, sir." Lou hurried back into the living room, and handed Gramps the will.

"Pen!" said Gramps.

He was instantly offered eleven pens, one from each couple.

"Not *that* leaky thing," he said, brushing Lou's pen aside. "Ah, there's a nice one. Good boy, Willy." He accepted Willy's pen. That was the tip they'd all been waiting for. Willy, then, Lou's father, was the new favorite.

Willy, who looked almost as young as Lou, though one hundred and forty-two, did a poor job of concealing his pleasure. He glanced shyly at the daybed, which would become his, and from which Lou and Emerald would have to move back into the hall, back to the worst spot of all by the bathroom door.

Gramps missed none of the high drama he'd authored, and he gave his own familiar role everything he had. Frowning and running his finger along each line, as though he were seeing the will for the first time, he read aloud in a deep, portentous monotone, like a bass tone on a cathedral organ:

"I, Harold D. Schwartz, residing in Building 257 of Alden Village, New York City, do hereby make, publish, and declare this to be my last Will and Testament, hereby revoking any and all former wills and codicils by me at any time heretofore made." He blew his nose importantly, and went on, not missing a word, and repeating many for emphasis — repeating in particular his ever-more-elaborate specifications for a funeral.

At the end of these specifications, Gramps was so choked with emotion that Lou thought he might forget why he'd gotten out the will in the first place. But Gramps heroically brought his powerful emotions under control, and, after erasing for a full minute, he began to write and speak at the same time. Lou could have spoken his lines for him, he'd heard them so often.

"I have had many heartbreaks ere leaving this vale of tears for a better land," Gramps said and wrote. "But the deepest hurt of all has been dealt me by — " He looked around the group, trying to remember who the malefactor was.

Everyone looked helpfully at Lou, who held up his hand resignedly.

Gramps nodded, remembering, and completed the sentence: "my great-grandson, Louis J. Schwartz."

"Grandson, sir," said Lou.

"Don't quibble. You're in deep enough now, young man," said Gramps, but he changed the trifle. And from there he went without a misstep through the phrasing of the disinheritance, causes for which were disrespectfulness and quibbling.

In the paragraph following, the paragraph that had belonged to everyone in the room at one time or another, Lou's name was scratched out and Willy's substituted as heir to the apartment and, the biggest plum of all, the double bed in the private bedroom. "So!" said Gramps, beaming. He erased the date at the foot of the will, and substituted a new one, including the time of day. "Well — time to watch the McGarvey Family." The McGarvey Family was a televison serial that Gramps had been following since he was sixty, or for one hundred and twelve years. "I can't wait to see what's going to happen next," he said.

Lou detached himself from the group and lay down on his bed of pain by the bathroom door. He wished Em would join him, and he wondered where she was.

He dozed for a few moments, until he was disturbed by someone's stepping over him to get into the bathroom. A moment later, he heard a faint gurgling sound, as though something were being poured down the washbasin drain. Suddenly, it entered his mind that Em had cracked up, and that she was in there doing something drastic about Gramps.

"Em — !" he whispered through the panel. There was no reply, and Lou pressed against the door. The worn lock, whose bolt barely engaged its socket, held for a second, then let the door swing inward.

"Morty!" gasped Lou.

Lou's great-grandnephew, Mortimer, who had just married and brought his wife home to the Schwartz menage, looked at Lou with consternation and surprise. Morty kicked the door shut, but not before Lou had glimpsed what was in his hand — Gramps's enormous economy-size bottle of anti-gerasone, which had been half-emptied, and which Morty was refilling to the top with tap water.

A moment later, Morty came out, glared defiantly at Lou, and brushed past him wordlessly to rejoin his pretty bride.

Shocked, Lou didn't know what on earth to do. He couldn't let Gramps take the mousetrapped anti-gerasone; but if he warned Gramps about it, Gramps would certainly make life in the apartment, which was merely insufferable now, harrowing.

Lou glanced into the living room, and saw that the Schwartzes, Emerald among them, were momentarily at rest, relishing the botches that McGarveys had made of *their* lives. Stealthily, he went into the bathroom, locked the door as well as he could, and began to pour the contents of Gramps's bottle down the drain. He was going to refill it with full-strength anti-gerasone from the twenty-two smaller bottles on the shelf. The bottle contained a half-gallon, and its neck was small, so it seemed to Lou that the emptying would take forever. And the almost imperceptible smell of anti-gerasone, like Worcestershire sauce, now seemed to Lou, in his nervousness, to be pouring out into the rest of the apartment through the keyhole and under the door.

"*Gloog-gloog-gloog-gloog-*" went the bottle monotonously. Suddenly; up came the sound of music from the living room, and there were murmurs and the scraping of chair legs on the floor. "*Thus ends,*" said the television announcer, "*the 29,121st chapter in the life of your neighbors and mine, the McGarveys.*" Footsteps were coming down the hall. There was a knock on the bathroom door.

"Just a sec," called Lou cheerily. Desperately, he shook the big bottle, trying to speed up the flow. His palms slipped on the wet glass, and the heavy bottle smashed to splinters on the tile floor.

The door sprung open, and Gramps, dumbfounded, stared at the mess.

Lou grinned engagingly through his nausea, and, for want of anything remotely resembling a thought, he waited for Gramps to speak.

"Well, boy," said Gramps at last, "looks like you've got a little tidying up to do."

And that was all he said. He turned around, elbowed his way through the crowd, and locked himself in his bedroom.

The Schwartzes contemplated Lou in incredulous silence for a moment longer, and then hurried back to the living room, as though some of his horrible guilt would taint them, too, if they looked too long. Morty stayed behind long enough to give Lou a quizzical, annoyed glance. Then he, too, went into the living room, leaving only Emerald standing in the doorway.

Tears streamed over her cheeks. "Oh, you poor lamb — please don't look so awful. It was my fault. I put you up to this."

"No," said Lou, finding his voice, "really you didn't. Honest, Em, I was just — "

"You don't have to explain anything to me, hon. I'm on your side no matter what." She kissed him on his cheek, and whispered in his ear. "It wouldn't have been murder, hon. It wouldn't have killed him. It wasn't such a terrible thing to do. It just would have fixed him up so he'd be able to go any time God decided He wanted him."

"What's gonna happen next, Em?" said Lou hollowly. "What's he gonna do?"

Lou and Emerald stayed fearfully awake almost all night, waiting to see what Gramps was going to do. But not a sound came from the sacred bedroom. At two hours before dawn, the pair dropped off to sleep.

At six o'clock they arose again, for it was time for their generation to eat breakfast in the kitchenette. No one spoke to them. They had twenty minutes in which to eat, but their reflexes were so dulled by the bad night that they had hardly swallowed two mouthfuls of egg-type processed seaweed before it was time to surrender their places to their son's generation.

Then, as was the custom for whomever had been most recently disinherited, they began preparing Gramps' breakfast, which would presently be served to him in bed, on a tray. They tried to be cheerful about it. The toughest part of the job was having to handle the . . . eggs and bacon and oleomargarine on which Gramps spent almost all of the income from his fortune.

"Well," said Emerald, "I'm not going to get all panicky until I'm sure there's something to be panicky about."

"Maybe he doesn't know what it was I busted," said Lou hopefully.

"Probably thinks it was your watch crystal," said Eddie their son, who was toying apathetically with his buckwheat-type processed sawdust cakes.

"Don't get sarcastic with your father," said Em, "and don't talk with your mouth full, either."

"I'd like to see anybody take a mouthful of this stuff and *not* say something," said Eddie, who was seventy-three. He glanced at the clock. "It's time to take Gramps his breakfast, you know."

"Yeah, it is, isn't it," said Lou weakly. He shrugged. "Let's have the tray, Em."

"We'll both go."

Walking slowly, smiling bravely, they found a large semicircle of long-faced Schwartzes standing around the bedroom door.

Em knocked. "Gramps," she said brightly, "breakfast is ready."

There was no reply, and she knocked again, harder.

The door swung open before her fist. In the middle of the room, the soft, deep, wide, canopied bed, the symbol of the sweet by-and-by to every Schwartz, was empty.

A sense of death, as unfamiliar to the Schwartzes as Zoroastrianism or the causes of the Sepoy Mutiny, stilled every voice and slowed every heart. Awed, the heirs began to search gingerly under the furniture and behind the drapes for all that was mortal of Gramps, father of the race.

But Gramps had left not his earthly husk but a note, which Lou finally found on the dresser, under a paperweight which was a treasured souvenir from the 2000 World's Fair. Unsteadily, Lou read it aloud:

" 'Somebody who I have sheltered and protected and taught the best I know how all these years last night turned on me like a mad dog and diluted my anti-gerasone, or tried to. I am no longer a young man. I can no longer bear the crushing burden of life as I once could. So, after last night's bitter experience, I say goodbye. The cares of this world will soon drop away like a cloak of thorns, and I shall know peace. By the time you find this, I will be gone.' "

"Gosh," said Willy brokenly, "he didn't even get to see how the Five-Hundred-Mile Speedway Race was going to come out."

"Or the World's Series," said Eddie.

"Or whether Mrs. McGarvey got her eyesight back," said Morty.

"There's more," said Lou, and he began reading aloud again: " 'I, Harold D. Schwartz . . . do hereby make, publish and declare this to be my last Will and Testament, hereby revoking any and all former wills and codicils by me at any time heretofore made.' "

"No!" cried Willy. "Not another one!"

" 'I do stipulate,' " read Lou, " 'that all of my property, of whatsoever kind and nature, not be divided, but do devise and bequeath it to be held in common by my issue, without regard for generation, equally, share and share alike.' "

"Issue?" said Emerald.

Lou included the multitude in a sweep of his hand. "It means we all own the whole . . . shootin' match."

All eyes turned instantly to the bed.

"Share and share alike?" said Morty.

"Actually," said Willy, who was the oldest person present, "it's just like the old system, where the oldest people head up things with their headquarters in here, and — "

"I like *that!*" said Em. "Lou owns as much of it as you do, and I say it ought to be for the oldest one who's still working. You can snooze around here all day, waiting for your pension check, and poor Lou stumbles in here after work, all tuckered out, and — "

"How about letting somebody who's never had any privacy get a little crack at it?" said Eddie hotly. " . . ., you old people had plenty of privacy back when you were kids. I was born and raised in the middle of the . . . barracks in the hall! How about — "

"Yeah?" said Morty. "Sure, you've all had it pretty tough, and my heart bleeds for you. But try honeymooning in the hall for a real kick."

"Silence!" shouted Willy imperiously. "The next person who opens his mouth spends the next six months by the bathroom. Now clear out of my room. I want to think."

A vase shattered against the wall, inches above his head. In the next moment, a free-for-all was underway, with each couple battling to eject every other couple from the room. Fighting coalitions formed and dissolved with the lightning changes of the tactical situation. Em and Lou were thrown into the hall, where they organized others in the same situation, and stormed back into the room.

After two hours of struggle, with nothing like a decision in sight, the cops broke in.

For the next half-hour, patrol wagons and ambulances hauled away Schwartzes, and then the apartment was still and spacious.

An hour later, films of the last stages of the riot were being televised to 500,000,000 delighted viewers on the Eastern Seaboard.

In the stillness of the three-room Schwartz apartment on the 76th floor of Building 257, the television set had been left on. Once more the air was filled with the cries and grunts and crashes of the fray, coming harmlessly now from the loudspeaker.

The battle also appeared on the screen of the televison set in the police station, where the Schwartzes and their captors watched with professional interest.

Em and Lou were in adjacent four-by-eight cells, and were stretched out peacefully on their cots.

"Em — " called Lou through the partition, "you got a washbasin all your own too?"

"Sure. Washbasin, bed, light — the works. Ha! And we thought Gramps's room was something. How long's this been going on?" She held out her hand. "For the first time in forty years, hon, I haven't got the shakes."

"Cross your fingers," said Lou, "the lawyer's going to try to get us a year."

"Gee," said Em dreamily, "I wonder what kind of wires you'd have to pull to get solitary?"

"All right, pipe down," said the turnkey, "or I'll toss the whole kit and caboodle of you right out. And first one who lets on to anybody outside how good jail is ain't never getting back in!"

The prisoners instantly fell silent.

The living room of the Schwartz apartment darkened for a moment, as the riot scene faded, and then the face of the announcer appeared, like the sun coming from behind a cloud. *"And now, friends," he said, "I have a special message from the makers of anti-gerasone, a message for all you folks over one hundred and fifty. Are you hampered socially by wrinkles, by stiffness of joints and discoloration or loss of hair, all because these things came upon you before anti-gearsone was developed? Well, if you are, you need no longer suffer, need no longer feel different and out of things.*

"After years of research, medical science has now developed super-anti-gerasone! *In weeks, yes weeks, you can look, feel, and act as young as your great-great-grandchildren! Wouldn't you pay $5,000 to be indistinguishable from everybody else? Well, you don't have to. Safe, tested super-anti-gerasone costs you only dollars a day. The average cost of regaining all the sparkle and attractiveness of youth is less than fifty dollars.*

"Write now for your free trial carton. Just put your name and address on a dollar postcard, and mail it to 'Super,' Box 500,000, Schenectady, N.Y. Have you got that? I'll repeat it. 'Super' *Box . . . "* Underlining the announcer's words was the scratching of Gramps's fountain pen, the one Willy had given him the night before. He had come in a few minutes previous from the Idle Hour Tavern, which commanded a view of Building 257 across the square of asphalt known as the Alden Village Green. He had called a cleaning woman to come straighten the place up, and had hired the best lawyer in town to get his descendants a conviction. Gramps had then moved

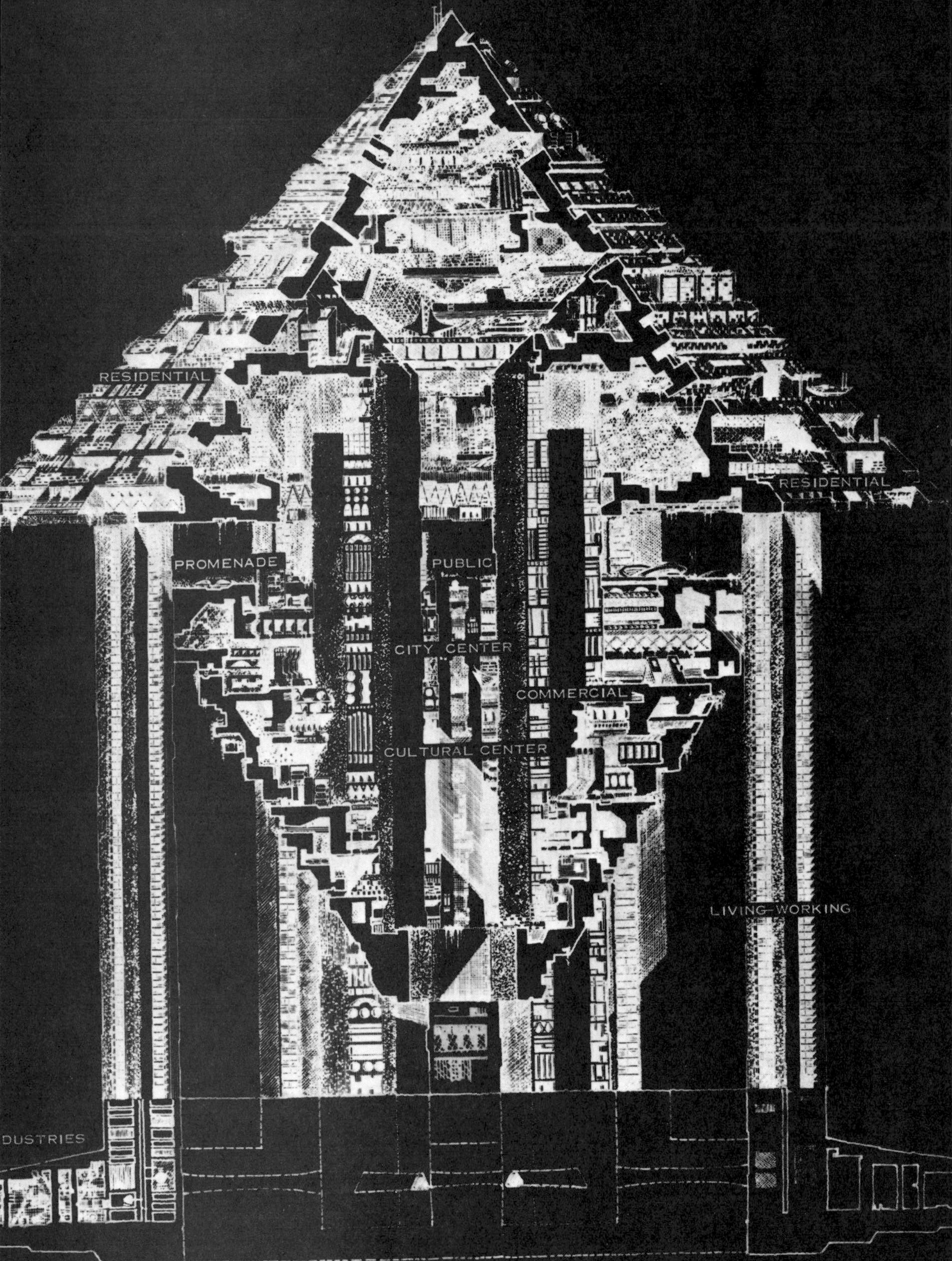
RESIDENTIAL
RESIDENTIAL
PROMENADE
PUBLIC
CITY CENTER
COMMERCIAL
CULTURAL CENTER
LIVING-WORKING
DUSTRIES

the daybed before the televison screen so that he could watch from a reclining position. It was something he'd dreamed of doing for years.

"Schen-*ec*-ta-dy," mouthed Gramps. "Got it." His face had changed remarkably. His facial muscles seemed to have relaxed, revealing kindness and equanimity under what had been taut, bad-tempered lines. It was almost as though his trial package of *Super*-anti-gerasone had already arrived. When something amused him on televison, he smiled easily, rather than barely managing to lengthen the thin line of his mouth a millimeter. Life was good. He could hardly wait to see what was going to happen next.